MW00478406

SHELTER FOR KOREN

BADGE OF HONOR, BOOK 14

SUSAN STOKER

This book is a work of fiction. Names, characters, places, and incidents are products of the author's imagination or used fictitiously. Any resemblance to actual events or locales or persons living or dead is entirely coincidental.

Copyright © 2019 by Susan Stoker
No part of this work may be used, stored, reproduced or transmitted without written permission from the publisher except for brief quotations for review purposes as permitted by law. This book is licensed for your personal enjoyment only. This book may not be re-sold or given away to other people. If you would like to share this book with another person, please purchase an additional copy for each recipient. If you're reading this book and did not purchase it, or it was not purchased for your use only, please purchase your own copy.
Thank you for respecting the hard work of this author.
Cover Design by Chris Mackey, AURA Design Group
Edited by Kelli Collins
Manufactured in the United States

CHAPTER ONE

Taco was glad he took the extra shift tonight of all nights. He'd already worked a forty-eight-hour shift, but one of the guys who was supposed to start work at five had a ballet recital for his little girl that he'd wanted to attend.

Knowing Adeline was going to invite him over to her house for dinner made it easy for Taco to decide to volunteer. It wasn't that he didn't love hanging out with his friends away from the station, but lately everyone had been trying to set him up with "nice women," and he was tired of it. After Jen, he'd written off dating for the foreseeable future.

He supposed that dating a serial-killing religious cult leader would do that to a man, though, so he didn't feel all that guilty about it.

Finding out he'd been such a horrible judge of character had shaken him...badly. He knew Jen hadn't really been getting along with the other women, which should have been his first clue, but he'd thought it was something that would improve over time. He should've known better.

He should've known when she was only interested in hanging out with him while Quinn was around… Quinn being her ultimate target.

The bottom line was that currently, Taco didn't trust himself when it came to women. And he wasn't ready for all the pity dates Sophie, Quinn, and the others were trying to throw his way.

So doing an extra night shift was much more preferable than going over to Crash's place to see which "absolutely beautiful, super-nice" friend would be there as well.

Taco didn't want beautiful.

He didn't want nice.

He didn't want to be set up.

He just wanted to be left alone.

Being single wasn't a bad thing, even if all his closest friends were married, engaged, or starting families of their own.

Brought out of his depressing musings by the emergency tones ringing throughout the station, Taco leapt up and rushed to put on his bunker gear. A good hard call was just what he needed to pull his head out of his ass.

He jumped into the front seat of the fire truck and reviewed the call notes on the laptop as they raced out of the station, sirens and lights blazing.

"Car versus semi," he told his teammates as they headed for the interstate. He continued reading from the call sheet as they raced toward the scene. "One person trapped. Semi driver seems fine and evacuated the truck without assistance."

Taco's mind raced through the different scenarios that might greet them. They'd have to be very careful. The trapped person was obviously in the car and could be suffering anything from a neck injury to internal bleeding. Time was of the essence and the sooner they got there, the better.

From what he understood from listening to the dispatcher as they sped toward the scene, the semi had run a red light and a Nissan had gone right under the trailer attached to the cab. Most semis these days had underride guards to keep cars from doing exactly what this one had, so obviously this was an older-model trailer. According to dispatch, the top of the car had almost been completely sheared off. From accounts of bystanders and witnesses, the hood wasn't smashed in and there was no gas leaking from the car, but it had apparently plowed under the trailer with almost enough force to make the Nissan a convertible.

The second the fire truck pulled up to the chaotic scene, Taco jumped out and ran toward the car. The sky-blue Nissan Altima was indeed wedged under the trailer, as dispatch indicated. Although it wasn't quite as clean as the reports had made it sound. There was glass and debris everywhere and the passenger-side door was bent beyond repair or use.

Visions of the occupant being decapitated ran through Taco's mind. He'd seen other accidents like this where the people inside the car had been killed instantly.

He crouched under the trailer and crawled on his hands and knees to the driver's side of the Nissan. The smell of burning rubber was strong under the eighteen-wheeler, as if one or both of the vehicles had tried to slam on their brakes at the last second. And even though he didn't see any gas, Taco could still smell it. He tried to put it out of his mind. The others would deal with that; it was his responsibility to see to the driver of the car.

The frame of the driver's side windows were bent downward, which, along with the impact, had most likely shattered the glass. He tugged at the door, but the metal was so badly warped he knew he'd need a crowbar, at the very least, to pry it open fully. More likely they'd have to use the jaws of life to get to the driver.

Managing to open the door just enough to see what he was dealing with, Taco peered inside the small crack. He saw the driver was a blonde woman. She was slumped over toward the passenger side of the car. Her seat belt was snug around her and he could see the steering wheel pressing down into her hips. He couldn't see her legs at the moment so he wasn't sure if they'd been crushed or not.

"Ma'am? Can you hear me?" he asked, not really expecting an answer—so he was shocked when the woman lifted her head and attempted to twist her body so she could see him. "No! Don't move," he ordered. "You might have a spinal injury. You have to stay very still."

She stopped moving immediately, much to Taco's relief. "I'm okay," she said in reply. "But I'm stuck."

Her voice sounded familiar, but Taco dismissed the thought. "Try not to worry, we're going to get you out."

"Not worry," she snorted. "Yeah, right. I'm stuck, I'm lying on broken glass, and I almost had my head torn from my body. Sure. I'll just lie here and think about eating bonbons while you do your thing."

He couldn't help it—Taco barked out a laugh. "Right. Although in my defense, I did say *try* not to worry. Now, does anything hurt?"

"Um…yeah?"

"You asking me or telling me?"

"Telling. And before you ask for specifics, at the moment, *everything* hurts."

Taco resisted the urge to chuckle again. Now wasn't the time or place. "How about this—does anything hurt way worse than the rest of you?"

"No. And before this truck tried to kill me, there was a seat belt cutter thing in the driver's side door. If it's still there, I wouldn't mind you getting this thing off. It feels as if it's strangling me."

Looking down to where she'd indicated, Taco was

impressed to see an orange emergency safety hammer. Somehow it hadn't flown out of the door upon impact. It had spikes on the end of the hammer head, which would easily break a window, and in the handle was a razor blade.

"I've got you," Taco said. He reached for the door handle and pulled on it with all his might. It made a horrible screeching sound as he yanked on it, but he was able to manhandle it open wide enough to get his shoulders and head through. Somehow, this woman had beaten a lot of odds. The last car-versus-semi accident he'd been to, the driver had been texting and ran right into the back of the trailer. The car had been crumpled beyond recognition and the passenger had died upon impact.

The woman had also been extremely lucky. She'd hit the trailer right in the middle, it didn't have under-ride guards, and he thought maybe the air in her tires had even been a little low. All of these things combined to give her the needed inches that allowed her to survive a horrific crash. And if she hadn't had the presence of mind to duck to the side, as well, her head would've been taken off right with the rest of the car.

It was truly amazing that she was still alive. The fact that she didn't seem to be badly hurt was literally a miracle.

Taking out his own seat belt cutting tool he always carried, Taco easily sliced through the material and wasn't surprised when the woman immediately slumped farther over the center console. He couldn't sit her up because of the truck above their heads, but now he could work on freeing her.

One of the other firefighters from Station 7 appeared next to him. Taco backed out of the car and together they used the crowbar Mick was carrying to pull both the driver's side door and the one right behind it completely off. They discussed their best course of action for a moment, then got into place, Mick at the front, with Taco climbing into the back seat as well as he could. It was a tight fit in the cramped space, but he'd worked in tougher spots.

"Ma'am?"

"Still here," she quipped.

Taco couldn't stop the smile that spread across his face. "Right. Here's what we're going to do. My friend Mick at your side is going to hold your hip still as we lower your seat to a reclining position. Then he'll ease you onto your back, and I'm going to hold your neck as he does. Once we have you supine, we can cut that steering wheel away, get you on a backboard, and pull you out. Sound good?"

"Oh, sorry…did you say anything other than getting me out?" she replied.

"Nope. All you have to do is relax. Let me and Mick do all the work. We won't drop you and we'll do our best to make this as painless as possible. But you need to let me know if anything hurts while we're moving you. I mean it. If you feel any pinching or shooting pains—or if you feel nothing at all—tell me immediately, and we'll stop and reassess."

"Okay. I can do this. Can I ask something first?"

"Sure."

"What's your name? I know Mick will be hanging on to my hips, but I didn't get your name."

Taco mentally smacked himself in the forehead. That was one of the first things he usually did. Introduced himself.

"I'm Taco. I'm with San Antonio Fire Station number seven."

"Taco?"

"Yeah, it's a nickname. What's your name?"

"Koren Garner. And I'm pretty sure we've already met."

Taco momentarily froze at hearing the name.

Yeah—he wasn't about to forget the name Koren anytime soon.

His sense of urgency, already high, kicked up a notch. And it didn't help when he heard raised voices from nearby talking about a ruptured gasoline tank on the semi.

"We have," he agreed. "Although if you were trying to get my attention, this probably wasn't the best way to go about it," Taco joked.

"Right, because when the semi appeared out of nowhere in front of me, I thought to myself, maybe if I go under this thing and get stuck, Quinn's handsome firefighter friend will be the one to respond and I can flirt with him during my rescue. Never mind the fact I smell like gas and might've decapitated myself. Any chance to snag a hot firefighter. Yup, that's what I was thinking all right."

Mick chuckled in front of him, and Taco shook his head with a grin. "All right, Koren, Mick is gonna do his thing. Remember, just relax. Let us move you." He nodded at Mick and the other firefighter pushed the button to recline the seat.

As Mick eased her up slightly, turning her slowly, Taco held Koren's head in his hands, supporting her. He and Mick gently eased her back until she was lying flat, looking up at Taco.

She had glass in her blonde hair and there was a scrape on her cheek, but otherwise she looked remarkably good for almost dying. Her blue eyes locked onto his…

And Taco swore he felt a bolt of lightning go through his body.

"Hi," she said softly. "We meet again."

He smiled, holding her head tightly. "Hi."

Now that she was lying down, there was a little more room between her hips and the steering wheel. Taco looked up at Mick. "I think we can scoot her out without messing with the wheel. The last thing we want to do is have to cut and risk a stray spark."

Mick nodded. "That's what I was thinking."

Koren blinked in surprise and tried to look down at Mick.

Taco held her head so she couldn't move. "What?"

"He's Australian," she said.

"I am," Mick said. "Hence the nickname. You know, Mick Dundee from that movie *Crocodile Dundee*."

"You're way too young to know that movie," she said.

"Like you aren't?" Taco retorted.

"It came out a year after I was born," Koren said.

"Which means nothing to me, really, as I can't say I have even the slightest clue when that thing first aired," Taco responded.

She winked. "I'm thirty-three. And if you wanted to know my age, all you had to do was ask. Like this... how old are *you*?"

"Older than you." Taco grinned. Then he turned when he heard someone at his side. Two more firefighters were standing there with a backboard. His attention went back to Koren. "All right, all kidding aside, it's time to get you out of there."

"Okay," she said, not taking her eyes from his.

"I'm going to lift you a bit and my buddies are gonna slip the backboard under you on the seat. Again, just relax, don't try to lift yourself in any way. Mick and I will get you on the board. Then it's just a matter of slipping you out the door. Got it?"

She tried to nod, but Taco still had too tight a grip on her head for her to move.

"Don't move your head, Koren."

"Sorry. Okay. I'm ready."

A shout went up from somewhere beyond the truck.

"Smoke!"

"Easy, Kor," Taco said when he felt her pulse leap under his fingers. "We got this. Ready, Mick?"

"Ready, mate."

"Okay, guys, bring in the backboard."

It took some maneuvering in the small, cramped space, but within just a minute and a half, Taco was kneeling on the ground next to Koren, fifteen feet away from her crumpled car and the tractor trailer. They were waiting for the mobile gurney to be brought over so they could transfer her onto it and take her to the hospital.

"You okay?" Taco asked.

"Yeah," she breathed. "Thank you."

"You're welcome."

"Here's her purse," Mick said from nearby.

Taco turned and took it from the big, burly fire-fighter. "Thanks."

Mick winked and rushed off to help someone else.

Taco looked back down at Koren, at a loss for words now that the rush of the rescue was already wearing off. He could tell she was well aware of how close she'd come to dying.

His thoughts were proven right when she took a deep breath and said, "I know this isn't the place or the time, but...wanna go out sometime? I *never* ask guys out but, you know, since I almost died, I'm giving myself a pass this once."

Taco hesitated. He wasn't ready. And he *really* wasn't ready to go out with someone who had a lot of the same features as his psycho ex.

He obviously hesitated too long, because for the first time, she looked away, her words tumbling out fast.

"Never mind. Forget I asked. Just blame it on adrenaline. I'm sure you're already taken. I mean, why wouldn't you be? You're beautiful." Then her eyes slammed shut. "And now I'm mortified."

"It's not you, Koren, I just—"

He was interrupted by two paramedics pushing a gurney. "Hey! Your ride to the hospital is here!" one of them said lightly.

Taco backed out of the way and watched as they lifted Koren onto the gurney. They carefully rolled her to the side and removed the backboard, handing it back to Taco. As they worked to buckle her in, Taco stepped up to the gurney, placing her purse between her lower legs.

Her eyes caught his for a second, before she looked away once more. "It was nice to see you again, Taco, despite the circumstances," she said somewhat formally, and with none of the flirtatious undertones she'd had earlier. "Thanks for getting me out of there."

"You're welcome. Koren, I—"

"Taco!" his chief called out. "Need you over here!"

Taco gestured that he'd be right there, and by the time he turned back around, Koren was halfway to the ambulance.

Running a hand over his short beard, Taco swore. Then, spinning on his heel, he rushed over to where his chief was standing to see what else he could help with.

CHAPTER TWO

Two hours later, Taco paced the fire station. They'd cleaned up the rest of the accident scene and when Koren's car was being put up on a tow truck, he'd once again realized exactly how lucky she'd been. By all rights, she should be dead. Most of the time he took accidents in stride. Death was as much a part of his daily routine as life. But something about seeing that mangled piece of steel sitting on top of the truck bed had made him anxious.

"Hey, Taco. Thanks for taking my shift last night. I owe ya."

Taco turned to face his friend. He looked at his watch and realized it was noon. "Sure thing, Slick. Anytime. How was the recital?"

"My baby girl was a star," Slick said.

"Uh-huh." He grinned. Of course he would say his

daughter was awesome, even if it turned out she had absolutely no grace or rhythm whatsoever.

"Anyway, I heard about that wreck this morning. Sounded nasty."

"It was."

"But the vic's okay?" Slick asked.

Taco nodded, but suddenly he felt uneasy. *Was* Koren okay? She seemed to be at the scene, but he knew more than most that sometimes after a bad wreck, a person could be walking around one minute and fall over with their heart not beating the next.

Taco made a split-second decision. "Have a good day," he said as he quickly headed for the door.

"See ya," Slick called out, but Taco wasn't listening.

He climbed into his older-model Chevy Silverado pickup truck and turned right out of the fire station, heading for the hospital.

Taco knew he was acting out of character, but he couldn't get Koren's face out of his mind. What if she had complications from the accident? What if she had a spinal injury? What if she was alone and scared? He didn't know anything about her, but he couldn't just go home and not find out how she was doing.

The drive to the hospital seemed to take forever, and Taco worked himself up thinking about everything that could be wrong with Koren. He hadn't had a chance to really look her over. She could have broken bones or maybe even a head injury. She hadn't felt any pain, but that could've been adrenaline. Were her legs broken? Her ankles?

He parked and jogged into the emergency room. He went right up to the reception desk and luckily recognized the nurse working there.

"Hey, Maria," he said as genially as possible.

She looked up. "Hi, Taco. It's good to see you."

"Same. It's been a while. So…I'm here about a patient who was brought in a few hours ago."

She raised her eyebrows in question.

"Koren Garner. She was in an MVA, I was first on scene."

"Ah, yes, Koren. I believe she's still here."

"Here? As in, the emergency room?" Taco asked incredulously. "She hasn't been transferred up to a room yet?" He'd been hoping to get Koren's room number out of the nurse. He didn't know what to make of the fact that she was still there. It could be good or bad.

"I heard you say my sister's name…is everything all right?"

Taco turned around to see a tall man with dusty-blond hair. He was standing with his arm around a slender red-haired woman.

"I hope so. I'm Taco, and I was the first firefighter on scene today. I just wanted to check on her."

The man held out his hand. "It's good to meet you. I'm Koren's brother, Liam. This is my wife, Kelle."

Taco shook both their hands…and couldn't figure

16

out why he felt somewhat disappointed that Koren wasn't alone. It was crazy. He should be *glad* she had family here. But a part of him had wanted to be the knight in shining armor swooping in and making everything better for her.

Stupid…so stupid.

Then another couple came up behind Liam and Kelle.

"Who's this?" the man asked.

"His name is Taco, and he helped Koren at the scene," Liam said.

The second man held out his hand. "Thank you so much. I'm Carter, Koren's other big brother. And this is my wife, Robin."

Taco shook their hands while mentally shaking his head. He shouldn't have come. Koren was obviously in good hands. She had her family.

Just then, Robin glanced over his shoulder before breaking away from their little group and rushing toward the double doors that led to the back.

Taco turned to stare in the direction she'd gone.

Koren stood there with an older couple he could only assume were her parents. There were also two other women with them too. Robin walked backward in front of Koren, speaking in low tones.

"You look surprised," Carter said. "I take it you didn't think she'd be discharged already?"

"Definitely not. If you'd seen her car, you wouldn't think so either," Taco said.

Kelle visibly shuddered. "I seriously can't imagine how in the world she managed to not only survive, but how she escaped with only a few cuts and bruises."

Then Koren was in front of him. She was wearing a pair of scrubs that were a little too tight. Her hair had been brushed and Taco wouldn't have known she'd been in a horrific crash only hours ago if it hadn't been for the slight black eyes.

"Hey," he said, suddenly feeling awkward.

"What are you doing here?" Koren asked with a tilt of her head and her brows drawn down in confusion.

"I wanted to make sure you were all right."

"I'm okay."

They stood in the middle of the waiting room, surrounded by her family, just staring at each other.

"I'm Gavin Garner, Koren's father," the older man standing near her said. He didn't offer his hand.

"And I'm Deena, her mom," offered the pretty blonde at his side. She smiled at him, keeping one hand on Koren's arm.

"Nice to meet you both," Taco said politely.

"And I'm Sue, and this is Vicky," one of the younger women said. "We're Koren's best friends. Thank you for what you do, and for coming by to check on her."

Taco felt ridiculous. Of *course* she had people who cared for her, who would be at her side in the hospital. Her friends had probably rushed to the ER the second they'd heard about her accident.

He dropped his eyes and took a step back. "Well, I

just wanted to make sure you were okay," he said again. "Take it easy for a while. You might feel all right now, but your body was put through the wringer. You'll feel it in a couple of days."

"Taco?" Koren asked.

He took another step back and looked around, not meeting her gaze, trying to figure out how to extricate himself.

"Hey, everyone, can you give me and Taco a moment?" Koren asked her family and friends.

Damn. Now Taco couldn't just turn around and leave. He watched as her brothers frowned, her friends smirked knowingly, and her parents simply looked concerned. But dutifully, they all stepped away.

Koren rolled her eyes and gestured for Taco to follow her over to an empty part of the waiting room. Reluctantly, he followed her until they were alone.

"Hi," she said with a small smile.

"Hey," he returned.

"Thanks for coming by to check on me."

Taco shrugged. "Sure. The hospital was on my way home." That was a lie. It was actually in the complete other direction.

"Oh. Well, I appreciate it anyway," she said.

"It looks like you've been well taken care of," he observed.

Koren smiled. "I called my mom and told her that I'd been in a little fender bender, and within half an hour, word had spread that I was on my deathbed and voila, everyone showed up."

"You were lucky," Taco said, not ready to joke about the accident yet.

"I know," she whispered. "Believe me, I know. All sorts of things went through my head in the seconds before my car slid under that tractor trailer." Koren put her hand on Taco's arm. "One of which was regret that I've always been too passive. I never speak up for myself or what I want. But I'm sorry for embarrassing you by doing so," she told him.

Taco knew exactly what she was talking about. "I'm flattered."

She blushed and huffed out a breath. "Right. Anyway, thanks again for checking on me. I'm fine. Maybe I'll see you around sometime."

She turned to walk away, but Taco's hand shot out and touched her upper arm. He didn't grab her, ever aware that she was probably sore and stiff from the accident.

"Yes," he said simply.

Koren's questioning gaze whipped up to meet his.

"I'd love to go out with you sometime," Taco said, clarifying. "And my hesitation wasn't because of you."

"I don't want you to say yes because you feel guilty or obligated," she responded.

"I'm not, I swear. It's just...the last woman I went out with pursued me, but it was for pretty nefarious reasons. She turned out to be a psycho serial killer."

Koren gasped. "*Seriously?*"

"Seriously."

"I'm so sorry! If it makes you feel better, I'm not. A serial killer, that is. I'm super boring and average. I can't stand to even kill the flies that somehow always find their way into my apartment. And once I found a nest of baby mice under my dryer. Sure, they were cute and all, but baby mice turn into adult mice, which aren't so cute or nice. I had to call Liam to come and get them out, and to set the traps for the adults. And when *those* were caught, my brother had to come back and get those too."

Taco smiled briefly, then sobered. "You look a bit like her. Blonde hair, blue eyes…I just… You caught me by surprise. I've been taking a break from dating, and I wasn't sure what to say—"

"I get it," Koren said. "I do. And it's okay. I *completely* understand. Just chalk it up to me almost dying."

Without thought, Taco reached out to gently cup her cheek in his hand. "You didn't let me finish."

"Sorry," she whispered, standing stock still and staring up at him.

"I'd decided not to date for a while…but there's something about you that I can't resist. You're funny, brave, and you make me laugh. There I was, hunched over in your wreck of a car, and I was *laughing*. That's never happened to me before. I'd love to take you out, Koren. But I've got some baggage. You're going to have to cut me some slack if I get weird on you."

"I understand," she said again. "And for the record, I've got two overprotective older brothers who would like nothing better than to see me become a nun, and two best friends who think I'm over the hill and have signed me up for every dating site known to man."

"I've tried my hand at a few of those," Taco said with a smile. "Can't say they worked out for me."

"Me either." Koren smiled. "But hey, maybe there's something to this connecting-with-a-hot-fireman-by-wrecking-your-car thing."

"You're the first woman I've ever even considered dating after meeting her on the job," Taco told her seriously.

"Well, *technically* we didn't meet on the job. Quinn introduced us in the grocery store, so it's okay."

When he didn't say anything, her smile dimmed a bit. "Like I said. Don't go out with me because you feel sorry for me. I'm perfectly happy with my life. I don't need a man, I'm capable of paying my own bills, changing my own lightbulbs, and last week I even replaced the bobber thingy in my toilet. All by myself."

"Baby mice?" Taco teased.

She grimaced, but said, "I've got two brothers for emergencies."

"Right." He took a deep breath. "You scare the shit out of me," Taco admitted.

"Me? I'm completely harmless."

He snorted. "You have no clue how wrong that statement is."

"Koren?" Carter called out. "You probably should get home to rest."

She rolled her eyes again.

Taco realized his hand was still on her cheek. "You're really all right?" he asked, knowing his time with her was almost up. He caressed her jaw with his thumb.

"Yeah. The doctor said I would be sore for a while, and I've got these nice black eyes forming, but I'm okay."

"I'm glad."

"Me too."

"Koren." Liam this time. "Time to go…"

Taco reluctantly dropped his hand and pulled out his phone. "Can I get your number?"

She recited it for him, and he punched it in. "I'm going to shoot you a text so you have mine too."

"Cool."

"Use it," he ordered.

"Yes, sir," she quipped.

"Time's up," Liam said as he strolled over. "Sorry…uh…Taco, but we need to get our sister home."

Taco understood what the other man was doing. Just what an older brother should—making sure Taco knew that Koren wasn't alone. That she had people who had her back. And that he'd better not mess with her. That part wasn't something Taco could have missed.

"Of course." Then he turned to Koren. "I'm glad you're okay."

"Thanks. Me too," she said.

Liam hooked her arm over his and turned her toward the exit. Taco didn't follow the entourage. He was slightly amused at the various comments he overheard, though.

"*Damn*, Kor. He's hot!" Sue exclaimed.

"Please tell me he was giving you his number when he got out his phone?" Vicky asked.

"What kind of a name is *Taco*?" Liam grumbled.

Kelle elbowed her husband in the side and hissed, "Hush!"

Carter didn't say anything, just eyeballed him for a brief moment before turning his back and following his sister out of the hospital.

But Koren's mom turned right before they were all out the doors, and she gave him a subtle thumbs-up.

Taco couldn't help it, he burst out laughing.

So far, Koren already seemed different as night and day from Jen, his psycho ex, that was for sure. He hadn't met any of Jen's friends, hadn't even known if her parents were still living or not. She'd worn buckets of makeup, never had a hair out of place, and was always impeccably dressed.

Koren was like a breath of fresh air. Saying what she thought when she thought it, rocking a pair of borrowed hospital scrubs and, even with two black eyes, knocking his socks off.

Yeah, it was safe to say Taco was interested. He didn't want to be, and hadn't planned on dating anyone for at least ten frickin' years, but damn. He couldn't resist Koren.

Waving goodbye to the nurse at the desk, he left the hospital feeling ten times happier than when he'd entered.

CHAPTER THREE

Koren breathed a sigh of relief when her friends and family finally left. It was after dinner and everyone had insisted on staying to make sure she was all right.

She had a headache and every muscle in her body hurt, but Koren knew how lucky she'd been. She'd seriously thought she was a goner. The only thing that saved her was the way she'd thrown herself to the side right before her car impacted the truck.

She had a ton of stuff to do, including a call to her insurance company to see what they'd give her for her car. She also had to catch up on emails from the lost day of work.

But right now, all she wanted to do was sit on the couch for a moment and soak up the peace and quiet. She loved her friends and family. They were well-meaning and it felt great to be able to call and have them there in a heartbeat. But they were also exhausting. They'd all come to her condo to make sure she had everything she needed. Her mom had made a turkey casserole after sending her dad to the store to pick up the ingredients. Sue and Vicky had wanted to talk about the "hot firefighter" who "couldn't take his eyes off her," and her brothers grumbled all night about how forward Taco had been, putting his hand on her face and all.

She'd done her best to pacify everyone, because that's what she always did as the peacemaker of her family, but inside, Koren was a mixed-up jumble of confusion and nerves. She couldn't stop thinking about Taco showing up at the hospital. Yes, he'd said that it was on his way home from the station, but she had a feeling he'd been lying.

After she'd asked him out at the accident scene, and he'd politely demurred, she was humiliated but had figured that was that. She should've kept her mouth shut, but no, she had to go and ask him out like a star-struck dummy.

She hadn't thought she'd ever see him again—and if she did, Koren had already planned to duck out of sight if possible. But then he'd shown up at the hospital, confusing the heck out of her.

At first she'd wondered if he'd assumed she'd be there pining away for him or something, or maybe pissed that he'd turned her down. And, if she was being honest with herself, she *had* done a little pining. But the presence of her loved ones had done a lot to pull her head out of her ass.

She was alive. And for a couple terrifying seconds today, she wasn't sure that was going to be a possibility.

Now she was finally alone.

She probably had a million work details to catch up on and trips to research and book, but she was too tired and hurting too much to even think about diving into that right now.

Shuffling into her kitchen, she opened her fridge to get a bottle of water and had to smile at the amount of leftovers that were stashed there. Her mom had gone a little crazy, wanting to make sure she had meals for the next few days.

Koren shook out one of the prescription, heavy-duty acetaminophen tablets Robin had run out and picked up for her, drinking half the bottle of water as she swallowed it. Recapping the bottle, she put it back in her fridge and shuffled to her bedroom.

After brushing her teeth, Koren stood naked in front of the mirror in her bathroom and examined her bruised and battered body.

There were bruises around her hips and across her chest from the seat belt. Her black eyes were already darker, and she had various other bruises on her arms and legs. Turning, she craned her head carefully to see her back. She had a bruise the size of a fist on her upper back. Koren didn't remember anything hitting her, but obviously something had.

There were a few cuts and scrapes, but again, she had no recollection of being sliced. With the amount of glass flying through the air, though, it wasn't surprising. She'd been so incredibly fortunate. There was no doubt.

As she continued to stare at herself, other thoughts creeped in.

No longer thinking about her wounds, Koren couldn't help but notice the way her stomach pooched out a bit. Her boobs sagged a little too much, and there wasn't even a hint of space between her thighs. She'd never thought of herself as fat, but looking in the mirror now, Koren couldn't help but wonder what Taco thought of how she looked.

Koren had never been called skinny in her entire life. She just didn't have the genes. She was average height at five-seven, and she had a perfectly average body to go with it. She wasn't fat, really; she just wasn't skinny. Yes, she had blonde hair and blue eyes, but she'd never come close to being what might be considered conventionally beautiful.

On those dating sites she'd mentioned to Taco, she'd received a total of five messages from men. She'd had to reach out to everyone else she'd talked to. No one would ever call her a bombshell, and it hadn't ever really bothered her before now.

Before Taco.

Disgusted with her line of thinking, Koren quickly turned away from the mirror. She pulled out her nightgown and slipped it over her head. She padded into her bedroom and climbed under the covers, sighing in satisfaction as she did.

She was drained. She loved her family, but they were extremely tiring. And listening to Sue's and Vicky's innuendos all afternoon had been just as arduous. They were both happily married, and they desperately wanted her to find a man of her own. But just because she was interested in Taco didn't mean they were going to live happily ever after.

She might find out he had some sort of terrible habit she couldn't overlook. Or he might decide she was a little too quirky for his tastes. More than one man had told her that her sense of humor went a little far sometimes. Wanted to know why she couldn't ever be serious.

Life was too short to spend it being grumpy and staid. She liked laughing. Liked having a good time. Drama was a huge turnoff for Koren.

Reaching for her phone on the nightstand, she turned onto her side and checked to see if she had any messages. She wasn't really expecting any, as those closest to her had been with her all day, so she was surprised to see the number three on the text-message icon.

Clicking on it, she saw the first message Taco had sent with his number while they'd been in the hospital. But there were two others from him as well. She'd obviously missed them while she'd been visiting with her family all afternoon.

Taco: Just wanted to check up on you. Make sure you got home all right.

The next message was sent ten minutes after the last.

Taco: That last message wasn't exactly the truth. I've been sitting here thinking about you and wondering how you're feeling. I keep seeing in my mind what your car looked like as I came up to it, and I'm still amazed that you're not only alive, but you had barely a scratch. I'm not a real religious guy, although I do believe in God, and I can't help but think there has to be a reason you're still here right now. I know you've got more than enough people there to make sure you have everything you need and to take care of you, but I still can't stop worrying. Thank you for having the guts to ask me out. As I said before, my hesitation was because I had told myself I didn't want to date, but you were so calm today, and every time you opened your mouth you surprised the hell out of me, and by the time I got you out, I wanted to know more. Okay, this message is way too long, but I wanted to make sure you knew that I didn't say yes out of pity or obligation. I like you, Koren, and I don't think I've ever been quite so intrigued by a woman before. Don't be a hero, take your pain meds. You're gonna need them. If this text hasn't freaked you out, I'll talk to you later.

Koren read Taco's message three times in a row before closing her eyes with a sigh. Yeah, she'd made the first move, but Taco had more than made up for his lack of initiative with his text.

Frowning, she tried to figure out what she should say back. Ignoring him didn't even cross her mind. She wasn't one to play games and she wasn't about to start now. Finally, she lifted her phone and began to type.

Koren: I got home and everyone stayed until after dinner. I didn't see your text until just now, which is why it took me so long to get back to you. Truth be told, I've been thinking about you too. I wasn't calm today, not in the least, but hearing your composed voice telling me that I was all right made me believe it. I was panicking until you got there. I'm sorry I made you uncomfortable when I asked you out. I hadn't planned on it, but the words just kinda snuck out. But, I'm not sorry I did it. Life is too short to not go for what you want. I was reminded of that today. And don't worry, if things don't work out, I'm not going to go all stalker on you. We might find that what-ever connection we're feeling (I'm feeling?) may only be because of the accident. I took a pill tonight, and I'll definitely continue to take them as long as I need to. Good night.

. . .

Hesitating a second before hitting send, Koren muttered "fuck it" and sent the text. She put the phone back on the nightstand and closed her eyes, willing sleep to come.

Two minutes later, her phone vibrated.

Surprised, Koren reached for it and read the short text Taco had sent.

Taco: We definitely have a connection. I was interested that day I met you in the grocery store.

His words made her smile. Koren remembered that meeting. Quinn, a woman she'd met in the grocery store previously, had introduced them, and she'd thought Taco was hot then, just as she thought he was hot now. She put the phone back on the table next to the bed and closed her eyes once more. She was asleep within minutes.

On the other side of the city, Nadine Patterson sat at a rickety table she'd found next to a trash heap and sorted through her notes. The trailer around her creaked and moaned and she could feel the wind coming through the cracks and holes.

But she didn't care about any of that.

Didn't care that she had a warrant out for her arrest for failure to appear on her DUI case.

Didn't care that the authorities had cleared her in the death of her son, because of *course* she'd had nothing to do with that.

All Nadine cared about was revenge.

Hudson Vines had killed her son.

She'd found his name when his picture had been in the paper the day after he'd killed her boy—and he'd been called a *hero*.

Some fucking hero. She knew the truth.

His one and only job was to rescue people from burning buildings, and he'd failed. He'd taken too long to go into her house and get her Stevie. Probably because he was fucking scared.

He was a coward—and he couldn't be allowed to continue as a firefighter. Other lives were at stake.

But the police had done nothing.

She'd have to prove to everyone that he had killed her son!

Stevie hadn't died because he'd had alcohol in his system, like the coroner said. He hadn't died because she'd left him home alone while she went and scored some meth. He was thirteen. Plenty old enough to handle a little beer. And she'd been leaving him home by himself since he was seven.

No—her baby had died because of that damn firefighter, Hudson fucking Vines!

He would pay.

She just needed a bit more information before she could put her plan in motion. She knew who his friends were, where they lived, where *he* lived…now she just had to discover the most important thing in his life. She had to take that away from him. Then they'd be even. He had to feel the pain she'd felt when the most important thing in *her* life had been ripped away. The pain she *still* felt.

Once she'd done that, her little Stevie could rest in peace.

Shuffling her notes around, Nadine took a swig out of the vodka bottle next to her, wincing as the liquid burned its way down. She noticed her hands shaking, and she knew the alcohol wasn't going to cut it for much longer. She needed something else. Needed just a bit of meth to keep her awake, so she could plan.

"He's gotta pay," she slurred as she stared at the names of the men and one woman Hudson Vines worked with most frequently at Station 7. "He'll be sorry he didn't try harder."

CHAPTER FOUR

Koren had exchanged a few texts with Taco over the last few days, but they hadn't pinned down a time and day for a date. It was making her nervous. Maybe he'd had second thoughts about going out with her.

She was feeling much better, and even the black circles under her eyes had faded. She covered the rest of the color with makeup and had decided today was the day she was getting out of the house.

Liam had picked up a rental car for her and dropped it off at her condo. Koren knew it was just an excuse to check on her, but she didn't mind. She didn't know when the check from the insurance company would arrive, but she'd see if Liam or Carter could go with her to buy a new vehicle when it did. Or maybe her dad. Gavin Garner might be in his sixties, but he was still a man to be reckoned with when it came to bargaining.

As she got into the small rental, Koren was already having second thoughts. She wasn't sure she should be doing what she'd planned, but nothing ventured, nothing gained. And Vicky and Sue had helped talk her into it.

Making sure the plate of cookies was secure on the seat next to her, Koren carefully pulled out of her neighborhood. This was the first time she'd driven since her accident, and even though she wasn't going far, she still felt a little nervous.

She drove cautiously, making sure not to go above the speed limit and to fully stop at all stop signs. Surprised at how close Station 7 was to her condo, Koren was pulling into their parking lot before she knew it.

There seemed to be a lot of vehicles there, including a Kia and a few pickup trucks as well. She parked and grabbed the plate of goodies and headed for the front door.

Koren had never been inside a fire station and wasn't sure of the proper protocol. She stood outside the door for a moment, trying to decide if she should just leave the cookies and run or if she had the guts to see this through.

Deciding she'd rather know now if Taco had just been humoring her or if he really did want to see her again, she knocked loudly on the door.

It took a few moments, but before she had to make

the decision as to whether to knock again or leave, the door opened.

A large Native American man dressed in a pair of cargo pants and a T-shirt with the Station 7 logo on it stood there. He had long black hair pulled back in a ponytail, and he nonchalantly crossed his arms and eyed her up and down before saying, "Can I help you?"

"Um...yeah. I'm Koren. I brought cookies." She hefted the plate a little, drawing his attention to it.

He smirked and dropped his arms. "Can't say I've ever met a cookie fairy before."

It took her a second, but Koren chuckled. "Sorry, apparently I haven't had enough caffeine today. I wanted to thank Mick and Taco for helping me the other day. I wasn't sure what they liked, and I didn't think a huge bouquet of flowers would go over as well as sweets."

When the large man just continued to stare at her, she went on nervously. "I don't know if they're allergic to anything, or if they're on any kind of diet. You know, like gluten-free, Keto, carb-free... These cookies are full of peanuts, carbs, *and* gluten, so they might not even like them, but I had to do something. It's not every day that you find yourself trapped under an eighteen-wheeler and have a couple of firefighters show up like your own personal guardian angels."

"From what I heard, sweetheart, your guardian angels weren't Mick and Taco. Those angels had worked overtime long before our guys showed up."

Koren nodded. "You're right. By all accounts, I shouldn't be standing here today. But I am. And I have cookies. If I'm not allowed to come in, can I leave them with you?"

The handsome firefighter shook his head as if berating himself. "Sorry. You're absolutely allowed inside. Come on." He held out a welcoming hand. "I'm Chief. Mick isn't on shift right now, but Taco's here. I'll even snag one or two of those cookies and put them aside for Mick, because if I don't, there's no way they'll last until the next shift."

Koren returned his smile and followed him into the fire station. There was a slight scent of smoke on the air, which she attributed to the nature of the job. She followed Chief, still gripping the plate of cookies as if it was the only thing holding her together.

She heard the group of people before she saw them.

The moment she stepped into a large, open living area, she stopped.

She'd expected a bunch of guys to be sitting around, eating pizza, maybe playing video games. But what she got looked like a casual dinner party or something. Yes, there were guys hanging out, but they were all doing so with women in their arms.

Koren recognized Quinn right away. She was sitting on the lap of the man she'd been with in the grocery store. The way he was looking at Quinn was beautiful. He gazed at her with such love, it was easy to see even all the way across the room.

Chief abandoned her at the entryway of the room and headed for a tall woman with white-blonde hair who was standing in the kitchen. He wrapped his arms around her from behind and the woman relaxed into him.

A pregnant woman was sitting sideways on the couch, and one of the firefighters had her feet in his lap, giving her a massage. Sitting in an oversized recliner was another man and woman—and a black lab. The woman had her eyes shut and seemed to be sleeping, from what Koren could see.

A behemoth of a man stood at the large table, wiping it down, and a diminutive woman was at the sink doing dishes.

But the second Koren's eyes met Taco's, everyone else faded.

He'd just come in from a back hallway and was staring at her with a look she couldn't interpret. Koren was so nervous, she wanted to turn and walk right back out. Instead, it seemed like time stood still as she waited to see what he would do.

If he seemed even one little iota upset that she was there, she *would* turn around and leave.

But after seeing surprise in his eyes, Koren was relieved when his mouth turned up in a smile. He immediately headed straight for her.

"Someone's here to see you, Taco," Chief said unnecessarily.

"Hey," Taco said as he got close. "What are you doing here? Are you okay?"

"I'm good. I brought cookies," Koren said, holding the plate up once more.

Taco's gaze brushed the plate, but his eyes came right back to hers. He examined her from head to toe before meeting her gaze once more. "You look good."

Koren knew she was blushing, but couldn't help it. She could count on one hand the number of times a man had told her she looked nice. She knew he meant good as in healthy—as in, not in hospital scrubs with two black eyes—but it still felt good.

"Thanks. I feel much better than a couple days ago."

"I should hope so," he said quietly.

"I hope I'm not intruding. I've been cooped up in my condo a bit too long and figured it was time I emerged from my cocoon. My eyes are at the stage where I won't frighten small children, so I thought I'd bring a little thank you to you and Mick."

"You didn't have to."

She knew he was going to say that. "I know. I wanted to."

"In that case…" Taco said, and lifted the edge of the aluminum foil. He leaned forward and inhaled deeply. Then he looked up at her. "Peanut butter and chocolate?" he asked.

Koren nodded. "And a few butterscotch and chocolate thrown in for good measure, as well."

"Shhhhh," he admonished, crowding her. "Don't let the others hear you."

"Too late!" a man called out. "Bring 'em here. You know the rule."

"Shut it, Squirrel!" Taco yelled back.

"What's the rule?" Koren asked.

Taco sighed. "Whenever someone brings us goodies, they're fair game for everyone."

Koren smiled. "Next time, I'll lace 'em with ex-lax."

Taco looked surprised again for a second—and she was about to tell him that she'd never do that, to him or anyone else—but then he smiled so broadly, Koren felt tingles shoot through her. "Deal," he whispered. Then in a normal voice, he said, "Come on."

He led her over to the kitchen. "You met Chief. This is his woman, Sophie."

"Hi," Koren said.

"Hi," Sophie returned. "And Taco, you can quit calling m-me 'his woman.' You know we got engaged two weeks ago when we visited his m-mom."

"What I want to know is when are all you guys actually getting *married*? We've got a roomful of engaged people, and I want a party, damn it," the blonde at the sink griped.

"Don't look at me," the woman on the armchair with the dog said sleepily. "Dean and I already did the deed before my surgery."

Everyone else started talking at once, explaining why they hadn't actually tied the knot yet.

Taco leaned into Koren. "That's Adeline. She used to have epileptic seizures at least once a day. Coco, her service dog, would warn her before she'd have one. That's how she and Crash met."

He motioned to the others in the room as he pointed them out. "That's Cade standing over there. His fiancée is Beth, she's our resident computer expert…and she's a recovering agoraphobic. She doesn't hang out here much, or anywhere really, but she's as much a part of this motley crew as anyone. Over there is Blythe and Squirrel, and you know Quinn and Driftwood. And Penelope and Moose are standing over by the table, arguing."

"They don't seem to like each other much," Koren observed.

"Actually, they love each other, but they're having a bit of an issue coming to terms with it."

She looked at him with one eyebrow raised.

He merely shrugged. "We're a bit crazy, and a lot loud, but I wouldn't trade this group of men and women for the world."

Just as he said the last word, loud alarm bells rang out.

Koren jumped what felt like ten feet, but Taco soothed her. "Easy, Kor. It's just the tones. I've got to go. Can you stay until I get back?"

She turned and looked up at him. She'd planned on just dropping off the cookies and being on her way. But how could she say no when he'd asked with such hope in his voice? She nodded.

Then he blew her mind by leaning down and kissing her cheek in a barely there caress. "Make sure Blythe doesn't eat all the cookies. She's got a wicked chocolate craving right now. You know...pregnancy hormones."

Then he was rushing out of the room behind the other men and Penelope.

Koren listened as the trucks started up out in the bay and then it was just her and the other women.

Sophie turned to her. "S-So...how do you know Taco?"

Hearing something oddly close to suspicion in the other woman's voice didn't exactly make Koren feel like the welcome mat had been rolled out, but she answered honestly. "I was almost decapitated, and he and Mick were the firefighters who showed up to extricate me from my car, which had been wedged under an eighteen-wheeler's trailer."

"That was you?" Adeline asked in disbelief. "I saw that on the news. Holy crap, I can't believe you're not in the hospital. Are you sure you're okay? Shit, please come sit down." She struggled to get out of the huge chair and out from under her dog, but Coco wasn't helping. She sat on top of her owner, panting happily.

"I'm fine," Koren tried to reassure her.

"Seriously," Blythe said. "I saw the pictures in the newspaper. The top of your car was sheared right off!"

"Yeah. I know. I was there," Koren said dryly.

"Come sit, Koren," Quinn ordered, patting the sofa cushion next to her. Then she turned to the others. "I met Koren a while ago in the grocery store. She was super nice when it seemed like everyone else in the store that day were being dicks."

Once again, Koren got the feeling that there were things being said beneath Quinn's words to the others that she didn't fully understand. She felt awkward and uneasy, but determined to stay until Taco got back. Besides, people generally liked her. She wasn't the kind of person who said shit just to piss everyone off. And, in her occupation, she had to be good at reading people and figuring out their moods.

Koren settled onto the couch next to Quinn and waited for the interrogation to begin. That's what it felt like, at least.

"You'll have to excuse our bad manners," Adeline said without a hint of shame. "The last woman Taco was interested in turned out to be…well…a bitch."

"You mean the psycho serial killer?" Koren asked, not beating around the bush. She didn't play games with men, and she refused to do so with her friends.

And if she was interested in a relationship with Taco, she wanted these women to be her friends. She also liked what she'd seen and observed of them so far. Liked how they teased each other and genuinely seemed to enjoy being in each other's company.

Everyone stared at her in surprise.

45

Koren shrugged. "Was I not supposed to bring it up? Taco told me that he hadn't had a good dating experience, and that I resembled her...at least my hair and eye colors. Rest assured, I am *not* her. I don't know who she is or what she did, but the only thing I murder is plants. I swear to God I can't keep one alive to save my life. My brothers gave me a cactus once, telling me all I had to do was water it once a month and it would live forever. I think it lasted like two months. Max."

"Jennifer Hale," Quinn said. "Her name was Jennifer Hale. She was the leader of The Edge Community Church. She kidnapped me because she thought I was marked by the devil, and she almost succeeded in burning me alive. She *did* succeed in murdering I'm not sure how many others to rid them of the devil inside *them*, as well."

Her words were flat and unemotional, but Koren saw the way she clenched her hands in her lap.

"Holy shit! Seriously? Why did she think you had the devil inside you?" Koren asked.

Quinn blinked in surprise. "Are you kidding?"

"No."

Quinn gestured to the birthmark on her face. "Because of the devil's mark on my face, of course."

Koren sat back, stunned. "Well, that's just stupid," she said hotly. "It's just a bunch of overactive capillaries! It's not like you did anything to *make* it happen."

There was silence following her pronouncement. Before Sophie declared, "I like her."

"Me too," Adeline said.

"Me three," Blythe echoed.

"Me four," Quinn said with a smile.

Koren stared at Quinn. "Are you okay?"

She nodded. "John got to me in time."

"John?" Koren asked.

"Driftwood. I call him John," Quinn explained.

"Oh. I don't even know Taco's real name. Should I be calling him that?"

"No!" four voices said at once.

Koren flinched in surprise. "Well…okay then."

Blythe explained, "Taco doesn't like his given name. We don't know why. But that bitch refused to call him Taco. Said it wasn't right. We tried to tell her how much he hated his name, but she wouldn't listen to us."

"She only dated him to get to me," Quinn said sadly. "He feels as if it's his fault that she kidnapped me because, you know, he brought her around and tried to help her fit in. But in reality, it's my fault *he* was put in that situation."

"Bullshit," Koren said without thought. Then winced. "Sorry. But seriously, it sounds like everything that happened was the psycho bitch's fault. But now I get why he wasn't exactly thrilled when I asked him out."

"You asked *him* out?" Adeline asked. "This I gotta hear."

Koren sighed. "Yeah, I'd just survived something I knew I really shouldn't have, and he was acting all concerned and stuff, and I just blurted it out. He let me down easy, but yeah." Now that Koren knew who Taco's ex was, she understood his reluctance a bit more. And she was beginning to think he really *had* only agreed to be nice. She wouldn't want to date again so soon if it had been *her* in the situation Taco had been in. If she'd dated a man who had gone after Vicky or Sue, she'd never forgive herself.

Quinn leaned toward Koren. "But then he said yes, right?"

Koren nodded. "He came to see me in the hospital and agreed to go out with me. But we haven't really talked since then. Only a text here and there. I thought maybe if I came by with cookies, we could set something up." She sighed and looked down at her hands.

Quinn reached out and covered Koren's hand with one of her own. Looking up, Koren saw the other woman staring at her with compassion.

"Don't give up on him," she said. "He's a good guy. Everyone who works here is. He's just gone through a lot and feels a ton of guilt as a result."

It felt a little weird getting dating advice from someone she didn't know all that well, but these women knew Taco a hell of a lot better than she did.

"I just… This is going to sound bad…but I'm not interested in dating someone who's just looking for a good time. You know? I'm thirty-three, and both of my best friends are married already. I want to find someone I can laugh with. Hang out with. I don't care if we don't have the same interests in movies or books. I just don't want to waste my time with someone who isn't looking for something long term."

"He's looking for something long term," Quinn reassured her.

"How do you know?" Koren asked.

"Look around you. Look at *us*. This is what he's surrounded by every day. His best friends, who are like brothers to him, are all engaged or married. And he told Sawyer he was envious. I think that's why he latched on to Jen as fast as he did, and why he tried so hard to get us to like her. Because he desperately wants what his friends have."

Koren bit her lip, then decided to just tell the women what she was thinking. "But…I'm really boring. I have no idea what Taco or anyone else could possibly see in me."

The other women burst into laugher.

Hurt, Koren pressed her lips together.

"S-Sorry, Koren, we're not laughing *at* you," Sophie said. "It's just that after everything that's happened, I think Taco would welcome a little boring."

That made sense. "Yeah, the ex-psycho girlfriend thing," Koren said.

"No. Not just that." Adeline took a deep breath. "Beth, Sledge's girlfriend, was kidnapped by a serial killer out in California and barely survived his torture. She's agoraphobic now, and was also a bit of a pyromaniac for a while."

"And Adeline was having seizures every day and could've died from them. Then her boss tried to rape her when they were at a business conference," Blythe explained.

"And Blythe was homeless," Sophie explained. "Then when s-she was trying to find her friend, Hope —who you'll probably m-meet at s-some point—a gang downtown almost killed her and S-Squirrel."

"And *Sophie* ran into a burning building that a doctor she worked with had set on fire. She almost died," Blythe explained.

Koren could only stare at one woman then the next as they explained their histories.

"So yeah, I think Taco would probably welcome some boring in the woman he's dating," Quinn finished.

"Holy crap," Koren breathed. "That stuff really happened to all of you?"

Everyone nodded.

"I don't know whether I should cross myself or rub myself all over you for luck," Koren said.

Everyone laughed.

"Wait until you meet our law enforcement friends' women," Adeline said. "Our stories sound kind of tame compared to theirs."

"I'm not sure what to say," Koren murmured.

"Do you have any scary exes?" Blythe asked.

Koren shook her head.

"Any terrible bosses?" Adeline asked.

"No, nothing."

"Your parents aren't devil worshipers? No hidden disabilities that could cause issues down the line?" Quinn asked.

"No. I'm perfectly average. I have two brothers—who I love, by the way. They're married and have perfectly normal, boring wives. Not boring, like I-don't-like-them boring. Just...*normal*. My parents are awesome, if not a little meddlesome, but I wouldn't have them any other way. Both sets of grandparents are still living, one set in Florida and the other in Alaska—don't ask; they like the cold weather. Now I'm *definitely* afraid I'm not interesting enough...should I make up a stalker or something?" Koren asked, only half-kidding.

"Good Lord, no!" Adeline said. "Be glad. I, for one, am thrilled that you've got no scary bad guys lurking in your past or present. I think it'll be nice for *one* of the guys to not have to deal with drama every time he turns around."

"Right?" Quinn said. "I swear, most of the time when I was first dating John, I felt like every single day he was fending off assholes who thought they had the right to say whatever they wanted to my face. I felt bad that he had to deal with that kind of thing. Be happy that you won't have any of that, Koren."

"I can't stand drama," Koren told them. "I'm also overly blunt. I'm the girlfriend who will tell you straight up if something you're wearing isn't right for you. Or if you have lettuce in your teeth, or if I hear about your man

51

cheating on you. And yes, I've totally done that last one before. My friend Sue's ex was a douchebag, and I told her without hesitation. I wasn't going to sit back and let her be the only one who didn't know what he was up to."

"I one hundred percent don't think our men would cheat on us," Blythe said, "but you're definitely the kind of friend I want. I think we've all had enough drama to last us a lifetime."

"Agreed," everyone said.

"So I guess that means you're in," Quinn said with a smile.

"I'm in?" Koren asked.

"Yup. We like you. But more importantly, we like you for Taco. Which is *not* what we thought about Jen. You'll be good for him. A nice, normal relationship with zero drama."

It felt good to be accepted by these women. Not that Koren *needed* to be. She had Sue and Vicky and her family. She had a job she loved, a condo she was doing her best to pay off. But somehow, being around the women who dated Taco's friends made her feel good. Like she was a part of something new.

"So, since that's settled, what do you do?" Adeline asked Koren.

Koren relaxed. Now *this* was something she could talk about. "I'm a travel agent who works from home. I'm associated with one of those online agencies. People email in looking for recommendations or for someone to do all the planning for them. I contact them and figure out what their budget is, and what they want, and I get to work finding flights, hotels, rental cars, activities…basically anything they want."

"Really?" Blythe asked, looking excited.

"Really."

"I'm obviously very pregnant, but I wanted to take Sawyer somewhere before this little nugget is born. Just the two of us. One last hurrah before we become parents. But we don't have a huge budget. Do you have any suggestions?"

"Do I have any suggestions?" Koren asked rhetorically. "Hell yes, I do. But I have some questions before I can get serious…"

The next hour was spent getting to know the women and helping Blythe figure out where she was going to take her fiancé. By the time they were finished talking, Koren had some great ideas, but figured she'd talk to Blythe about them when she was alone. She got everyone's phone numbers, and she promised Blythe in particular that she'd be in touch with her soon about trip options.

They all heard the sound of the trucks returning to the bays, and Koren followed suit and stood when the others did. The other women greeted their men as they came back into the room.

Feeling a little weird about still being there, and not knowing exactly where she and Taco stood in regards to their relationship—or non-relationship, as the case may be—she hung back by the couch.

She watched as Taco grinned at his friends, then looked around the room. When he saw that she was still there, he smiled broadly and headed for her.

"Hey," he said when he got close. "You stayed."

"Yeah. Me and the others were talking," Koren told him.

"Things go okay?" he asked.

Understanding where the question was coming from after learning how Jen had acted with the other women, and why, she said, "Yes. Great, actually. They're all awesome and funny."

The relieved expression on his face made Koren want to go and beat the shit out of Jen.

"Any cookies left?" he asked.

Koren chuckled. "We were so busy talking, we didn't even bust into them."

"Good. More for me," he quipped. Then he reached out and grabbed both her hands. His voice lowered, and suddenly it felt as if they were the only two people in the room. "You really are doing okay after the accident? No residual side effects?"

"I'm still sore," she admitted. "And the bruises from the seat belt are pretty horrific. But I can't get too upset, considering it saved my life."

When Taco frowned, and she figured he was two seconds away from wanting to see the bruises for himself to make sure she was all right, she quickly said,

"I'm good, Taco. Promise. Especially when I think about how *not* good I could be right about now."

"True." He looked into her eyes for a moment longer, then dropped her hands. "How about a cookie?"

Koren tried to tamp down the disappointment. She'd hoped he'd been about to ask her out for their first official date. But remembering his history, she simply nodded. "Absolutely."

Taco kicked himself after he'd seen Koren out. The other women were taking their leave as well, and she made it clear that she wasn't exactly comfortable staying when everyone else left...not that he could blame her.

So he'd walked her out, and they'd had some general conversation about her rental and when she expected to get a check from her insurance company so she could purchase a new car. Then he'd taken a step back and waved at her like a dork as he said goodbye.

Koren hadn't seemed upset, but *he* was...with himself. He'd kissed her hello, but couldn't do the same when she was leaving? And he'd been too much of a chicken to even bring up when they might meet for their date.

"Dude, what was that?" Driftwood asked when they were back inside.

"What was what?" Taco asked, trying to feign ignorance.

"Don't give me that bullshit," his friend said. "You fucking *waved* goodbye."

Taco collapsed onto the couch and rested his head on the back cushion. "I don't know. I just...I can't get what Jen did out of my head. What if Koren's like her? What if she's just pity-dating me? Did one of you somehow set me up? Did you tell her what happened and encourage her to ask me out?"

"Fuck you," Sledge said without heat. "We wouldn't do that to you."

"So, you think we orchestrated that huge accident because a car crash would be a good time for her to ask you out?" Crash asked sarcastically.

Running a hand over his short beard, Taco sighed. "No, of course not. Shit, sorry. I'm just having a hard time believing someone like her would want to go out with me."

"Why?" Penelope asked, sitting next to him. "You're good-looking, you have a steady job so you aren't a deadbeat. You have great friends...you're a hell of a guy."

"Hey," Moose complained softly from her other side.

Penelope jabbed an elbow into his ribs, but didn't take her eyes from Taco's.

"Jen was a bitch. Plain and simple. She used you. It sucks. But that doesn't take one thing away from the man you are. Besides," she said, using her ace in the hole. "Everyone liked her. You think *Quinn*, of all people, would welcome anyone who even remotely rubbed her the wrong way? No way in hell. And Blythe might seem quiet, but I've heard her go off about Jen. It's not pretty. I chatted with every one of the ladies before they left. They like Koren. And she's into you, Taco. The only question is, are you ready to do something about it?"

"I...I didn't think so," Taco admitted. "But every time I see her, it gets a little harder to say goodbye."

"Do you just want to fuck her, or is there more?" Penelope asked.

"Jeez, Tiger," Moose complained. "Cut him some slack."

Penelope turned to glare at the big man next to her. "No. I get it. It was a blow to his ego to have Jen only want him to get to Quinn. But if all he wants is someone to make him feel like a 'man' again," she put up her hands and used them as quotes, "then he should go to The Sloppy Cow and have Erin set him up with one of the bar bunnies. I don't know Koren very well, but it's obvious she didn't come here with a fucking plate of cookies, dressed in a pair of well-worn jeans and a nice, modest top, just to try to seduce Taco."

"What would she do if she *was* trying to seduce me?" Taco asked, smiling now.

Penelope shrugged. "I don't know. As I said, I don't know her very well, but I'd guess her jeans would probably be tighter and her shirt would be a lot more low cut. Look, all I'm saying is, be careful. You know how *you* felt after being used by Jen the bitch; don't do the same to Koren."

She had a point. Taco hadn't thought about it that way. He definitely hadn't considered dating Koren just for sex. In the short time he'd been around her, he liked her. She had a funny personality, and he actually felt calm in her presence. He couldn't say that's how he felt when he'd been around his ex.

"I hear you," he finally told Penelope.

"Good." She looked at her watch. "I'm going to go take a nap. And if any of you yahoos wake me up before the tones go off, I'll have to hurt you. Or sic Smokey on you."

Everyone watched as she marched out of the room toward the back hallway and the bedrooms.

"She's getting worse, not better," Sledge observed quietly.

Moose sighed. "I know. She stopped going to therapy, saying it wasn't helping."

"She can't go on like this," Crash warned.

"I *know*," Moose repeated and abruptly stood up. "I don't know how to help her. She won't *let* me help her. It's maddening and frustrating. I'm just afraid that one of these days she's going to break, and it'll be too late to help her at all."

"PTSD doesn't manifest itself the same way in

everyone," Chief said without censure. "One person's path is never the same as someone else's."

"I'm aware of that," Moose said a little testily.

"Maybe she needs to talk to the SEALs or Deltas who were there when she was rescued in Turkey," Squirrel suggested.

"Or maybe she needs to hit rock bottom before she can even think about clawing her way back out," Taco warned.

Without a word, Moose left the room and headed for the back bedrooms. They all knew he was going to talk to Penelope, and that now probably wasn't the best time, but no one stopped him.

The rest of the afternoon and evening were slow as far as calls were concerned. By the time the sun was making its way above the horizon the next morning, Taco had made a decision.

He liked Koren. He'd been prepared to wait years before dating again, but something inside told him if he didn't give Koren a shot, he'd lose his chance—and regret it for the rest of his life.

He wasn't supposed to be on duty when she'd had her accident.

She shouldn't have survived it.

But he was. And she did.

Maybe it was God's way of apologizing for what Jen had done.

Taco didn't know. But he was done being wishy-washy about going out with her.

Maybe they wouldn't get along. Maybe they'd find that they didn't click so well after all. But if he didn't at least try, he'd never know.

The second Mick and the others arrived for their shift the next morning, Taco did what he'd been thinking about for at least an hour before he'd taken a fitful nap.

He was going to go see Koren.

Nadine Patterson sat in the strip mall across the street from Station 7. She wrote down every license plate of every vehicle that entered and exited the parking lot. She didn't have a lot of computer skills, but one of the guys she got her drugs from had a friend who'd been feeding her the information she wanted.

Flipping a page of the notebook on her lap, Nadine checked to make sure she had descriptions of all the cars as well. When she saw *his* Silverado pull out of the lot, she quickly put her notebook to the side and started her car. Pulling out a few cars behind him, Nadine followed.

When he didn't turn toward his house, she grinned.

Hudson Vines really was one of most boring men she'd ever had the misfortune to know. Most of the time he went straight home from work. He went grocery shopping and sometimes visited some of the other asshole firemen he worked with.

But today he was taking a route she hadn't seen him take before.

Looking behind her to make sure she wasn't being followed, Nadine tried to ignore the anxiety she always felt when it had been too long since she'd had a hit. Her regular dealer hadn't shown up the night before, and she hadn't had time to find an alternate source for her stash.

After she found out where the asshole was going, she'd remedy that. She was getting tired, needed the rush the meth gave her. Then she could start putting things into motion. Hudson would suffer, but first she'd terrorize him—*and* all his friends.

The man would rue the day he hadn't tried harder to save her son.

CHAPTER FIVE

Koren startled badly when someone rang her doorbell. Looking at her watch, she saw that it was only nine in the morning. She hadn't heard from Vicky or Sue that they were coming over, and they should be at work anyway. Her parents also usually called before they visited.

Figuring it was someone selling something, she ignored it, turning back to her computer. She was researching a trip to Hawaii for a couple who wanted to go there to celebrate their thirtieth anniversary.

When the doorbell rang again, Koren sighed and pushed back her chair. She looked down at herself and shrugged. Maybe the sweats, T-shirt (without a bra), and fuzzy slippers would scare away whoever it was. She hadn't even brushed her hair after getting out of bed.

Jogging downstairs and crossing to the door, Koren

looked through the peephole—and gasped. She put her back against the door, as if that would somehow change the situation.

She couldn't open the door looking like *this*. Letting Taco see her au natural wasn't going to happen. No way.

But she couldn't just pretend she wasn't home. That was rude. And one thing Koren wasn't, ever, was rude.

She cracked her door open, leaving the safety chain on.

"Hi," she said through the crack.

Taco smiled. "Hey. Sorry about showing up unannounced. Can I come in?"

Koren looked down at what she was wearing, then scrunched her nose and said, "I'm not exactly dressed for company."

"I don't care."

Dang it. He was supposed to apologize and say he'd come back later. "Um…" She frantically tried to think up another excuse. "I just started working, and I've got about a hundred emails to wade through."

"I won't take long."

She huffed out a breath. *Now what?*

"If you don't want me to come in, just tell me," Taco said calmly. "I wanted to talk about our date, but if you've changed your mind about that too, all you have to do is say the word and I'm outta here."

"No!" Koren blurted. "I haven't changed my mind."

Her voice lowered, as did her eyes, as she mumbled, "But if I let you in right now, *you* might."

"Are you okay?" he asked, stepping closer to the door. "Are you hurt?"

"I'm fine," she told him.

"Then why won't you let me in?" he asked.

Sighing, Koren said, "Because I look like I just rolled out of bed…maybe because I *did* just roll out of bed. I haven't showered, haven't even brushed my hair yet. I'm wearing ratty old sweats and my slippers. I'm barely passable on my best days, but I'm pretty sure if you look at me right now, I'll never see you again."

"Open the door," Taco said in a tone Koren hadn't heard from him before.

Still, she hesitated.

"Please," he added.

Sighing, and having a feeling she'd regret it, Koren shut the door so she could undo the chain, then slowly opened it once again. Maybe this was good. If he saw what she looked like now, he wouldn't have any surprises later, right?

She didn't know what she'd expected him to do, but pushing into her foyer and slamming the door with his foot wasn't it. His gaze was penetrating as he stared at her, and Koren instinctively took a step back. Then another.

He stalked forward, matching her step for step. She saw his gaze go from her hair, to her chest, down to her feet, then back up to her face.

But she couldn't read what he was thinking. God, she should've at least kicked off the slippers she'd had forever. She was such a cliché.

"Taco?" she asked when he didn't say anything, just continued to move toward her. Her back hit a wall near the kitchen, and she stared up at him when he didn't stop. He walked right into her space. She put her hands up instinctively, and they rested on his chest. She wasn't sure if she wanted to push him away or pull him closer.

He smelled delicious. Like he'd just showered. His hazel eyes glittered with some emotion she couldn't read. He had a short beard, just enough to cover his jawbone, and Koren's hands itched to move upward and touch it. Would it be rough or soft? She'd never been with a man with a beard before. She never thought she'd be attracted to someone with facial hair, but on Taco, it was sexy as hell.

He brought his hands up and speared them into the hair on either side of her head, gently forcing her head back so she had no choice but to look him in the eye. Her fingers curled on his chest, and she vaguely had the thought that he was all muscle under the black T-shirt he was wearing.

"You think seeing you like this is gonna make me bolt?" Taco asked.

Koren knew she was breathing faster, but she couldn't seem to control it. "Um…yes?"

He huffed out a breath, and Koren could smell peppermint, as if he'd recently brushed his teeth.

"You haven't been with that many men, have you?"

She felt the blush blossom in her cheeks. What kind of a question was that? She wasn't a virgin, but she definitely hadn't had many long-term boyfriends. How could he tell? And it wasn't exactly a polite question.

"Don't answer that; you don't have to. But I hope to God you haven't opened your door to anyone else while looking like this."

She panicked for a second. Jeez, was she *that* hideous?

"Because this is a dream come true for *any* man."

Um... What? But Koren couldn't get her mouth and brain to work together. She could only stare up at him in surprise.

"Sure, men like to see their women all dressed up. Wearing a slinky black or red dress, high heels, a little makeup. I can't deny I like that too. But right now...I'm looking at the sexiest thing I could ever imagine."

He moved one of his hands so it cradled her nape. His thumb caressed the sensitive skin of her neck, making goose bumps spring up on Koren's arms. His other hand slowly ran down her arm—surely feeling how affected she was—before it rested behind her, on the small of her back. His hand felt huge against her, heavy.

Had he called her *sexy*? Koren was so confused.

"You have no clue what I'm talking about, do you?" he asked.

Koren shook her head. "No. In fact, I think you must've hit your head after I left the station. Do you feel okay?"

His lips quirked, but he got serious again immediately. "Your hair is all mussed, like you truly did just climb out of bed. Your face is devoid of any makeup, so I can see the real you. Your clothes are relaxed and comfy. *You're* relaxed and comfy, from the oversized T-shirt down to your fuzzy slippers. And all I can imagine is waking up next to you and looking over and seeing you just like this."

Koren knew her mouth was hanging open, but she couldn't seem to close it.

"I see you're gettin' it. You look delightfully mussed, Koren. There's only one thing missing."

"What?" she whispered.

Taco's eyes flicked down to her lips—and then he was kissing her. His hands holding her tightly against him, but not so tight that if she protested, he wouldn't let go. Koren knew down to the marrow of her bones, if she put the slightest pressure on her hands, to push him away, he'd immediately back off.

But she didn't want him to back off. If anything, she wanted him closer.

She fisted her hands, crushing his shirt in her fists and pulling him toward her.

His head tilted one way and hers tilted the other.

His tongue twined with hers, playfully at first, then more seductive. She could feel his rock-hard body against her own. His mustache and beard tickled her face. It was an odd feeling, but she liked it.

She whimpered in her throat and raised a leg without thought, trying to get closer to him. To absorb him into her.

But he pulled back, nipping at her bottom lip as he did.

Koren dropped her leg and stared up at him. He was still holding her, the hand at her back pressing her against him, the fingers at her nape feeling like a brand.

"*That's* what was missing," he said with satisfaction.

"What?" she asked again, licking her lips.

He groaned and shut his eyes for a moment. Koren could feel his length against her lower belly. He was hot and hard...and for the first time in her life, she finally understood what lust was. She'd been attracted to her past lovers and boyfriends, but she'd never felt anything like *this*. Like she'd die if she couldn't feel him inside her in the next ten seconds. Her panties were soaked—from a *kiss*. That hadn't ever happened before either.

She bit her lip to try to keep herself from doing something really embarrassing...like sinking to her knees and begging him to let her take him in her mouth.

His eyes opened, and the heat she saw in them made

her panic for a second, wonder if she'd said the words out loud.

He brought his hand forward and ran his thumb over her lips. "*This*. Kiss-swollen lips."

Koren didn't know what to say. Her mind was blank. He'd short-circuited her brain.

"Barely passable on your good days?" he asked. "I seriously don't understand women. I can't speak for other men, but I'm not looking for a supermodel, Koren. I want someone who I'm not afraid to muss up. Who I can kiss without getting lipstick all over myself. Who can eat a doughnut and not worry about whether or not it'll go straight to her hips. I want a woman who is comfortable enough in her own skin to hang out in a T-shirt and sweats and doesn't have to be perfect all the time."

"I had a Pop-Tart for dinner last night, does that count?" she asked quietly.

Taco smiled. "Perfect," he whispered. Then he took a deep breath and stepped away from her. Or at least he tried to. Koren clung to his T-shirt, not letting him go.

"What did you want to talk about again?" she asked softly.

"I wanted to see when you were free to go on our date. I was an idiot yesterday, and I should've asked you then."

"I get it," Koren reassured him. "If I had an ex like yours, I would be just as gun-shy."

"You have a lot of exes?" he asked.

She shook her head.

"Good," he said, and his gaze flicked down to her mouth again, before meeting her eyes once more.

"Tonight?" she asked.

Satisfaction lit his expression. "Perfect," he said. "Five?"

She liked that he was anxious to see her again. She usually worked until around six, but she'd definitely make an exception to stop early today. "Sounds good."

Neither moved.

Finally, she asked, "What should I wear?"

Taco took a deep breath, then said, "This?"

Koren chuckled. "Um, *you* might like me looking like a slob, but I'm not sure anyone else would be impressed."

"Not a slob—comfy," he corrected. "And I don't give a shit about anyone else."

It was a good answer. "Seriously, Taco. Are we talking jeans and a nice top, a skirt and a nicer top, or that little black dress you mentioned?"

"You have a little black dress?" he asked, his eyebrows rising.

"Well, no. But I could go buy one today if I needed to. I'm sure Vicky or Sue would take a long lunch and go with me."

Taco grinned. "You'd do that for me?"

"What? Go shopping?" she asked. "Unlike most women, I don't particularly like to shop, but yeah, if you said you were taking me somewhere fancy and I needed to dress up, I'd dutifully go and find an appropriate dress and something classier than the ten-dollar flip-flops I have with sparkly flowers on the thongs."

His eyes drifted down to her feet. "I'm gonna want to see you dressed up one of these days," he said. "But tonight, I'm thinking jeans will be more suitable."

"Okay," she said. She willed her fingers to let go of his shirt. She looked down and saw that she'd wrinkled the hell out of the material. She tried to smooth it, with no luck. "Sorry," she mumbled.

Taco chuckled. He covered one of her hands with his and pressed it against his chest. "You have a lot to do today?"

She shrugged. "A decent amount. I'm still catching up from the time I took off after the accident."

"You'll take it easy?"

Koren nodded.

"I should let you get back to it," Taco said, but didn't remove his hand from the small of her back.

"You want coffee?"

He groaned.

"What? You don't drink coffee?"

"Of course I do. But I don't want to do anything that might make you uncomfortable, and right now I'm thinking awfully hard about kissing you again."

Koren bit her lip.

"Fuck, sweetheart. Don't look at me like that. Maybe if you were wearing regular clothes, I'd stay. But if I sit across a table from you, with you looking like you do, I'm not sure I'd be able to control myself."

"I trust you," Koren said softly.

"And that means the world to me," Taco said. "Do me a favor?"

"Sure. What?"

"Don't answer the door looking like you just crawled out of bed if it's not me on the other side, okay?"

"Taco, I don't think you understand. No one cares."

"You're wrong. They care. You're entirely too irresistible, looking like you do right now. I think I proved that."

"It's not like I've had any other guys back me into my house and kiss me until my toes curled," she protested.

"Your toes curled?" he asked softly.

Knowing she was blushing again, Koren shrugged shyly.

"Okay, now I'm *really* going. I'll be back at five," Taco said. Then he dropped his hands and took a giant step back from her. He looked her up and down once more and took another deep breath. Then he backed away toward her front door. "Lock this behind me," he ordered.

"I will." Koren followed him at a distance as he kept backing up. He reached behind himself and grabbed the handle of the door when he got near enough.

"I want this to be exclusive," he said abruptly.

Koren frowned in confusion.

"Us," he gestured back and forth between them, "dating. I want to be the only one you're seeing."

"Oh…of course. I don't date more than one man at a time. Um…do you? With women, I mean? Are you seeing someone else?"

He huffed out a chuckle. "No. So…it's settled. We're exclusive."

Koren nodded.

"Good. And for the record, this'll be the last time I leave without giving you a goodbye kiss. I don't think my heart could take kissing you again right now. Besides…I'm giving you time to get used to me."

"*This* is giving me time to get used to you?" Koren asked incredulously.

He grinned. "Yeah. See you tonight." Then he turned and strode out the door toward his pickup.

Koren watched until he pulled out of her driveway and headed down the street. Then she shut the door and leaned against it again. She brought her fingers up to her mouth and traced her lips. Smiling, she screeched and did an impromptu little dance right there in her foyer.

CHAPTER SIX

Taco pulled into Koren's driveway at five minutes 'til five. He'd been driving around the neighborhood passing time for the last ten minutes. He didn't want to be too early. He'd spent the day doing errands and looking forward to getting to know Koren.

Now that his brain had gotten past the blockade of wanting to date someone, he was one hundred percent all in. And seeing Koren in her house looking like she'd just tumbled out of bed had been a huge wake-up call for him.

He'd *never* seen Jen looking like that. She'd always worn makeup, day and night, and he'd never seen her with a single hair out of place.

And when he'd kissed her, she'd never, *ever* reacted the way Koren had.

He could still remember the way her hands clenched his T-shirt, how the material tightened against his back. She'd been as into that kiss as he'd been. And it had been one of the hardest things he'd ever done to pull back and step away from her.

She had no idea of her appeal. None. And that in itself was a huge turn on. He'd been honest with her; he didn't want his woman to be coveted by every man they came into contact with. He knew himself. It would drive him crazy trying to make sure everyone knew she was taken.

Koren was perfect, as far as he was concerned. She wasn't beautiful in the traditional sense. She wasn't tall and boney like most models, and she had a lot of laugh lines around her eyes and healthy curves on her body that the masses might not fawn over. But *all* those things increased the appeal for Taco. She made him think of relaxing evenings at home, cuddling on his couch. The laugh lines around her eyes drew attention to the fact she'd led a happy life. He definitely got the impression she wasn't afraid to be herself.

And that's exactly what he wanted. Someone real. A woman without secrets. Someone who would support him, and who he could support in return. He wanted someone who wouldn't be afraid to go mudding one day and out to a fancy dinner the next.

Taco was well aware he also wanted what all his friends had found. Beth, Adeline, Sophie, Blythe, Quinn...even Penelope...they were all very similar. Down to earth, supportive, but with ambitions and goals of their own. He didn't want to marry someone who thought the man should be the sole breadwinner in the family. He wanted a partner.

And he had a feeling that Koren just might be that person. It was too early to know for sure, but some of the signs were there.

Feeling at peace with his decision to date again, Taco knocked on her door. It opened within seconds, as if she'd been waiting for him.

Not able to help the comparison that sprang to mind, he remembered always having to wait on Jen. He'd never been invited to her home, and she was always late in meeting him when they went out.

"Hi," she said somewhat shyly.

She looked great. Jeans with a dark purple V-neck shirt that showed off a hint of cleavage. When he looked down at her feet, he grinned. "I take it these are the infamous sparkly flower flip-flops?"

She returned his smile and held out a foot. "One and the same."

"I like 'em," Taco told her.

"It's a good thing, because you'll probably be seeing them a lot. They're comfortable and somewhat dressy, so I wear them anytime I can get away with it."

Taking a step toward her, Taco leaned close. Her hands came up and grabbed hold of his biceps as his lips brushed hers.

She sighed, and Taco could smell the minty scent of her toothpaste. She also smelled like peaches. He wanted to bury his nose into the space between her shoulder and neck, but he controlled himself. He loved the way her fingers tightened on his arms when he pulled back, as if she wanted to hold him close.

Once again, thoughts of Jen reared in. She'd frequently turned her head when he'd tried to kiss her. As if she couldn't bear his touch. And she *never* gave any indication that she actually liked him being near. Unlike Koren, who seemed to grab hold of him whenever he got within reach.

"Ready to go?" he asked.

"Yeah. I just need to grab my purse. Taco?"

"Yeah, sweetheart?"

"I…thank you."

"For what?"

"For giving us a shot. It's been a long time since I've been this excited about going out with someone. And I'm not saying that to pressure you. I mean, we might find that we don't click, or that we don't have enough in common. I know you weren't all fired up to go out with anyone after that bitch, and I don't blame you, not in the least. But thanks for taking a chance on me."

"I won't lie," Taco said. "You're a surprise. I was all ready to be done with dating for the foreseeable future. But there's something about you that I'm drawn to. And I admire you for having the guts to go after what you want. I have a feeling that we're going to click quite nicely."

She licked her lips, and Taco wanted to lean down and taste them once again. She turned to get her purse, and Taco waited by the door, undecided. He wanted to follow her inside again. Back her up against the wall and take everything he'd been thinking about all day. The kiss he'd stolen earlier had been hotter than anything he'd experienced in recent memory.

He could easily imagine her looking at him exactly the same way she had after he'd kissed her...but from next to him in his bed. Hair mussed, no makeup, just her.

He didn't tell her this morning, to avoid freaking her out...but something seemed to overcome him the second he'd seen her, after she'd opened the door. A vision of Koren in his kitchen, wearing exactly what she'd been in that morning, cooking breakfast for him —and their three kids.

It was just a flash, but it had been so vivid, so *real*, that Taco'd had to touch her. Had to kiss her. It was completely unlike him, but equally unavoidable.

He knew those thoughts were crazy. They'd just met, for God's sake. But he couldn't help but feel as if she was important to him for some reason. That she'd been put in that car, at that crash, so he'd find her again. Why, he hadn't figured out yet. But Taco wasn't a stupid man. He knew quality when he saw it. Why some other man hadn't snatched Koren up and put a ring on her finger yet, he had no idea. But he'd be damned if he didn't snatch her up now.

No, he certainly wasn't about to pop the question anytime soon; Jen had taught him to be extremely cautious. But from what he could tell, Koren was pretty much the opposite of that bitch in every way. And that was what he needed. Wanted.

"I'm ready," she said, appearing in front of him.

Without a word, he stepped out of her condo and watched as Koren locked her deadbolt before she turned to him with a smile.

Just to make small talk, he said, "This is a nice area."

"Yeah. My dad helped me with my house search. I know it's a condo, but I can't stand doing yard work, and here, it's all taken care of for me. I've got awesome neighbors too, which is a bonus."

"I never really thought about getting a condo. I don't particularly like yard work either, but I can't stand the thought of having someone share a wall with my place." He shrugged. "Fire hazard and all that. I rented an apartment for years, but was never comfortable with it. I finally bit the bullet and bought a house a few months ago."

She chuckled. "Yeah, I thought about the whole sharing a wall thing too, but honestly, the pros outweighed the cons for me. And I don't really cook, so it won't be *me* who's causing the place to go up in smoke."

Taco eyed the building. It looked like there were eight or nine condos in a row, in one huge building. Then there was a break, and another six or seven condos. The buildings across the street were a mirror image to this one. The condos were two or three stories tall, and looked like they had plenty of room. There were a few kids' toys in a yard down the street, and for the most part, things were quiet and peaceful. It definitely had its appeal.

"You don't cook?" he asked as he followed her to his truck.

She shrugged. "I *can* cook. I just don't enjoy it. My mom can stay in the kitchen all day making dinner and dessert. I'd rather order out or stick a pizza in the oven or something. My brothers' wives love cooking, though."

Taco helped her into his truck and walked around. When he climbed inside, he continued the conversation. "What if I told you I was having some friends over and wanted you to help me put something together?"

Koren was silent so long, Taco finally looked over at her. She was staring at him with an unreadable look on her face.

"What?" he asked.

"I'm not sure what you're fishing for," she admitted.

"It's just a question," he said a little defensively.

"I don't think it is. But fine. If you said you'd invited a bunch of people over and *asked* for my help, I'd first want to know what your friends liked to eat. Were they a beer-and-pizza kind of crowd, or did they prefer something from the grill? Then I'd probably go to the grocery store and pick up a bunch of easy appetizers. I'd suggest that we keep things simple and get paper plates and napkins, because they're easier to clean up. I might even suggest that you ask your friends to bring stuff over too. Someone could bring chips, someone else a dessert, that sort of thing. Then I'd *help* you prepare what needed to be prepared. But if you expected me to slave away in the kitchen all day while you did…whatever…then I'd be pretty pissed."

Taco grimaced. "Sorry. You're right. It was a loaded question, and I didn't even realize it. Your answer was perfect."

After a moment, she said, "I take it that's not what happened with Jen."

"Not even close," he confirmed.

Koren looked down at her hands, then took a deep breath. "Look. I can cut you some slack because she really did a number on you, but I'm not her. And there are only so many times I can reassure you of that. I can't be afraid every time I'm with you that I'm going to say or do something that will remind you of her. It's not fair to either of us. I'm me. I can't say I'm perfect or that I won't do something that's going to irritate you, but I'm not interested in you because of some ulterior motive. I'm attracted to you, Taco. I don't know what else to say or do that will make you believe that."

"I know you're not her," he said. "I can't say there aren't times when I don't compare you to her. But, Kor, I've already come to realize there *is* no comparison. You are head and shoulders so far above her, I'm kicking myself for staying with her as long as I did."

Koren nodded.

"And, for the record, I didn't sleep with her. And I only kissed her twice. That's all she would let me do. She didn't seem to like me touching her, I never met her family or friends, never went over to her place. I was just so stuck on the idea of having a girlfriend, I didn't open my eyes and see what was right in front of my face. And your idea of a dinner party sounds heavenly. It was a perfect answer. I'll try not to be a dick for at least the rest of our date."

She smiled at that, and Taco relaxed a fraction. He hadn't meant to put her on the spot, but she was absolutely right for calling him out on it. Koren wasn't Jen. Period.

"I'm a toucher," Koren admitted. "I can't imagine not touching and being touched. If you don't like that, or if it makes you uncomfortable, then let me know. I can try to curb it, but I'm not sure I'll be all that successful, if this morning was any indication."

Taco put his right hand on the console between them. She looked at him, then down at his hand, then back up to his face. Then she slowly brought her left hand up and placed it in his.

Wrapping his fingers around hers, he used his thumb to brush back and forth over the back of her hand. "I like you touching me, Kor. And I don't care if you do it in front of my friends, either."

"Do you have family?" she asked.

Taco sighed. He didn't really want to get into the crap relationship he had with his parents this early in their date, but it was probably better to get it out of the way. "Yeah, but I don't talk to them much."

"Brothers? Sisters?"

He shook his head. "No. I was an only child. And nothing I did pleased my father. He was super strict, and the harder he pushed me, the more I did the opposite of what he wanted me to do. I joined a local volunteer fire department when I was in high school, and he hated that I spent so much time at the station, shooting the shit with the guys."

"What did he want you to do?" Koren asked.

"I think he wanted me to follow in his footsteps and work in finance. But I hated math. Hated accounting. Sucked at it. I didn't particularly like school all that much. We fought throughout most of high school. I managed to graduate, but my grades were shit."

"And your mom?"

Taco shrugged. "I think she was disappointed because my *dad* was disappointed. She never really said much one way or the other."

Koren's lip curled, and Taco couldn't help but grin. "You don't like that." It wasn't a question.

"I mean, I think it's great that she supported her husband, but moms are supposed to always want the best for their kids. If they want to be a trash collector, she should give them the tools to be the best damn trashman the city has ever seen. And if he wants to be a professional skydiver, an accountant, or the President of the United States, it's her job to be as supportive as possible."

Her words seemed to patch a hole in his heart that Taco hadn't even realized was there. He'd always felt a little resentment toward his mother for not sticking up for him when his dad harangued him for his low grades. Neither had come to the fire station when he'd been honored as junior firefighter of the year. And neither said a word when he'd been recognized by the city for doing CPR on one of the lunch ladies when she'd collapsed at school.

"You're going to make a great mother."

"Damn straight I am," Koren said with a smile. "What'd you do after you graduated?"

"Moved out, of course," Taco told her. "I worked for a landscape business right after I graduated. Long enough to know that wasn't what I wanted to do for the rest of my life. So after I saved up enough money, I moved from Illinois down here to Texas. One of the guys I worked with at the volunteer fire department hooked me up with a friend down here. The rest is history, and here I am."

"And you don't talk to your parents? Do they know how amazing you are and how many lives you're changing and saving?"

Taco shrugged. "I send them a Christmas card every year and they do the same for me."

"Well, they're missing out," Koren said firmly. "It's their loss. I can't imagine not talking to my mom at least once a week, and I'm sure she feels the same. I know I'm not doing what they think I should be doing with my life, but they love me and would support me no matter what I wanted to do."

"What do they think you should be doing?"

"I don't know. Something more glamorous than working from home for an Internet travel agency, for sure. But I like it. I like making people happy and trying to solve problems if they call in the middle of their trip with an emergency. Just recently I had to help a family get home after the island they were vacationing on was directly in the path of a hurricane. It was touch and go there for a while, but I managed to get all five of them on the last flight off the island."

Taco smiled over at her. "I bet that felt good."

"Of course it did," she said with a smirk. "Because I rock." She sobered. "I know you kinda already met them, but I'm going to introduce you to my folks again. No, don't get weird on me," she said quickly when he wrinkled his nose. "No matter what happens with us, they'll be your champions, Taco. They're good people, and they're really great at building people up rather than tearing them down. Of course, you might not want them in your life once you *do* get to know them. They're kinda nosy."

He chuckled. He'd immediately balked at the idea of getting to know her parents, but the more he thought about it, the more curious he became. Koren was down to earth, friendly, not stuck up in any way, compassionate, and a whole host of other adjectives he probably didn't even know about yet. From what he'd seen of them at the hospital, he had a feeling they were probably awesome.

"I can't wait to officially meet them."

"Hey, Taco?"

"Yeah?"

"Can you tell me why you go by a nickname?"

It wasn't something he talked about much; even his friends' women didn't know the story behind why he hated his real name. But this was Koren. Even though their first date hadn't officially started yet, he was willing to try to be an open book for her.

"Every time I hear the name Hudson, I think of my father. He was always so condescending when he spoke to me. 'Hudson,'" he mimicked, "'You need to do better in school. How will you join my firm if you don't? Hudson, this isn't acceptable. Hudson, you should stay home and study instead of hanging out with those reprobates at the fire station. Hudson, if you leave this house, don't expect me to welcome you when you come crawling back.'"

"I'm sorry," Koren whispered, squeezing his hand.

"Thanks. Anyway…when I first moved down here, one of my roommates brought tacos home for dinner for the rest of us. We weren't exactly swimming in cash, but they were super cheap, so he bought a lot. I ate so many, they joked about me turning into a taco. The nickname just stuck."

"Hmmm," she said.

"What?"

"I don't mind the nickname. I mean, it's the only name I've ever known you by, but…crud. Never mind."

He pulled into the parking lot of the restaurant he was taking her to and parked. Then he turned to her and said, "What, Koren? You can say anything you'd like to me."

"Fine…but remember, you insisted. I just can't imagine being in the middle of an orgasm and crying out, 'Oh, Taco. Right there, Taco. That feels amazing, Taco.'"

Silence filled the cab for a beat as he watched her turn bright red.

He reached over and put his hand behind her neck, turning her so she had no choice but to look at him. The position was awkward, as he hadn't let go of her hand, but he leaned in so he had her complete attention. "My middle name is Robert. When we're alone, you can call me Rob. In bed, out of it, if you need to send me some secret signal that all isn't right in your world…I'm Rob. I'm not ashamed of my nickname. It's just who I am now. But when I'm so deep inside your body that you can't feel anything but me, when you can't *think* about anything but me, you call me Rob."

Taco knew he might be pushing his luck. This was their first date, but the second she'd mentioned sex and him in the same breath, he was a goner.

Koren licked her lips, and he felt her free hand

come up and grasp the sleeve of his shirt. He loved how she did that. He didn't think she realized she was doing it, either. Holding him tight as if she had no intention of ever letting go. It was such a refreshing change from the way his ex had always acted...as if he'd had the plague.

He pushed any and all thoughts of Jen out of his head. He was with Koren, and there wasn't anyone else he could imagine wanting to be with. Jen wasn't welcome here.

"Okay," she said breathlessly.

Taco fought against his base instincts for a moment —and lost. His head lowered at the same time he put a bit of pressure on the back of her neck. But he needn't have bothered. She tilted her chin up and met him halfway.

The second their lips touched, the same feeling of rightness he'd felt that morning when they'd kissed engulfed him again. Her tongue immediately came out and tangled with his. There was no hesitancy in her kiss. No first-date awkwardness. It was as if they'd known each other their entire lives.

When he felt his dick stir, Taco pulled back. As much as he wanted her, he didn't want to rush into things. Which was new for him since his last relationship. Previously, he'd never felt a desire to hold back when it came to his needs. But with Koren, he wanted to savor every small milestone. Including their first date.

"Ready?" he asked softly.

"Ready," she confirmed.

Squeezing the back of her neck lightly, he dropped his hand. His sleeve pulled a bit when he sat back, and Taco smiled.

"Sorry," Koren said a little ruefully, as she smoothed the fabric.

A sense of déjà vu hit him. Yes, she'd done the same thing that morning with his T-shirt, but it was more than that. It felt like a deeper memory, somehow.

Taco had never considered himself fanciful. He was a take-it-as-it-comes kind of man. But with the vision of her in his kitchen, cooking for him and their kids, and now this, he couldn't dismiss the signs the universe was sending him.

To cover up the feeling of rightness filling him, he said, "Come on, Kor. Let's get something to eat."

And with that, they climbed out of the truck and headed for the Mexican restaurant.

Two hours later, Koren's stomach hurt from laughing and her face was sore from smiling so much. Taco was a charming and funny dinner companion. They'd been seated in a booth and he'd taken the seat across from her. She'd ordered a strawberry margarita but he'd stuck to iced tea, since he was driving. They'd talked about everything from her brothers and their wives, to the funniest calls he'd been on.

The time had passed by in a blink, and she definitely didn't want the night to end. She couldn't remember a time when she'd been this relaxed with a guy. She felt this comfortable ease around Vicky and Sue, but never a man.

"You want another?" Taco asked, nodding at her empty glass.

She shook her head. She wasn't much of a drinker and she was already a bit tipsy from the one drink she'd had. It was a *big* glass, but still.

"You want anything else to eat?"

"I think between the two of us, they're more than ready to see us go," she teased. "If you're Taco, then I must be 'Chips and Salsa.'"

He chuckled and leaned his arms on the table. "You can't know how refreshing it is to be with a woman who isn't afraid to eat what she wants."

Koren rolled her eyes. "See, guys *say* that, but then when they've been together for a while, he starts with little comments... 'Are you sure you need a second helping? Maybe you don't need dessert.' Then before you know it, he's making salads for dinner and leaving pamphlets around the house for Weight Watchers."

"Not me," Taco said adamantly. "I won't lie, I want my woman to be healthy so she lives a nice long life. But eating chips and salsa on occasion doesn't mean you need to go on a diet. Regardless, I think you're just about perfect, Koren."

She blushed, but forged on. "So you're saying that you wouldn't want someone like *her* on your arm?" She indicated a slender woman standing at the bar. A man had his arm around her and they were clearly in love.

Taco didn't turn his head. "No."

"You didn't even look," Koren protested.

"I don't need to. Because whoever's standing there, she isn't you."

It was a good answer. A *really* good answer.

"Come on," Taco said abruptly. "There's something I want to show you."

Koren eyed him with raised brows. "Is this where you take me back to the truck, park in a secluded spot, and tell me what you want to show me is in your pants?"

He burst out laughing. "No." He stood next to the booth with his hand outstretched.

Scooching over, Koren took it and let him help her stand. "Okay, but I'm reserving the right to smack your face indignantly and tell you that I'm not that kind of girl if you do."

"Noted," Taco said with another chuckle.

She walked a little ahead of him to the door and when his hand rested on the small of her back, she couldn't help but remember the way it had felt when he'd had it there earlier this morning. When he'd used it to hold her against him as he'd kissed her.

It was safe to say she enjoyed Taco's hands on her, and if he wanted to show her what was in his pants, she probably definitely wouldn't smack him.

He kept his hand on her back as they made their way through the parking lot to his truck. He opened the passenger door for her, and she was more than aware of his eyes on her as she climbed into the seat.

"Are you looking at my ass?" she asked sassily when she was seated.

"Yup."

She blinked. "You're supposed to say, 'Uh-uh, no way.'"

"Why would I say that when I was? I mean, you've got one hell of an ass, Koren." Then he winked at her and slammed the door.

She tried to hide her smile as he walked around the truck, but knew she hadn't managed it when he got back in and said, "And you like me looking at your butt. As much as you like looking at mine. Don't think I didn't notice where your eyes were when I went to the restroom."

She couldn't deny it. Taco in a pair of jeans was definitely stare worthy. And she'd wanted to claw the eyes out of the other women in the restaurant who'd noticed as well.

"No comeback?" he asked as he started the engine.

Koren shook her head and pantomimed zipping her mouth shut.

Taco grinned and concentrated on the road. They

drove for about twenty minutes in an easy silence. Koren was glad Taco didn't feel the need to talk incessantly. She didn't mind being alone with her thoughts, and there were a lot of times she didn't bother turning on the TV or radio at home, preferring the silence to unnecessary noise.

When he pulled down a dirt road, she looked over at him. "So you *are* going to pull the down-your-pants trick?" she asked, feigning disappointment.

"Nope. But I'll warn you, Crash is the one who's the expert at awesome dates. Make Adeline tell you about their first date sometime. It was epic."

"Can't you tell me?" Koren asked.

"Nope. Especially not right now. You'll be all disappointed in what *we're* doing and you'll wonder why I can't be as awesome as Crash."

"That's not what I'm thinking," Koren said softly.

They bounced their way down the road and eventually came to a stop. "We're here," he announced.

"Where's here?"

But Taco merely smiled and got out of the truck.

Koren got out on her side and Taco was there immediately with a steadying hand. She would've told him that she was fine, but with the rocky ground and the drink she'd had, she was happy for the assistance.

He walked her down a rough path and just when she was about to ask where in the world they were going, she gasped.

Somehow they'd gone up in elevation and she

hadn't even noticed. They were on a small hill, and the lights of downtown San Antonio shone brightly in the distance.

"Look up," Taco said softly.

She did. Wavering on her feet, she shot out a hand to grab on to something, which was stupid because they were in the middle of nowhere, but Taco didn't let her down. He took a step closer and got behind her. He wrapped his arms around her waist and clasped them together over her stomach.

She was surrounded by him, and it felt amazing. She closed her eyes and soaked in the feeling.

"Beautiful, isn't it?" he asked softly.

"Uh-huh," she said absently.

Taco chuckled and she felt it rumble against her back. "You aren't even looking," he chastised.

Koren opened her eyes and gazed upward. The stars twinkled above their heads, looking bright in the darkness of their surroundings.

"I found this place one night when I was just driving around, bored. I couldn't sleep and I thought I'd turn around. I saw the little path and got curious. I'm guessing teenagers use this place as a make-out spot or something, but I've never seen anyone else here. It's not exactly the Marfa lights, but I thought you might like to experience it with me."

Koren had heard about the Marfa lights. They were out in west Texas, and most people thought they were UFOs or something else unexplainable. She'd never really felt the need to go see them, and standing here with Taco felt ten times better.

She crossed her arms and grabbed hold of the sleeves of his shirt. They stood like that for a long time. Neither spoke, just absorbing the moment.

Eventually, Koren shivered.

"Cold?" Taco asked, his warm breath wafting over her ear, sending another shiver through her. "I didn't think it was that chilly out. I'm sorry," he apologized and loosened his arms around her.

Koren refused to let go of his sleeves. "I'm fine. I always get cold after I eat. Something about the blood going to my stomach to digest the food. And there's a lot of chips and salsa to digest tonight," she quipped.

He chuckled and wrapped his arms around her again. She could feel him against her back. A solid strength that she had a feeling would protect her from anything and everything. It was an odd thought to have on a first date. But she couldn't deny how she felt. Part of it was probably because of how they'd connected at her car wreck. But most of it was just him.

Without giving it much thought, Koren let go of his sleeves and turned in his arms. Before he could ask what was wrong, she'd snuggled back into him. Her hands gripped his shirt at his back and her head rested on his shoulder. Her flip-flops gave her another two inches in height, just enough to be almost eye-to-eye with him.

"Koren?" he asked, his hands coming to rest on her hips.

"I'm okay," she said. "I'm just enjoying being here with you."

"Ditto."

After a moment, Koren decided to do what she'd been thinking about since before dinner. She moved her hand up behind Taco's neck, as he seemed to like to do to her, and touched her lips to his.

She licked his bottom lip. He opened immediately, and she swept her tongue inside. He tasted like the tea he'd drank right before they left the restaurant.

And she wanted more. Needed more.

Going up on her tiptoes, she pressed her body to his and gripped both his neck and the shirt at his back with tight fingers.

But instead of kissing her harder, he pulled back a fraction. His lips brushing against hers as he spoke. "I'm not going anywhere, Kor. Easy."

She didn't want easy. She wanted him as out of control as she felt.

"Shut up and kiss me," she ground out.

And then he was.

If she thought their earlier kisses were hot, they were nothing compared to the way he took her mouth just then.

He didn't just kiss her…he made love to her mouth, using his lips and tongue to mimic the act. Koren had never been taken as thoroughly as she was right then. It was a claiming. One she was more than happy to acquiesce to.

When he pulled back, he rested his forehead on hers. They were both breathing hard. One of his hands had slipped under the waistband of her jeans and she could feel his fingers against the crack of her ass. He'd wrapped the other around her back to anchor her to him.

The hand at his neck had dropped to grasp his biceps and the other one was under his shirt—and she had a feeling that she'd left fingernail marks on his back. But she wasn't sorry. Couldn't be, because it was obvious *he* wasn't.

"God, your hands feel so good," were the first words he said after he'd disengaged from her.

"Did I hurt you?" she asked quietly.

"Never. Knowing you want me so bad that you can't hold on tightly enough is a hell of a turn on."

Koren bit her lip, not sure how to respond to that.

He groaned. "And you biting your lip isn't helping. I need to get you home."

"Don't wanna," she mumbled.

He chuckled. "We can't stay out here all night. We'll be a bug feast."

He had a point. Bugs freaking loved her. Taking a deep breath, she pulled back so they were looking at each other. "Thanks for bringing me out here. It's beautiful."

"You're welcome, sweetheart."

Then he slipped his hand out of her pants and guided her back up the trail to the truck. Once again, on the way back to her condo, they were silent. He walked her up to her door and waited until she'd unlocked it and turned to him to speak.

"I had a good time," he said.

"Me too."

"I'm off tomorrow," he hinted.

She smiled. "Want to come over for dinner?"

"I thought you'd never ask."

She laughed, then sobered. "Is this weird?"

"What?"

"This," she said, gesturing between them. "Us connecting so fast."

He shrugged. "Maybe. But I don't care. Do you?"

"Not really."

"Good. I'll see you tomorrow evening then. Around five again?"

"Sure."

"Want me to pick up something on my way?" he asked.

"Yes."

"What?"

"Anything."

"Okay. I'll text you and let you know to make sure it meets with your approval."

"Sounds good."

"Come here," Taco said and pulled her into him.

Koren stumbled slightly and fell against his chest,

but he held her secure and was kissing her before she could take a breath. It was short and sweet compared to their last kiss, but no less profound.

"See you soon," he said, righting her and making sure she was steady on her feet before taking a step back.

"Bye, Taco."

"Bye."

Once again, Koren found herself closing her door and leaning against it. Every time she saw Taco, she fell harder. He wasn't anything like the men she'd dated in the past. He was...more. In every way. And she liked more.

CHAPTER SEVEN

Six days later, Koren's cell phone rang.

"Hi, Koren. It's S-Sophie."

"Hi," Koren said as she moved the phone from one ear to the other. "Everything all right?"

"Yeah. I'm having an impromptu thing at m-my house tonight and wanted to invite you."

"Oh," Koren said, the disappointment easy to hear in her voice. "My friend Vicky is coming over for a few drinks. I haven't seen much of her lately."

"Let m-me guess…a certain firefighter has been taking up all your s-spare time?" Sophie asked.

Koren wanted to deny it, but Sophie was right. Every night that Taco hadn't been working, he'd spent with her. They'd gone out to eat again, stayed in at her place, and she'd even been over to his house. It was almost scary how well they clicked. Things were moving quickly with him, but it felt right. "I'm sure I don't know what you're talking about," Koren said in an overdramatic voice.

Sophie laughed. "I don't blame you. Our guys are pretty awesome. Anyway, s-since they're all working tonight, we thought we'd have our own little get-together. You're welcome to bring Vicky if you want to."

"Really?"

"S-Sure. Why not? The m-more the m-merrier."

"What should I bring?" Koren asked.

"Just whatever you want to drink. Beth is in charge of the grill, and I've got a m-million hamburgers and hotdogs we can eat."

Koren frowned. "Is that smart?" she asked quietly, as if Beth was sitting in the next room and might over-hear her.

"What? Oh! Actually, Beth is the best person to have in charge of the grill. S-She's extra careful with fire now and s-she never lets the flames get too high and burn our dinner." Sophie chuckled. "S-Say you'll come."

It felt good to be invited. "I'll talk to Vicky, but I'm sure she won't have a problem with it. What time?"

"Yay!" Sophie exclaimed. "Whenever. I think Adeline's coming s-straight from work. Blythe worked in the library this m-morning, but s-she s-said s-she was going to take a nap before s-she came over. I s-swear that kid is s-sucking out all her energy. Beth will come over once everyone else is here and Quinn is on her way now. Oh, and Penelope will be here too."

"Really?" Koren asked. "I was under the impression that she always worked the same shifts with the others."

"S-She does usually. But for s-some reason, s-she asked the chief to s-switch her s-schedule around. M-Moose was none too pleased."

"So she and Moose are dating?" Koren asked. She'd seen the two together, and it kind of looked like they were dating, but since they'd been arguing at the time, she wasn't sure.

"Not really. I m-mean, they are and they aren't. It's complicated."

"Right."

"And I'm not s-saying that to blow you off. It really *is* complicated. I don't think any of us really know what's going on with those two."

"Maybe I can ask some stupid new-to-the-group questions tonight and find out," Koren said.

"Yes!" Sophie exclaimed loudly, then laughed. "I knew you'd be an awesome addition to the group. Call your friend and I'll s-see you later."

"Want me to text when I'm on my way?" Koren asked.

"No need. S-See you s-soon."

"Later." Koren hung up and found herself smiling. She liked Sophie already.

Koren texted Vicky and asked if the change of plans was okay, and got an immediate, "Hell yeah!" response.

For the rest of the afternoon, Koren took care of the

pending requests for quotes and service that had come in overnight and that morning. Then she spent half an hour finalizing the details on some options for Blythe's short romantic getaway. Time was quickly ticking, and if she and Squirrel didn't go on vacation soon, their baby would arrive and they'd lose their chance.

Vicky was coming over to the condo around five-thirty, and then they'd head over to Sophie's. She was going to follow Koren, because she needed to get home by eight to tuck her little boy in. Koren would never give her grief for that because Vicky and her husband had tried for years to have a child, and when her son was finally conceived, Koren had cried with joy right along with Vicky. Her son was the center of her world, and while Vicky was no longer able to spend as much time with her as they both wanted, Koren wouldn't change a thing about her best friend's new life.

It was getting close to five-thirty when Koren's phone vibrated with an incoming text.

Taco: Heard you're heading over to Sophie's tonight.

She wasn't sure if he was happy or not about the fact she was going to be spending time with the other ladies. She didn't think he would be upset; in fact, he'd been telling her for a few days that the others wanted to get to know her better, and they'd accused him of monopolizing her time.

Koren: Yeah. She called earlier. I assume you're not texting to scold me for not asking your permission.

Taco: Hell no. First, you're a bit too old for getting permission to go "play" at a friend's house. And second, I'm thrilled.

Koren: Thrilled, huh?

Taco: Maybe that's not the right word. I'm very happy that you're getting along with them. They didn't like Jen...for good reason.

Koren hated his ex, and hated even more that he was obviously still affected by what she'd done.

Koren: Well, I like them...what I know of them. And I get to meet Beth tonight. She kinda scares me.

Taco: LOL. She scares me too sometimes. But honestly, she's mostly harmless. And there's no one I'd rather have at my back if the shit hits the fan.

Koren: Is there a chance of shit hitting the fan?

Taco: No! I'm done with drama. All of it.

Koren: Good. I'm allergic to drama.

Taco: Something happen?

Koren: Nothing recent. But when I was in high school,

one of the cliques decided to spread a rumor about me that wasn't true. It was extremely hurtful and it stuck with me a couple years. Kids can be really cruel. I've avoided drama at all costs since then.

Taco: I'm sorry you had to go through that.

Koren: *shrug* It seems like a rite of passage. But I decided then and there to do whatever it takes to stay away from drama or the people who cause it.

Taco: Then it's a good thing I'm drama free.

She wasn't so sure about that. After all, his ex was currently in jail for killing several people and trying to kill his friend's fiancée. And she was making a huge exception by befriending all the other women. They'd all definitely had their share of drama. But it was in the past, and she was counting on it staying there.

Koren: A very good thing.

Taco: Have fun. Will you text me when you get home?

Koren: Sure. You be safe tonight.

Taco: Always. Talk to you later.

Koren: Bye.

She really liked how attentive Taco was. He wasn't smothering, didn't insist that she text him whenever she left her place when he was working or anything crazy like that. He just wanted to know she was safe. And that felt good. Yes, her parents, brothers, and friends worried about her, but Taco's concern was different.

Putting the phone down, Koren finished up with what she was doing and logged off her computer. She changed into a pair of jeans and a comfortable T-shirt and put on a pair of plain flip-flops. By the time she was ready to go, Vicky had arrived.

She gave her friend Sophie's address and soon they were on their way. By the time they got to the house, there were several cars parked on the street. They headed for the door and it opened before they even got there.

"Hi!" Sophie greeted them warmly. "It's great to s-see you again. And you m-must be Vicky! Come in, m-make yourself at home. Ice and glasses are in the kitchen."

Koren smiled and followed the bubbly woman into the house. Sophie made introductions for Vicky, and when she was done, she said, "Beth and Penelope aren't here yet, but they're both on their way. I've got s-some finger food in the kitchen, help yourself."

The second she was out of earshot, Vicky leaned in and said, "She certainly has a lot of energy."

Koren chuckled. "Yup. From what I understand from Taco, though, she wasn't always like this. I think her confidence has come from having friends like these and from her fiancé."

"Well, I like her."

"Me too," Koren said with a smile, relieved that Vicky was already taking to Sophie. It wasn't that she hadn't thought her friends wouldn't get along with Sophie and the others, but thinking it and seeing it firsthand were two different things. And if Vicky liked the women here, then Sue would too.

With a smile, Koren turned toward the door when she heard it open. Her smile died, replaced with a gasp when she saw who'd entered. It was Penelope—and she was leading a donkey.

Blinking to see if her vision cleared, Koren watched Quinn head over to greet the newcomers.

Koren had never seen a donkey so small. He was adorable! She and Vicky hurried over to the crowd at the door to meet the little guy.

"Hi," Koren said to Penelope. "This is my friend, Vicky."

"Good to meet you," Penelope said with a smile. "This is Smokey, and he's my PTSD service donkey. Well, not officially, but that's what I call him. Sophie's nice enough to let me bring him when I come over."

"Can I pet him?" Vicky asked.

"Of course." Penelope then went on to tell them the story of how she'd found the donkey burning in the middle of a forest fire. "We figured he belonged to a rancher nearby, but when we were driving away, Smokey ran after our truck crying in the most pathetic way. I couldn't leave him."

Koren ran her hand over Smokey's head. "I wouldn't have been able to either. He's so cute."

Just then, Coco, Adeline's black lab, came over and nosed Smokey's snout. The donkey lifted his head up and down and brayed loudly, scaring the crap out of Koren. She took a huge step back, and noticed that Vicky had done the same.

Penelope and the rest of the women merely laughed.

"He's been looking forward to seeing Smokey since we got here," Adeline said with a chuckle. "Wanna play?" she asked the duo.

Smokey brayed and Coco barked.

"Well, come on then," Adeline said and headed for a sliding glass door in the living area. She let the two animals out and closed the door behind them.

"Aren't you afraid they'll run off?" Vicky asked.

"The yard is fenced on the front and s-sides, and the woods out back are dense," Sophie told them. "But they'd never wander away. They love their people too m-much."

"And they know that you're going to give them left-overs," Adeline said with an eye roll.

"That too," Sophie agreed.

Koren was smiling at the easy way the women teased each other and genuinely got along, as Quinn came up to her. "I'm glad you could come tonight."

"Me too."

"And just so you know, we didn't invite you over to

grill you, or to make sure you really fit in or anything. I admit that we're all a little leery after the whole Jen thing, but we enjoy your company."

"Thanks."

"Wait—you aren't sure Koren fits in?" Vicky asked.

"It's fine," Koren said, putting her hand on her friend's arm. When Vicky got riled up, it wasn't good.

"No, seriously. I want to know why they'd think that. Because you're the most laid-back, easygoing person I know. You pretty much fit in with *anyone* because you don't have a judgmental bone in your body. The other day, you helped a woman in a motor-ized cart in the grocery store when everyone else was ignoring her. You constantly take customers that your co-workers won't just because they're not from America and have thick accents that can be hard to understand. You even stuck up for Quinn in the grocery store when you overheard people talking about her birthmark. I think it's you who needs to be grilling *them* and deciding if they fit with who you want to hang around with."

Silence followed Vicky's impassioned speech, and Koren wasn't sure if she should apologize, cry, or laugh.

"You forgot to include that she recently planned a getaway for an LGBT group because they were having trouble finding a travel agent willing to do the research required to find a safe place for them to vacation. And after she met Adeline and Coco, she went online and made a donation to a service dog organization to sponsor training a puppy. And she spent hours looking up information on stuttering, homelessness, and agoraphobia, trying to understand all of us so she wouldn't accidentally say something offensive."

Koren turned to look at the newcomer in shock.

"Beth!" Adeline shouted and went to greet her at the door.

Beth didn't take her eyes from Koren's. "Yeah, I researched you. And I'm really sorry. But after everything that's happened lately, I couldn't in good conscience *not* do a little digging. Erin was kidnapped by that psycho guy so he could hunt her. There was Milena and Sadie's shit, Hope and Blythe were *both* homeless…and don't even get me started on the stuff I've had to deal with in regards to Penelope's SEAL and Delta friends. Everyone here has had firsthand experience with someone lying about who they really were. I'm probably the last person who can talk, since I totally deceived Cade during my stint with pyromania, but I wouldn't be able to handle it if something happened under my nose again."

Koren got it. She did. She wasn't thrilled that Beth had used her computer skills to look into her life, but she understood why she'd done it.

Blythe wasn't quite as understanding. "That wasn't cool, Beth."

Beth opened her mouth to respond, but Adeline

beat her to it, turning to Koren. "Did you really donate to a service dog charity?"

Koren nodded. "Yeah. I mean, I've been lucky enough to not have any need for something like that, but I got to thinking about all our veterans who come home from overseas and have a hard time integrating back into society. Or about someone like you, whose dog literally changed your life for the better. I don't make a ton of money, but I wanted to do something to contribute."

Koren felt Vicky grab her hand in support. She didn't exactly feel like she was being interrogated, but it was close.

Beth walked over to Koren. Then she did something completely surprising—she put her arms around her and hugged her tightly. Koren couldn't do anything but return the embrace.

"I really am sorry," Beth said quietly into her ear.

Then she pulled back and turned to the others. "Koren's good. We're all good. I'm gonna be out back with the ass and mutt, lighting a big honking fire if anyone needs me."

She marched across the room and out the sliding glass door. They could all hear Coco and Smokey greeting Beth as if they hadn't seen her in years.

"Well...Beth has s-spoken," Sophie quipped. "Welcome to the family, Koren."

"She's *not* our spokesperson," Adeline said a little

grumpily. "I didn't need her to tell me that it's okay to like Koren."

"Me either," Blythe put in. "I'd like to think after all that time on the streets, I'm a pretty good judge of character. And let's face it, none of us liked Jen from the start."

Koren kind of felt like she was listening in on a conversation she shouldn't be.

"Koren was super nice to me the first time I met her in the store. These asshats did what asshats do, made fun of my birthmark, and she was quick with a nice word. And believe me, I needed it that day," Quinn said.

"She's also standing right here," Vicky said in irritation. "And can hear you."

"I've never seen Taco act like he has the last couple weeks," Penelope said quietly. "I don't care what your browsing history is or how many charities you donate to. That's all superficial stuff. What I care about is Taco. And his happiness. And he's happy. *Really* happy. And he definitely wasn't when he was with Jen. So, for that alone, I'm happy to welcome you to the fold."

Koren swallowed hard. She'd already hung out with Quinn, Sophie, Adeline, and Blythe, but hadn't spent much time with the female firefighter. And to have her endorsement seemed like quite an accomplishment. "Thanks."

"You're welcome. Now, whose turn is it to watch Beth and make sure she doesn't start a bonfire to rival the ones that Texas A&M used to build in the eighties and nineties?"

"How do you know about that?" Adeline asked. "You aren't old enough."

Penelope smiled. "I have my ways."

Sophie rolled her eyes. "Whatever. And I think s-since you brought it up, you get to go babysit Beth. I mean, she's definitely the best when it comes to grilling, but still…"

"Gladly," Penelope said, winking at Koren and heading for the back deck.

"Now that *that* awkwardness is done, I need a drink," Sophie said.

As everyone headed for the kitchen for drinks and snacks, Quinn approached Koren. "Are you okay?"

"Yeah."

"I'm sorry about Beth. Don't be mad at her."

"I'm not mad. I get it, I do."

"Taco's gonna be pissed when he hears," Quinn said.

Koren blinked in surprise. "How will he hear about it? I'm not going to say anything, if that's what you're getting at."

"Oh, nothing around here is a secret. Guarantee he'll hear about it eventually, and that he won't be happy. He's just as protective as the rest of our guys, and hearing that Beth invaded your privacy, partially because of him, isn't going to sit well."

"I understand why she did it."

Quinn shrugged. "Even so… Anyway, enough of that. It's drink time!"

"Vicky and I drove," Koren protested as she followed behind Quinn.

She shrugged. "You can stay here tonight if you have to."

Surprised by the impromptu invitation, Koren just stared at her. "Really?"

"Sure," Quinn said. "Sophie loves it when people stay the night. I think it has to do with the time she almost died while Chief was on duty. She always feels better when she's not alone in the house."

"Oh Lord," Vicky said under her breath. "Another drama?"

Quinn heard her and chuckled. "Right? But this wasn't anything that anyone else did…unless you believe Chief's Native American beliefs that it was the work of a skin-walker."

"I think I'll have that drink after all," Koren said.

"Me too," Vicky echoed. "My husband will come and get me if necessary."

* * *

After dinner, and after Beth did *not* burn the burgers and hotdogs, Koren was sitting on the couch next to Penelope.

Vicky'd only had one drink and had gone home to put her son to bed. Beth had also left a bit ago, saying without embarrassment that she'd reached her limit of "out of the house time."

Blythe had been overjoyed with the ideas Koren had given her for the mini getaway with Sawyer. She said she'd think about them and get back to her.

Now, Smokey was asleep at Koren's feet, and the remaining women were playing a card game at the table behind them. Koren wasn't as comfortable with Penelope as she was with the other women, but she was going to make her best effort to get to know her better.

"I was surprised to hear you'd be here tonight," Koren said. "Taco said that you haven't been around as much lately. He's worried about you."

Penelope shrugged. "That's nothing new."

Koren wasn't sure *which* wasn't new. People worrying about her, or that she hadn't been around the fire station and the guys as much. She didn't know Penelope's story. The others had hinted that it was tragic, but then again, all of the women's histories seemed to be tragic.

"So…you and Moose?" Koren tried again.

Penelope huffed out a breath and looked down at Smokey. She absently rubbed the donkey with her foot. "Nah."

"Really? Because even me, a newcomer, can see there's something between you guys."

"I'm not good for him," Penelope said quietly. "Did you know Sledge is my brother?"

"Beth's fiancé? Really?"

"Yeah. I signed on to be a firefighter because of him."

Koren struggled to understand Penelope's abrupt topic change. "So, you don't like it?"

"It's not that. It's…" Her voice trailed off. Then she said, "Have you ever wondered what your purpose in life is?"

"Yeah, of course," Koren answered immediately. "I mean, I'm a pretty good travel agent. I can find really good deals and most of my clients have no complaints, but I'm not sure I'm changing the world or even making the tiniest of differences. But it pays the bills." She shrugged.

"I've seen too much," Penelope said quietly. "I used to think I was lucky. That I'd survived when others didn't for a reason. But as time goes by, I'm having trouble figuring out what that reason is."

Koren was a bit alarmed now. She wasn't really equipped for a conversation like this. It sounded like perhaps Penelope needed professional help, but the last thing she wanted was to blow her off. If she needed to talk, Koren would listen. "I don't know your story, but—"

"You don't know my story?" Penelope interrupted, her eyes wide.

"Um…no."

"Wow. Color me shocked," the other woman said with a small chuckle. "I think you're the only one in the entire country."

Koren shrugged. "I don't really do gossip. I don't like drama."

"Then you're friends with the wrong people," Penelope stated.

Koren had no reply for that.

Penelope sighed. "I'm sorry. I'm being bitchy. What happened to me doesn't matter. But I'm a different person now, and it seems as if everyone wants me to be the *old* Penelope. But the harder I try to find her, the more she seems to slip away."

"Maybe you need to forget about being the old Penelope and embrace the new Penelope," Koren suggested. "I mean, the things that happen in our lives shape us, for good or bad. And we either embrace those changes or go crazy."

The other woman nodded. "Yeah."

"I'm probably the worst person to talk to about anything remotely having to do with tragedy, as I've lived a charmed life, and I know it. But I think life is about more than what we've lived through. It's also about how we see ourselves. We have two choices there: we can see ourselves as *others* do, or we can say 'fuck that' and see ourselves as we truly are. Strong, powerful, kick-ass women."

Penelope was silent, and Koren suddenly felt like she'd overstepped. Or she'd at least been somewhat overly impassioned.

But then Penelope whispered, "What if you can't see

yourself at all? If you've lost her?"

Koren opened her mouth to speak, when Coco suddenly bounced up from his spot on the floor next to Smokey and began barking ferociously at the sliding glass door.

"What in the world?" Adeline said. "He never acts like this. Coco! No! Down!"

But the dog didn't stop. He began to scratch at the door as if his life depended on it. Then Smokey got into the act, throwing his head back and braying.

The noise in the room was deafening. Adeline and Penelope went to the door to see what the animals were so upset about.

"I don't see anything out there. No wild animals or anything," Adeline said in confusion.

As Adeline held Coco back, Penelope opened the door and looked to the left—and then said, "Oh, shit. Sophie, call 9-1-1. Your shed's on fire." She slid the glass closed, turned to Adeline, and ordered, "And you call Crash." Then Penelope ran for the front door.

Koren gaped at the others, then she, Blythe, and Quinn followed Penelope, close at her heels. The second they went out the front door and turned right, they could see the kind of glow that only comes from a fire, lighting the darkness on the far side of the yard. The flames growing stronger and brighter in the night sky as they watched.

Penelope ran fast for someone her size, and she disappeared around the side of the house and out of view. By the time they rounded the corner, Penelope was frantically trying to get the faucet turned on.

"We've got this. Go!" Koren shouted, pushing Penelope out of the way.

Nodding, the firefighter began unraveling the hose and heading toward the shed, which was almost completely engulfed.

Koren cranked on the faucet as the other women helped Penelope stretch out the hose.

The second Koren turned to look at the fire, she knew the hose wasn't going to do much. The flames were shooting high out of the shed's roof and the sound the fire was making was definitely scary. But she quickly realized Penelope wasn't actually spraying the water on the shed anyway, she was soaking the grass around it and trying to wet down the trees, bushes, and the fence as well.

Sophie came running out of the house then, holding the phone to her ear. "Did you s-see any dogs around?" she yelled frantically.

Koren was confused.

But apparently the others weren't. "No, nothing. It's not that. It's all good, Soph."

"Dogs?" Koren asked Blythe.

"I'll tell you later," the other woman said.

Just then, a huge explosion sounded from the shed and a fireball shot up in the sky.

"Holy shit!" Quinn exclaimed.

"Probably the lawn mower engine!" Penelope yelled. "Everyone get back!"

They all backed up about five feet.

"What did Crash say?" Penelope asked Adeline.

"They're comin'!"

And a second later, they heard the sirens.

"Thank God," Blythe said.

One second they were all standing there watching Penelope do her best to keep the fire contained to the shed, and the next they were surrounded by firefighters in full bunker gear.

Moose—easy to pick out because of his size—headed straight for Penelope. He took her by the arm and leaned in to say something. She shook her head, and Moose physically ripped the hose out of her hands and pointed back to where the rest of the women were standing.

She glared at him then spun and stomped away. Past the group watching, straight into the house. Within seconds she was back, leading Smokey. Without a word or a look to anyone, she skirted around the fire trucks, got into her PT Cruiser, and sped away.

"Well, shit," Adeline said.

"Something's definitely wrong there," Blythe commented dryly.

Koren kept her mouth shut. It wasn't just that she was new to the group and didn't want to speculate on something she didn't know anything about. It was more because of the conversation she'd had with Penelope. The woman was hurting. Deeply. And it was only a matter of time before she broke.

She felt the hand on her back before she heard Taco. "You okay?"

"Yeah." She looked up at him—and melted a little inside. Wearing his gear, he reminded her of the day she'd seen him on the job for the first time. She was so proud of him and what he did for a living, and not just because he'd saved her.

Taco nodded and got to work. She stepped back and watched as the fire in the shed was put out within minutes. The hoses on the truck, along with the high pressure, were obviously much more effective than the small garden hose had been.

When the shed was nothing but smoldering ruins, Sledge took all the women aside. "What happened?" he asked.

"Coco went crazy," Adeline said. "Barking and clawing at the window. I've never seen him do that before. Then Smokey joined in. Penelope saw the fire first. We called 9-1-1, and you guys, and then she came out here to do what she could until you got here."

It was a succinct version of the events of the evening.

"Is anyone hurt?" Sledge asked.

All five of them shook their heads.

"Good."

Chief came up then and, without a word, took Sophie in his arms. They clung to each other for a long moment before he took her face in his hands and asked, "Coyotes?"

"None. I asked. No one s-said they s-saw any."

He nodded. "Good. I've been careful, and the guys all have my back. This wasn't because of me."

Koren frowned. "Of course it wasn't," she blurted. Everyone turned to look at her, and she blushed. "I mean, you weren't even here," she said lamely.

Chief's lips quirked.

"When Sophie and Chief were dating, she saw a coyote one night, and later that evening, she almost died of carbon monoxide poisoning," Taco explained quietly, snaking his arm around her waist. "Chief concluded it was a skin-walker, something that his people believe in. Now, we do our best to make sure Chief doesn't come into contact with any dead bodies; in his culture, they're known to hold evil spirits."

Koren nodded even though she was still confused. She'd go home and look up skin-walkers and coyotes and make the connection later.

"Sorry about your shed, man," Crash told Chief.

The other man shrugged. "There wasn't anything in there that can't be replaced. I'm just glad the women are all right."

"What *was* in there?" Squirrel asked.

"The usual. Lawn mower, weed eater, other gardening odds and ends."

"Gas?" Driftwood asked.

"Of course."

"Was it wired? Like for electricity?"

"Yeah. I even had a small fridge in there with cold drinks for working in the yard."

"Hmm. It could've been a short in the cord or something," Crash said. "But I'll call the fire investigator tomorrow just to be sure."

"Sounds good," Chief said. Then he leaned close and told Sophie, "I know you miss me when I'm gone, but this is going a bit far, isn't it?"

She giggled. "S-Shut up. But it *is* good to s-see you."

Taco tightened his arm around Koren's waist and led her away from the others. When they were out of earshot, he asked, "You really okay?"

"Yeah. That was a little scary, but Penelope was awesome."

Taco frowned and turned his head to look at where her car had been parked.

"She's hurting," Koren said softly.

Taco looked back at her. "I know. We all know."

"Can't you guys convince her to go see someone or something?"

"She was, then she quit. Moose is trying to get her to continue. But she's putting distance between all of us and herself."

"You can't let her," Koren said, shaking her head. "She needs you guys. Make Sledge do something. He's her brother, she can't refuse to talk to him."

"I'll say something to him," Taco told her. Then he

bent his head and nuzzled the side of her neck. "You smell good."

Koren giggled and pushed his head away from her. "Your beard tickles. And you stink."

Smirking, Taco bent her backward over his arm and playfully rubbed his head and beard over as much of her neck and face as he could.

Koren shrieked and laughed even as she tried to shove him away.

Then he stopped, but didn't set her upright.

Koren remained pliant in his arms. She grabbed hold of his bulky bunker jacket and stared up at him. "Taco?"

"Just counting my blessings," he said softly before kissing her tenderly. He finally brought her upright, but Koren didn't let go. "You'll drive safe going home?" he asked.

She nodded. "I only had one glass of wine and that was hours ago."

"Good. Text me when you get there?"

"Of course."

The other guys were rolling up the hose they'd used to put out the fire and getting ready to go.

"I'm glad you boys weren't too far away."

"Me too."

"I'll talk to you later."

"I'll call tomorrow."

"Okay."

"Can I come over when I get off shift the day after

tomorrow?" Taco asked.

She beamed. "Yeah. I'd like that." And she would. She'd been spending a great deal of time with Taco, and every day that went by, the more she fell for him.

"Me too," he said. Then he kissed her once more before gently peeling her fingers off his sleeve with a grin. "Fuck, I love that you always grab hold as if you never want to let me go."

"Reflex," she teased.

Taco grinned and merely shook his head as he backed away.

Koren watched as he turned and jogged over to the truck. He helped his friends get the fire truck ready to go again, then they were gone.

"Good Lord," Blythe said, one hand resting on her pregnant belly.

"What?" Quinn asked.

"We have some hot-ass men," Blythe said.

It took a second for her words to sink in, but as soon as they did, the women all burst into laughter.

Koren followed them inside with a smile on her face. Things sure weren't boring around this crew, that was for sure.

Nadine Patterson stood up from behind the tree where she'd been hiding. Luckily, firefighter number one's yard backed up to a wooded area. Otherwise she may not have gotten away without being seen. The damn dog had obviously seen or smelled her.

It hadn't been hard to get into the shed, the stupid Indian didn't even keep the thing locked. She scrounged around until she found a greasy rag. She carefully poured gasoline from a tank in the corner on it until it was soaked. She wanted the fire to look like it was an accident, at least at first glance. She didn't care if investigators figured out that it was arson at some point though. She shoved the rag under the back side of the refrigerator next to the wall and set the end alight. She waited until she was sure it would catch, then exited the shed as silently as she'd entered it.

Nadine stood behind a tree nearby and watched as the small building quickly caught fire. She slunk from one tree to the next, loving the scent of smoke on the air. It reminded her of the night she'd lost everything— but it also signified that she'd finally get closure soon.

She'd set herself on a path she wouldn't deviate from. *Couldn't* deviate from. Stevie was watching. Judging. She had to do this for him. She'd gathered as much information as possible about everyone Hudson Vines knew, and it was finally time.

And she didn't miss the way Hudson had gone straight to the woman he'd started seeing recently...*Koren*. Such a stupid name. It was like whore and corn at the same time.

Nadine hated how happy Hudson looked. That was unacceptable. He would be as miserable as she was by the time she'd finished with him. That much was certain. If he thought he'd get to live happily ever after, he was wrong. *Dead wrong.*

Feeling as if she was on top of the world, or at least at the peak of her high from the meth she'd scored and shot up earlier that night, Nadine rubbed her hands together.

Soon. His time was coming soon...she was saving the best for last.

CHAPTER EIGHT

"Hi!" Taco said. "Come in." He held the door open and couldn't help but run his eyes up and down Koren's body as she brushed past him and came into his house. She met him there so they could go car shopping. She'd finally gotten the check from her insurance company and was going to replace the rental she'd been driving around.

"This could've waited until tomorrow," Koren told him. "I mean, you just got off shift."

It had been a week since Chief's shed had gone up in flames. The fire investigator had agreed that it had most likely started because of a short in the cord that led to the mini fridge, but he couldn't say definitively. Sophie had sworn that she hadn't seen any coyotes or other suspicious animals around, but the women had all been busy inside, so it's possible they'd missed it.

Chief had already made plans to go back to the

reservation and have another cleansing ceremony. Taco knew he wasn't put out by the idea—since he and Sophie were planning on getting married while they were there.

He was thrilled for his friend. It seemed as if everyone was planning a wedding or, in Squirrel's case, getting ready for a baby. Taco knew if he wasn't dating Koren that he'd probably feel a lot more upset about literally everyone moving on with their lives, but he was content. Koren made him feel that way.

"Taco?"

"Sorry. It's fine. You need a car. You can't keep paying for that rental now that your insurance company has given you the check."

"You're not too tired?" she asked, her brow furrowing.

Taco reached out and grabbed her around the waist and hauled her close. She screeched, but laughed as she held on to him for balance.

He waited for it…and smiled when he felt her fingers scrunch his T-shirt. He'd never take that for granted. Ever.

"I'm not too tired. I don't think I'll *ever* be too tired to hang out with you. You need a car; I can help you negotiate. I can take a nap later while you're working."

She looked at him and bit her lip. "If you wanted… you could nap at my place while I'm catching up."

"Absolutely." He'd never pass up a chance to spend time with her. And while they'd fooled around plenty on her couch and at his place, he'd never been in her bed. The thought of sleeping where she did, of smelling her peach scent on her sheets, was appealing.

"What's that smile for?" she asked suspiciously.

Taco leaned down and kissed her hard and fast. "Nothing."

She rolled her eyes. "I don't trust you as far as I can throw you."

The smile fled from his face. "You can trust me."

She obviously realized he'd taken her words to heart. "I didn't mean it that way. I was teasing."

"I know, but seriously, you can trust me."

She studied him for a moment, then nodded.

"Good. How about we go and get this taken care of. The faster we get you a car, the faster I can be in your bed."

Koren chuckled and shook her head in exasperation. "I swear no matter how old boys get, they always have one thing on their minds."

"News flash, Kor. When I'm around *you*, that's one of the only things I can think about."

Instead of laughing at him, her smile dimmed.

"What?"

"You probably shouldn't have super-high expectations when it comes to that."

Taco felt her fingers tighten on the material of his shirt. She was nervous about having sex with him? Unacceptable.

"With the way I get hard just looking at you, I don't think we're gonna have a problem."

She dropped her eyes, and Taco frowned. He put a finger under her chin and lifted her head. "Hey, what's wrong, sweetheart?"

"I just...I'm not anything to write home about, and I'm worried you're going to be disappointed."

Knowing he was taking a gamble, Taco grabbed hold of one of her hands, disentangled it from his shirt, and slowly brought it down to the front of his jeans. "I don't know where you got the idea that you aren't pretty, because every time I see you, spend time with you, *this* is how I get. You don't even have to do anything, Koren. You smile and I get hard. You laugh, I get hard. You get pissy with me, and yeah, I get hard. When we get to the point where it feels right for both of us to move our physical relationship to the next step, I have absolutely no doubt that you're going to blow my mind."

"You can't know that," she protested, but she didn't move her hand away.

"Close your eyes," he ordered.

Her lids immediately dropped. And of course that turned him on even more. He felt his dick twitch. Koren's lips opened and she panted slightly, but she didn't open her eyes, and she still didn't move her hand.

"It's a good thing I have my own room at the station because at night, after we talk on the phone, I can't help but touch myself. Just the *memory* of your voice makes me hard. Do you ever touch yourself when you think about me? Do you get wet? For me, it doesn't matter if we're talking about something as harmless as car shopping or the trips you've organized, my body reacts to your voice; it recognizes you as its own. And my *very* favorite thing about you isn't your voice, or your ass, or your tits—though they're great. It's the way you hold on to me as if you can't bear not to. No one in my entire life has felt that way about me. Ever."

A small noise left the back of Koren's throat, but she didn't move.

Taking an even bigger chance, Taco brushed the backs of his fingers against one of her tight nipples.

She gasped, but didn't shrink away. In fact, she arched her back and pressed herself harder against him.

"When you get me in bed, sweetheart, I'm not going to be able to think of anything but how amazing you feel. You won't have to do anything to have me wrapped around your little finger because I already am."

"Taco," she whispered before her eyes opened. She moved the hand from between his legs and brought it up to cover his own, on her breast. "I'm not a virgin, of course. I've had sex. But I've never really enjoyed it much. Never really understood what all the fuss is about. But last night, after we talked, I did just what you said. I was so wet, and I started fantasizing about you, and before I knew it…I was coming."

Her cheeks were pink, and Taco wanted to drag her into his room and put them both out of their misery. But he was enjoying this too much. He loved dragging out the anticipation of making love with her. He'd never done this before. He'd been all about getting to the good stuff as fast as possible, except with Jen. But with Koren, the foreplay *was* the good stuff.

Taco twisted his wrist and took her breast into his hand. Even through her bra, he could feel her nipple stabbing into his palm.

"Will you help me make sure you're pleased?"

It was a bit of an awkward statement, but he understood what she meant. "Kor, you aren't going to have to do much of anything to please me."

"You know what I mean," she said, biting her lip.

"Only if you do the same."

She snorted and glanced down at his hand on her breast before saying, "I don't think you're going to need much direction."

"I'm not a virgin either, but none of the women I've been with have been *you*. None have meant as much to me as you do. I'm just as nervous as you are, Koren. The fact that you haven't enjoyed sex is scary as hell. I want to be the man to show you what you've been missing, but that's a lot of pressure. You're going to have to talk to me, help me make sure you're enjoying it."

"So we're going to talk throughout?" she asked with a little scrunch of her nose.

It was fucking adorable.

He grinned. "Talking can be sexy."

She looked skeptical.

"You'll see." Then with one last caress of her breast, he dropped his hand, loving the sigh of disappointment that left her lips. "Ready to go get you a new set of wheels?"

She grimaced "No. I hate car shopping. Dad offered to go with me, but he has to talk about every single thing and haggle them to death. I just want a good price for a car so I can get on with my day."

"I've got your back, Koren."

"Thanks."

He reached down and grabbed hold of the hand that still had his T-shirt held fast. "Let's go before all this talk of sex makes me forget about car shopping at all."

She rolled her eyes.

"Hey, I *am* a guy, as you so eloquently pointed out."

"You're not going to do something weird like sniff my sheets, are you?"

Taco wasn't sure what to say because he'd totally planned on smelling her sheets.

"Fine, but I draw the line at masturbating while you're in there."

He swallowed hard, and when her eyes flicked to the fly of his jeans, he knew she saw how much he liked the prospect of doing just that. "Today...I'll promise. But *after* today, all bets are off."

He held on to her as he grabbed his keys and headed for the front door.

Koren knew she'd blushed all the way to the Nissan dealership. She wasn't used to talking about sex, especially not with a guy. Sure, she, Vicky, and Sue had talked about it plenty, but having Taco so nonchalantly discuss how he'd masturbated after talking with her on the phone, and not even get embarrassed by his hard-on, was...weird. And refreshing.

But all thoughts of sex, what Taco was going to be doing in her bed later, and how good his hand had felt on her breast fled when they were greeted by a smarmy car salesman. She would've preferred to have gotten the one woman saleslady, but it appeared she was too busy flirting with one of the mechanics to greet them.

They'd just spent half an hour listening to the salesman talk about how great the Altima was and about their financing. She knew how great the Altima was, it had literally saved her life, but the thing that really irritated Koren was how the salesman was talking to Taco...not *her*. At one point, Taco had even told the guy that he wasn't the one buying the car, she was. But it didn't seem to help at all.

They'd gotten a tour of the latest model and were

currently sitting at a desk while Melvin—yes, that was really his name—went over the function of every single knob and button.

Koren hated confrontation. Loathed it. But at the moment, she hated Melvin more.

Scooting her chair back, ignoring how it made a screeching noise as it scraped against the floor, she stood up and simply walked out of the cubicle without a word.

"Guess she needs to use the restroom, huh?" Melvin said with a nervous chuckle.

Koren heard Taco say, "If I had to guess, I'd say she's had enough of your bullshit," before she was out of earshot. She ignored the other salesmen and woman saying goodbye and pushed open the door of the showroom. She stomped to her rental and by the time she'd sat and closed the door behind her, Taco was climbing into the passenger side.

Koren immediately started the car and pulled out of the parking spot. "Why can't Amazon sell cars? Seriously. Guys like Melvin are why people don't like car shopping. God! What a *douche*."

"I tried to tell him that I wasn't the one buying the car," Taco said.

"I know. And I appreciate it. He wouldn't even look at me. He just kept trying to sell *you* the car. I'll be the first to admit that I don't know a lot about vehicles, but he didn't even consider the fact that I'm the one paying, so maybe he should try to sell it to *me*."

"So what now?" Taco asked, putting his hand on her thigh.

Just the weight of his hand calmed her somewhat. Sighing, Koren said, "There's another Nissan dealership on the other side of San Antonio. I didn't want to go all the way over there, but Melvin left me no choice. You don't think he'll call and warn them I'm on my way, do you?"

Taco chuckled. "No. Are you sure you want another Altima? What about an Accord? Or a truck? Maybe a Humvee?"

"I'm sure." Koren glanced over at Taco before bringing her attention back to the road. "An Altima saved my life. Literally. There's no way I want to push my luck and get something different."

He didn't call her silly or try to talk her into something bigger again. "Do you want me to stay in the car this time? Maybe if you go in by yourself, you'll have better luck."

Koren blew out a breath. "No. I don't trust myself to buy a car on my own. And that sounds stupid. I mean, I'm thirty-three years old, but I just know they'll somehow screw me if I don't have a guy with me. I *hate* car shopping."

"You're not giving yourself enough credit," Taco said. "You're smart. You saw through Melvin's bullshit in two seconds. But I get what you're saying. We'll just see how things go, and if you want to leave, we'll leave."

"I don't like being rude," Koren mumbled. "But I

will when I have to."

"It was hot," Taco said.

"Oh, no," Koren told him, holding up a hand. "Do *not* go there. I'm pissed off and need to hold on to this mood to deal with another car salesman. Don't get me all hot and bothered, because then I might cave and put up with more antiquated, sexist bullshit."

Taco burst out laughing. "Right. Gotcha. But I'm reserving the right to bring up how much you're turning me on right now at a later date."

Koren merely shook her head and concentrated on merging onto the interstate.

* * *

Three hours later, Koren was beaming as she drove home in her brand-new dark purple Nissan Altima. The salesman helping them had been amazing. When Taco had said in no uncertain terms that he was only there to keep Koren company, the salesman focused all his attention to her. He'd patiently answered all her questions and hadn't even blinked when she wanted to test drive three different cars to make sure they all drove the same and the Altima was really what she wanted.

She was now the proud owner of a two-year-old Altima that she'd gotten for a steal. With the big down payment, thanks to the insurance check, her monthly payments were extremely manageable.

"You look pleased," Taco said after a while.

"I am," Koren said, smiling over at him. "Thank you for going with me."

"You're more than welcome."

"I'm sure you had better things to do all morning than this."

"Nope," Taco said. "Any time I get to spend with you is perfect. Doesn't matter what we do."

She felt the same way about him, but hadn't admitted it. "Ditto," she said softly.

"Want to stop for lunch?"

Koren glanced at her watch and grimaced. "I really need to get home and get some work done. People are super impatient nowadays. If I don't answer their inquiries within an hour, they'll go to someone else."

"You don't have to explain, Koren. I understand. How about if we get you back to your place, then I'll go out and grab us some takeout?"

Her heart fluttered in her chest. She'd never dated someone as considerate as Taco. Generally, the men she'd dated hadn't really understood how important her job was to her. How it wasn't just something she was doing as a hobby from home. She earned a damn good commission because of how dedicated she was to her work.

"That sounds great," Koren told him.

She carefully parked her new baby in her driveway and they went inside. She handed her keys to Taco and threw her purse on the counter. She headed for her laptop, which was currently on the dining room table, and was about to pull out a chair and sit when Taco took hold of her arm.

"Koren," he said hesitatingly.

"Yeah?"

"I didn't think this through. My truck's at my place."

"So?"

"I don't have a car to go get us something to eat. I'll just make something here, if that's okay."

Koren frowned at him. "You can use mine."

He stared at her without saying a word for a full thirty seconds.

"Taco? What's wrong?"

"That's your *new* car," he finally said.

"Yeah? And?"

"You'd let me drive it?"

Koren finally understood. "Taco, you drive those big ol' fire trucks. I trust you. Of course you can drive it."

She watched as he swallowed hard. "You didn't even hesitate though. You just handed over your keys."

Koren snuggled into him. She lay her head on his shoulder and her hands gripped his T-shirt at his back. "Yes, it's my new car. And yes, it would suck if it got wrecked again. But the bottom line is that it's just a hunk of metal. I trust you to not drive like a crazy man. And I'm hungry."

She felt him chuckle and looked up at him.

"Thank you, Kor. I'll be careful with her."

"Her?"

"Of course. Cars are always feminine."

"Oh, jeez. *This* I gotta hear," Koren teased.

"The outside of your car might not be as beautiful as a Lamborghini or Porsche," Taco said, "but if you treat her right, she'll purr just the same. She's mine to take care of and protect, and in return for giving her what she needs to stay healthy and at peak performance, she'll stand by me, support me, and get me to where I want to go. It's a give-and-take kind of thing."

Koren couldn't keep the smile from her face. "First of all, none of that explains why you think cars are female. But secondly…are we still talking about cars?"

Taco shrugged and returned the smile. "Of course."

"Do guys get secret classes on things like this? On saying the right thing at just the right time?"

"I'll never tell," Taco said with a smirk.

"One thing…I don't need protecting," Koren told him.

He nodded. "I don't necessarily mean from people barging into your condo with a gun or something. Just in general. Like today from Melvin. He wanted to rush out after you, but there was no way I was gonna let that happen."

She stared at him in surprise. "He did?"

"Yup."

"You know I *do* support you, right?" Koren asked. "I love how dedicated you are to your job."

"My shifts can be a pain in the ass."

"Yeah, they can be, but honestly, I like my alone time. It doesn't bother me to have you gone for a day or two at a time, know why?"

"Why?"

"Two reasons. One, because when I get to see you again, it's the best feeling in the world."

His face softened.

Koren hurried on. "And two, because I know without a doubt if I needed you, *really* needed you, you'd be there. You'd leave work and come straight to me."

"I absolutely would."

"I know we haven't been dating that long, and we haven't gone all the way, but—"

"Gone all the way?" he teased. "Seriously?"

"Fine. We haven't had sex yet—"

"Made love," he corrected.

"Stop interrupting me," Koren grumbled.

"Then say what you mean," Taco returned.

"Fine, I know we haven't *made love* yet, but you're important to me."

"Ditto."

"And I trust you."

"Same," Taco reassured her.

"So take my car and get me something to eat," Koren finished.

"Anything you're in the mood for?"

Carnal images flashed through her brain, but she knew he wasn't talking about that.

As if he could read her mind, his gaze dropped to her lips. "Damn, woman. You're killin' me."

"Puffy tacos from Henry's?" Koren asked.

"You got it. And good choice," Taco said.

"I thought you'd approve."

Then Taco took her face in his hands and held her gently. "After Jen, I never thought I'd get here."

"Where?"

"Here," Taco said, nodding his head at her. "Being with a woman who could make me laugh one second, and the next, make me want to throw her down onto the nearest piece of furniture and ravage her. I've been a bachelor for a hell of a long time, but now the only thing I can think of is when I'll get to talk to you, see you, touch you. You've changed my life, Koren. And I couldn't be happier about it."

It was a hell of a compliment, and Koren wasn't sure how to respond. He'd changed her life too. She'd never really been jealous of Vicky and Sue, just a little envious that they'd found good men who'd made them happy. Now she had her own.

"I'll be back soon," Taco told her, before leaning down and kissing her hard. It was a short kiss, but not lacking in passion. "Now, stop slacking and get to work."

She chuckled. "Yes, sir."

As Koren sat down to check her emails, she couldn't help but marvel over her luck.

CHAPTER NINE

Taco wasn't nervous at all to officially meet Koren's parents. In fact, she was way more anxious than he was. Of course he wanted them to like him, but the bottom line was that even if they didn't, he wasn't giving up Koren. She was amazing, and he knew a good thing when he had it. He'd dated enough women to know that what they had together was precious. So while he hoped he got along with Mr. and Mrs. Garner, ultimately, it wouldn't make a difference in his choice.

He'd never had a good relationship with his own parents, so that was probably influencing his thoughts now. Though he still hoped things went well tonight because Koren was super stressed about it.

"Relax, Kor. It's going to be fine."

"I know. They're good people, they'll see how awesome you are and it'll be great."

"Then what's wrong?"

"I've never done this," she blurted.

"Done what?"

"Brought someone home before. Someone important."

Taco grinned and pulled her across the console. He kissed her forehead. "I'm flattered."

She rolled her eyes. "You're just possessive," she countered.

"That too."

"My dad is awesome, but whatever you do, don't talk politics. He can go on for hours and he's definitely opinionated. And ignore my mom when she starts talking about how she wishes she had more grandchildren. And their cat is old and grumpy, so don't be offended if she won't come to you for pets. Don't take it personally. And if you use the downstairs bathroom, the toilet squeaks when it flushes. Dad's been meaning to get to that forever, but I don't think he has yet. And Mom—"

"Shhhh," Taco interrupted. "It's going to be great, you know how I know?"

"How?"

"Because they love you. And you love them. You respect them and you told me yourself that your mom is still one of your best friends. How could I *not* like them?"

Her shoulders relaxed and she took a deep breath. "You're right. You're so down to earth, you aren't going to freak out if Mom gets out one of my baby albums."

"Exactly. Take a deep breath," he ordered.

She did.

"And another." He waited until she'd exhaled. "Good. Feel better?"

"Yeah. Thanks."

Taco leaned in and nuzzled the skin behind her ear for a moment, waiting until he felt goose bumps break out on her arms. "And if you stay nice and relaxed tonight, I'll reward you…later."

Her hand came up and took hold of his sleeve. Taco didn't even care if she wrinkled it beyond repair. Every time he looked down, he'd see the evidence of how she liked to touch him.

"Yeah?" she asked. "Maybe it needs to be the other way around. If you're good tonight, I'll make sure it's worth *your* while later."

Her words brought erotic images to mind. The last time she'd spent the night with him, he'd brought her to orgasm with his hand. She'd straddled his thigh and rode him, and with a little extra stimulation on her clit, through her clothes, she'd exploded.

It had been hot as hell…and just another chink in his armor when it came to her.

"Deal," he said immediately.

"How about a good luck kiss before we go in?" Koren asked.

"Making out in your parents' driveway? I'm shocked, Miss Garner," Taco teased.

"That's me, Miss Shocker," she quipped before grabbing him behind the neck and pulling him to her.

He gave her what she wanted. He devoured her mouth as if it was going to be the last time he'd ever get to kiss her. When he pulled away, he was both delighted and dismayed to see her red, swollen lips. Hoping her parents would be clueless as to why their daughter was flushed, he kissed her on the forehead and said, "Come on, Kor. Let's do this."

Twenty minutes later, after the initial introductions were made and Koren had settled a bit when everyone seemed to be getting along, Taco was on the couch with his fingers intertwined with Koren's as they sat and chatted with her folks.

Just as she'd said, they were a bit old fashioned, but very down to earth. It was obvious they only wanted the best for their daughter.

"How long have you been a firefighter?" Mr. Garner asked.

"It seems like my entire life," Taco said. "I was a junior volunteer in high school and when I moved to Texas, volunteered while I got the necessary schooling to be hired on by the city."

"We appreciate what you did for Koren," her mom said. "You know, when she was in that wreck. She said that you were very calm and didn't panic at all. We didn't get a chance to really talk to you at the hospital, so I wanted to make sure I said it tonight."

Taco shook his head. "I actually didn't do much at all."

"Not true," Koren said with a shake of her own head. "He does this all the time, Mom. Downplays what he does. He and his friends are amazing. I never really thought much about it until it was *me* needing help. He works for two days straight, and it doesn't matter if the call comes in the middle of the night, if it's for a huge fire, or just a lonely little old lady who wants someone to talk to, they go without a single complaint."

"It's my job," Taco said, a little uncomfortable with the praise.

"See?" Koren said with a smile.

"If you could do something else, anything else, what would it be? Pretend that you had the education needed and you could automatically be awesome at it... what would you do?" Koren's dad asked.

That was easy. "Be a firefighter. Honestly. I never really dreamed of being a pilot or doctor or anything. When I was little, a house caught fire on my street. I sat on my front steps and watched it for hours, how chaotic the scene was, and how the firefighters seemed so capable despite the frenzy. They hooked up their hoses and ran into that house without hesitation. It was fascinating and awesome. I wanted to be them."

"Good answer," Gavin Garner said.

"What about you, honey?" her mom asked.

Koren shrugged. "I don't know. I like what I do. Is it my dream job? No. But I have a super-flexible schedule and can work from home. If I ever have kids, that's important to me. I don't want to see them for only a few hours after five-thirty, when I get home from a nine-to-five job, until they go to bed at night. I want to be there for them. And working from home would let me do that."

"Do you want children, Taco?" Deena Garner asked.

"Don't answer that!" Koren exclaimed, holding up her hand. "Mom, we talked about this."

"What? I'm just curious," she said with a sly grin. Her mom shook her head, but let the topic drop.

Gavin got up not too much later and headed out to grill the steaks they were having for dinner. Deena headed for the kitchen and before Koren could follow her, Taco stole a kiss.

"Told you it would be fine," he said after he'd forced himself to let go of her.

She rolled her eyes at him, but she smiled before heading into the kitchen.

Taco went out to talk to her dad and they had a nice, easy chat about nothing in particular. The area, the best restaurants, and the best places to go for a hike. Then they re-entered the house and sat down for dinner.

Taco was actually having a great time. Koren's parents were funny and obviously still deeply in love. They teased each other a lot, and Gavin and Deena even whipped out a small photo album she'd obviously pre-planted near the table just to torture their daughter.

Seeing Koren as a teenager was hilarious. She, of course, thought she was hideous, but Taco loved seeing her smiling and happy in the photos. She sportingly shared a story about a homecoming dance she'd gone to where her date had spent the evening flirting with another girl. Koren had dumped his ass and, because she'd driven, left him to find his own way home.

Just after they'd eaten dessert, an amazingly wonderful strawberry cheesecake, Taco's phone rang with a text. He knew it was Sledge's number, as he'd programmed a special tone just for him in case of emergencies, since he was in charge of their crew at the station.

"Saved by the bell," Koren muttered.

Taco grinned as he looked down at his phone.

Sledge: *Car fire. Fully involved. Crash's house.*
Taco: *On my way.*

He turned to Koren. "I need to go."

Without asking why or complaining, Koren stood. "Sorry, Mom and Dad."

"No, no, it's fine. Go. We'll catch up with you later," her mom said.

"Everything okay?" Gavin asked.

Taco shrugged. "Probably. Just need to check on a friend." He didn't want to go into detail right now. He needed to get to Crash and Adeline's place. Sledge didn't say whose car was on fire, but if it was Adeline's brand-new Volvo, Crash was going to lose it. He'd wanted Adeline to have something safe and stylish. He'd thought about what to get her for ages and finally settled on the Volvo. Adeline loved it, and she'd be devastated as well.

They quickly said their goodbyes and were in his truck and heading for the scene in minutes.

"I'd drop you off at your place, but I really want to get there and make sure everyone is all right."

"It's fine. I'd rather go with you anyway," Koren told him. "I'll stay out of your way."

"I'm not worried about that," Taco told her with a small smile.

She returned it.

"Oh, and…" He paused dramatically.

"Yeah?"

"I loved your baby pictures."

Koren smacked him on the arm. "Shut up."

"Seriously, your parents are awesome. I can definitely see why you are the way you are. They're gracious, sweet, and I love how much they're concerned about your well-being."

"Sorry about the third degree you got about your intentions toward me over dinner," Koren said.

"I'm not. I'd be more concerned if they *hadn't* grilled

me. They love you and want the best for you. It's obvious."

"Yeah."

They were quiet the rest of the way to Crash's house as Taco concentrated on getting them there fast but safely. When they got close, the lights from the emergency vehicles were visible from blocks away. Taco had to park way down the block from his friend's house. He quickly walked around his truck and put his hand on Koren's back as they made their way through the police cars and fire trucks.

They immediately saw Crash and Adeline, along with the rest of the Station 7 crew—except for Moose and Penelope—hanging out in a group in the front yard. Taco headed right for them.

"Is everyone all right?" he asked as he neared.

Crash nodded. "We're good." Adeline was standing in front of him, and he had one of his arms slung diagonally across the front of her body. She was holding Coco's leash with white knuckles.

"What happened?"

"We were eating dinner, and we heard something out front. Coco went crazy and when I looked out there, we saw the back end of my Civic on fire," Crash explained.

"It's yours? Not the Volvo?" Taco asked.

"Hers was in the garage," Sledge offered.

"Any ideas about how it started?" Taco asked.

It was Chief who shook his head this time. "I've

already talked to the fire investigator, but it's too soon to tell."

"Any guesses?" Taco pressed.

"Are you the owner?" a voice asked. Taco turned to see a sheriff's deputy standing behind them.

"Yes," Crash said.

"When the flames had been knocked down enough, we saw some lettering on the back windshield of your car. I just need to make sure that you didn't write them on there yourself."

"What? No, nothing was written on my car."

"Right. If you can come and see?" the officer asked.

"Stay here," Crash ordered Adeline.

"I want to see what it says too, Dean," she protested.

Crash took her shoulders in his hands. "Please, stay here. I'll bring you up to date as soon as I can."

"I'll stay here with you," Koren said. She squeezed Taco's hand, then moved closer to Adeline. "We need to let them do their thing."

"Okay, but come right back here and talk to me," Adeline warned Crash. "I mean it."

"I will. Thank you." Crash kissed Adeline tenderly and followed the deputy to the back of his car.

Taco and the other men followed behind him as well.

"Motherfucker," Crash said under his breath.

Taco tilted his head and squinted until the words written on the glass finally made sense.

. . .

Are you sorry?

"Does that mean anything to you?" the deputy asked.

Crash ran a hand through his hair. "Maybe."

When he didn't elaborate, the deputy looked a little impatient. "And?"

"My wife had a...thing...with her boss a while back. He assaulted her in a hotel room up in Dallas. She pressed charges, and we haven't heard anything from him since he was sentenced, but it's possible he was paroled, has stewed in jail and is still pissed."

"What's his name?" the deputy asked, getting his notepad and pen out of a pocket.

Taco wandered nearer to the car, followed by Squirrel and Driftwood. The firefighters were still putting water on the tires to make sure they were out.

"Car fires usually start in the engine," Driftwood said. "I'm not saying they don't start other places, just that it's unusual."

"Jesus, let's just hope there's not a dead body in the trunk," Squirrel muttered.

"Don't even say that," Taco admonished. "Oh, shit... Is that a flare?"

"Where?"

"Stuck under the back tire," Taco said, pointing.

Without a word, Squirrel turned and headed back to the deputy, probably to inform him of what they'd seen.

"So this really could be Adeline's old boss?" Driftwood asked.

Taco shrugged. "I guess."

Chief approached. "Does that flare mean I should be more worried about my shed burning down?"

Taco hadn't even *thought* about that.

A whistle pierced the air, and they all turned to see Sledge motioning them over.

As Taco walked toward his friend and the impromptu meeting he was obviously calling, he glanced over to Adeline and Koren. They were standing shoulder to shoulder, and their attention was fixed on the car.

Gritting his teeth at this latest unwelcome event, Taco gathered around Sledge with the others.

"It looks to me like someone may be targeting fire-fighters," Sledge said, keeping his voice low but not beating around the bush. "It's possible it could be Adeline's previous boss, but we just don't know. Chief, I've asked the deputy to get with the fire investigator and re-investigate the fire at your house. Everyone else needs to stay on alert. So far, torching material possessions is just an annoyance rather than anything more life threatening, but the fire at the shed could've spread to the trees if Tiger hadn't been there to help subdue it until we arrived. And this…setting fire to a firefighter's car in his driveway? Doesn't exactly give me warm and fuzzy feelings."

"What's the plan?" Squirrel asked.

"Look for anything out of the ordinary. I think we have to assume whoever is doing this knows where we live," Sledge said.

"Come on, this could all be a coincidence," Driftwood argued. "Two fires don't automatically mean someone is targeting *us*."

"Are you willing to gamble Quinn's life on that?" Sledge asked with a hard look. "Maybe it'll be your *house* next. And she could get hurt by association. I'm not willing to put Beth's life at risk for anything. If this turns out to be a personal vendetta against Adeline, fine, we'll shut this shit down and deal with it. But if it's someone who has a thing against *us*? We all need to stay on our toes."

"Has anything happened to the others on the other shifts?" Taco asked.

"I texted Mick, and he said he hadn't heard of anything," Sledge said. "Which makes me all the more leery about this shit."

"And we have no idea if our women are safe, do we?" Chief asked.

Sledge hesitated, and Taco's stomach churned.

"I'm not sure of anything at this point," Sledge admitted. "All I know is that my oh-shit meter is pegged and I'm not feeling good about this."

"What am I supposed to be sorry about?" Crash asked. "It doesn't make sense. It makes more sense for it to be about Adeline. And Chief's shed could've been an unfortunate coincidence. I still don't think we should panic at this point."

"I agree," Taco said. "But that doesn't mean I don't think it's worth keeping our women close for the time being." Even though they were having a serious conversation, he couldn't help but feel how right it was to think of Koren as "his woman." He'd never really thought of anyone else that way.

He looked over and saw that Koren and Adeline had sat down on the grass with Coco between them. Both looked worried and stressed out, and Coco was doing his best to console them. The two women were holding hands and leaning toward each other, obviously taking comfort in each other's presence.

"Could this be related to Jen?" Taco blurted. Then more thoughts crowded into his brain. "Or what about that doctor at the hospital that was fired? He was really pissed off at Sophie. And should we tell the cops to check into that gang Blythe had issues with? Lord knows we've had our share of people who might be pissed at us over the last year or so."

No one said anything for a long moment.

"Shit," Chief said. "I'll talk to the deputy."

"No, I'll do it," Sledge said. "And Taco is right. This could be any number of people. Let's not do anything crazy at this point though. Until we know more, we really know nothing. While I definitely don't like the look of that flare, that doesn't mean unequivocally that someone has it out for us. Be careful, tell the women to be careful, and we'll carry on as normal. But let's encourage them to check in more often when we're on shift. If they have errands, maybe they can team up and go in pairs or groups. If this *is* a vendetta against us, let's not make it easy on whoever it is."

Everyone nodded and Taco made his way back over to where he'd left Koren.

She immediately stood when he approached. "Is everything okay?" she asked nervously.

Taco wrapped an arm around her shoulders and pulled her into him.

She came willingly.

And, as he was coming to expect, her fingers gripped his shirt at his sides.

"Everything's okay," he assured her, even if he wasn't one hundred percent positive about that.

"This wasn't an accident," Adeline said from next to them.

Crash walked up and said, "Come on. We'll talk inside." He grabbed hold of Adeline's hand and took Coco's leash at the same time.

Taco felt Koren turn her head, but she didn't pull away from him. "I'll talk to you later, Adeline."

"Definitely. Remember what I said," Adeline replied, then let Crash lead her into their house.

"What'd she say?" Taco asked.

He didn't think she was going to answer. But after a beat, Koren said, "Just that she'd never seen you look so content."

Taco wasn't surprised everyone else noticed. "That's

because it's been too long since I've been this happy." He kissed her temple. "Come on, I want to get home too. It's been a very long day."

He realized just how tired she was when she didn't respond. He turned her, but kept his arm around her shoulders. She wrapped her arm around him and they walked side by side down the street to where he'd left his truck earlier that evening.

Taco still had a hundred questions about what had happened to Crash's car and what was really going on, but at the moment, he just wanted to get Koren home safely.

CHAPTER TEN

It was easy to remain undetected with all the chaos outside the firefighter's home. Nadine didn't stay to watch the police and fire investigator do their thing. She didn't care what they found; it wasn't as if she was trying to hide the fact that she'd set the fire. Not anymore.

Her eyes stayed on Hudson Vines and his girlfriend. She had a few more things up her sleeve before her *coup de grace*.

Absently, she scratched at the scabs on her arms as her gaze followed her nemesis. She needed another hit, but before she left, she watched as Hudson opened the passenger side door for the woman with him. He kissed her tenderly before she hopped inside.

"Enjoy your whore while you can," she muttered.

The second the truck was out of sight, Nadine turned and headed back through the neighbors' yards to get to her car parked two blocks over. A dog barked from nearby and the cicadas were loud, but she heard none of it. She was busy thinking of the perfect revenge.

It took her two tries to get the key into the ignition, but that didn't really register either. She needed more meth. She'd smoked her last rock before setting the car on fire. As she drove, she picked up her phone and dialed her dealer's number, not noticing that she almost side-swiped a parked car in the process.

When he answered, she simply said, "I need more."

"Nadine, I just gave you a rock."

"I know, but I need it!"

"You got money?" he asked.

Nadine didn't answer.

"I'll take that as a no. You know what I want in exchange. I'll be at your trailer in an hour."

"I need something sooner," she whined.

"An hour. I got shit to do," he said, then hung up.

Nadine clicked off her phone and gripped the steering wheel with both hands. She hated what she'd become, but she needed the drugs now more than ever. They helped her forget. Without the numbing bliss, as she drove toward the trailer, Nadine's mind automatically drifted to the past...and how far she'd fallen.

"Honey...I'm pregnant!" Nadine said.

"*Really? Oh my God! That's so awesome!*" Preston exclaimed. "*I love you so much...*"

Shaking her head, Nadine scowled. Yeah, Preston had loved her *then*, when things were going well. But after Stevie was born, he'd found fault with everything she did.

"*All I'm asking is that you do a bit of housekeeping while I'm at work,*" Preston said when he got home.

"*I'm doing the best I can. It's hard to keep up with Stevie. I got the laundry done today.*"

"*Do you want a fucking cookie, Nadine? Jesus, look at this place. There's toys and shit everywhere. The kitchen's a disaster. Honest to God, I have no idea what you do all day. You're not working, your only job is to make sure my son doesn't hurt himself, and look,*" he threw out a hand, "*he could choke on those toy pieces over there! All this damn food on the floor isn't exactly sanitary either. And look at yourself.*" His gaze went from the top of her head to her toes. "*You've let yourself go. You're fat, you're dressed like a slob. I want to know what happened to the beautiful Nadine I married.*"

"*You asshole!*" Nadine said. "*You want to try staying home and watching Stevie? It's not as easy as it looks.*"

"*Whatever. Clean yourself up. Jesus. If you're so damn tired, I'll take Stevie and we'll go out to eat. Hopefully after*" *you pick up this pigsty, you'll be asleep by the time we get back so I don't have to see you again tonight."*

And with that, Preston put his briefcase on the floor and went to pick up their son.

Nadine gripped the steering wheel so hard her knuckles turned white. What a *dick*. It wasn't as if she hadn't tried to keep him happy. She'd tried everything to lose the extra weight she'd gained, and when a normal diet hadn't worked, she'd turned to more extreme measures. She'd started smoking weed...but instead of helping her lose weight, it gave her the munchies, and she'd put on even *more* pounds instead of taking them off.

"If you really want to lose weight, darlin', smoking weed isn't gonna do it," said the man she'd been getting her marijuana from.

Nadine frowned. "Well, no shit, I know that now."

"Weed'll make you feel good, and you won't give a shit what your old man says, but if you really want to win him back, you're gonna have to lose that baby weight."

She scowled harder. "Fuck you. What else do you have for me then?"

The dealer just laughed as he reached into his pocket. "You're hot, Nadine. But you could be so much hotter. Here, this one's on the house."

Nadine looked at the small blue-white rock in his palm. "What is it?"

"Ice."

She had no idea what that was, but she didn't want to look stupid. "Oh."

The dealer rolled his eyes. "I've got some time. I'll show you how it's done."

Nadine hesitated. She only had two hours before she had to meet Stevie at the bus stop. She'd never not been there when he got home, and she didn't want to start now. He was the best thing that had ever happened to her.

And Preston...

He was definitely fucking around on her. But she wasn't ready to let him go. Wasn't that why she'd started smoking pot in the first place? To try to lose weight so he'd be attracted to her again? If this ice stuff could do what the weed obviously hadn't, then she could get her husband back and they could all be a happy family again.

"Okay," she agreed.

She watched carefully as the dealer put the chunk into a small glass pipe, then used a lighter to heat it up. She saw the rock slowly melt into a liquid. He turned and smiled at her, then concentrated on what he was doing. Once the drug started to solidify again, he handed her the pipe.

She looked at him in confusion.

"I'm gonna heat it up again. Once it begins to smoke, inhale slowly. Don't hold it in, exhale immediately."

"That's it?"

"That's it."

The second the smoke built up in the pipe, she sucked it into her lungs. She didn't feel anything. Turning to the dealer, she shrugged.

He laughed. "It takes a few minutes. Here, take another hit."

She did.

Ten minutes later, Nadine felt a euphoria like she'd never felt before. It was beautiful. She felt as if she could take on the world. She had more energy than she'd had in a long time.

"Feels good, doesn't it?" the dealer said, running his hand up and down her arm in a slow caress.

"Yeah," Nadine said, nodding and grinning like a fool.

"Trust me, you're gonna love this. You aren't gonna feel like eating, which is where the weight loss comes in. You'll have the energy to clean your house ten times over, so your old man'll have nothing to complain about when he gets home."

"Awesome," Nadine said.

"Now...that one was free, but how about showing me some gratitude?"

"What? How?" She should've been alarmed, but at that moment, she felt too good to worry about anything.

"Just a kiss, baby. Just a kiss."

A kiss. She could do that.

When she kissed the man ten years younger than her, Nadine didn't feel a sexual spark of any kind. But he sure seemed pleased.

"When you need more, let me know. We can work out a deal, I'm sure," he said with a smile.

"Awesome," Nadine said again. *Then she headed out the door to pick up her son from school.*

Thinking back on that first high, Nadine felt sad. It had been so beautiful. She'd felt deliciously happy and slightly numb for hours. She'd cleaned the house from top to bottom, and even Stevie being a whiny little brat hadn't bothered her. Of course, the next day had been hard. And the next even harder. She'd been more depressed than she had in a long time. And she'd eaten everything she could get her hands on.

It hadn't been long before she'd called her dealer again.

The second time she'd done meth had been just as good as the first.

Then she'd done it again.

And again.

It soon got to the point where she needed a hit every morning.

Then her dealer had shown her how to shoot it instead of smoke it, which was great because it was faster, and there wasn't a chance that Preston would smell the smoke.

But she hadn't been careful enough.

.   .   .

"What's this?" Preston asked as he came out of the bathroom holding a used syringe.

Nadine froze—and couldn't think of anything to say.

"Are you doing drugs?" he asked, the anger clear in his tone.

"What if I am?" Nadine said. "It's not like you care."

He sneered. "You're disgusting!"

"Really, Preston? Because you didn't think so when I was sucking your dick last night! You told me to lose weight. I did. You told me to keep the house clean. I did. I don't know what you're so pissed about."

"I'm done," he said, heading for their closet.

"Done with what?" Nadine asked.

"You. I'm moving out."

She just stood there staring after him. Nadine knew she should feel something, anger, disappointment, sadness, but because she'd recently taken a hit, she felt nothing. And nothing felt awesome.

She'd managed to make it through her job at the nursery today without a hit, but it had been a close call. She'd started working part-time at the greenhouse when Stevie was old enough to go to school. She hated the job, really, but it gave her the money she needed to buy the meth she'd become so reliant on to make it through the day.

"Go ahead! Move in with the secretary you've been fuck-ing!" she yelled. "I don't care. But you aren't taking Stevie."

Preston came out of the closet after several minutes and headed for the bathroom.

"Did you hear me?" she yelled. "You aren't taking my son!"

Preston reemerged from the bathroom a minute later, and the look he threw at her was full of scorn. "I don't want anything that will remind me of you."

"Good. Get out!"

"I should've done this a long time ago. Who knows how much of my money you've used for whatever shit you're putting in your body. Good luck finding enough to live on. That shitty part-time job won't cut it. You'll never get another dime from me."

"We'll see about that," Nadine told him, suddenly calm. She wasn't stupid. She'd been collecting evidence against her husband for years now, just in case. She had cold, hard proof of his affairs.

After he left, she checked to make sure he hadn't taken the syringe she'd carelessly left on top of the trash can that morning, and smiled to realize he hadn't. He might try to bring up her drug use in court, but he had no proof. None. She was a model wife—and she was going to take him to the cleaners.

Nadine pulled up to the trailer she'd begged her dealer to let her use after her house burned down. She managed to turn off the ignition, but was too tired to get out. She should get inside. Eat something...she couldn't remember when she'd last eaten, but first, she'd rest for just a bit.

. . .

"Stevie! I'm headed out for a bit."

When her son didn't answer, she knocked on the door to his room. "Stevie?"

"I heard you, Mom."

"I'll be back soon."

"Sure. Whatever."

Nadine hesitated. Stevie had been withdrawn and sullen lately, but from everything she'd read, that's how thirteen-year-old boys were. And she knew he was upset because he'd wanted a pair of expensive sneakers, but she'd had to tell him no. She didn't have any extra money to buy the shoes. The cash she'd gotten from Preston in the divorce had seemed like a fortune at the time, but somehow she'd managed to go through it in less than three years. Yes, the courts were making Preston pay child support every month, but that money was practically gone before it hit her account. Spent on the drugs her body so desperately needed.

Feeling jittery and knowing she needed a hit so she wouldn't crash, she told herself that it would only take an hour or so and she'd be back. Stevie was more than old enough to stay home by himself now. She no longer had to hide the fact she left her child alone, like she used to when he was younger.

"Love you!" she called out to Stevie through the door.

There was no response.

Shaking her head, she turned to head down the hall. Seeing the bottle of vodka sitting on the kitchen table, she

169

made a detour and grabbed it. She took a long swallow before putting it back down. The burn of the liquor settling in her stomach went a long way toward making her feel better. She'd be okay now until she could get to her dealer's.

Nadine pried her eyes open and stared blindly at the dilapidated trailer in front of her. She missed her house. Missed having money. When she was flush, she'd let her dealer and his friends fuck her on *her* terms. Now that she had nothing—and he knew it—she had to do what he wanted, when he wanted, in order to get what she needed.

And she *needed* the drugs. Her teeth were rotten from years of use, but she didn't care. She was skinny. She saved a shit load of money because she didn't often feel the need to eat. But she didn't really care about any of *that*, either.

Her reason to try to keep going was gone. She was living only for revenge at the moment. That's all she cared about.

So she'd let her dealer fuck her in the ass, as long as she got a rock in exchange. It didn't matter. Nothing mattered but making sure the person responsible for her son's death paid the price.

She felt great. Euphoric. Like she was on top of the world. She didn't care about her stupid ex-husband and his new wife. Didn't care that the bitch was pregnant, that Preston was bragging to anyone and everyone about how happy he was.

Fuck him.

Swerving so she didn't hit the person who'd stepped right out into the crosswalk in front of her, Nadine ignored the sound of horns blasting. Idiot drivers.

Frowning, Nadine pulled down her street. Why were there so many flashing lights? They were hurting her eyes.

Pulling as close to her house as she could, ignoring the thump as she ran over something, Nadine didn't even notice that she'd pulled onto a neighbor's lawn.

Flames were shooting out of the roof of her house. Out of the windows. Smoke rose into the sky, visible in the flashing lights from all the emergency vehicles.

Her drug-addled mind couldn't process what she was seeing.

She got out of her car and stumbled. She couldn't take her eyes off the man who'd just emerged from her house.

He was carrying Stevie.

A limp Stevie.

She heard him say, "He's gone. We were too late," before placing him on the ground. Then he stood and turned his back on her son.

Rage burst to life inside her, which was unusual. In all the years she'd been doing meth, she'd never felt much of anything except euphoria after a hit. But now her heart raced, and a feeling of hatred so deep and dark rose within her.

He wasn't even trying to save him! The fireman was late to the fire—and it had killed her son. He killed her son!

She memorized the man's features, knowing in that instant it was now her mission in life to destroy him.

She rushed up to him and got in his face. "You killed my baby!" she screamed.

The firefighter took a step backward, but she wasn't going to let him get away. He had to admit what he'd done.

"You should've been faster! You took too long to get to him! He's dead because of you!"

The firefighter held his hands up. "Stand back, ma'am," he ordered.

"No, you did this! It's your fault!"

He just looked down at her arrogantly. So much like Preston. He didn't care. He didn't have one ounce of feeling inside him. He'd let her baby die.

"You need to step back for your own safety," an officer said as he took hold of her arm.

"He killed my son!" she yelled.

"Come on," the officer said.

Nadine fought him. She was strong, she could take him. She continued to yell at the firefighter, even as another cop came up and started to talk to him. Then he turned his back on her. That was unacceptable.

She fought with everything she had, and it took four cops to finally pin her down and get her inside the back of a police car. Right before they slammed the door, she screamed, "You're going to regret this! Mark my words. You. Will. Regret. Killing. My. Son!"

. . .

Nadine startled when a knock sounded at her window. Looking up, she saw the smarmy face of her dealer.

"It's about time," she said grumpily as she rolled down the window.

"Believe it or not, I don't live to serve you," the man said with a smirk. "But now that I'm here with my bud, you can serve us both."

"Whatever. Did you bring it?" Nadine asked.

He held up a small baggie containing a few rocks. There was enough there to last her through what was left of the night and into the next day. Her mouth watered at the thought of the high that was waiting. She reached for the bag.

The dealer snatched it back. "Uh-uh. Payment first."

Sneering, Nadine climbed out of the car and immediately tripped and landed on the ground on her hands and knees. The men didn't help her up, merely laughed as she got to her feet. Not caring, Nadine led the way to the trailer. There wasn't much inside. A bed. A desk. A beat-up old sofa. That was about it. But she didn't need anything else. Now that Stevie wasn't there, she didn't need anything at all.

Feeling sadness start to creep its way in, Nadine shook her head. No, she wasn't going to be sad. Or feel guilty. Nope. What happened to her son *wasn't* her fault.

But the words of the cops on that horrid night wouldn't stay out of her head.

"Your son had a blood alcohol level of over .2. Do you know what that means?" the officer asked.

Of course she knew. She wasn't an idiot. But all Nadine could think about was getting out of the room so she could get to her dealer. She felt sick and needed some meth. Badly.

"Yes, sir."

"It means that he was most likely unconscious when the fire started. Passed out drunk. The fire investigator believes it started in the kitchen. Probably sparked from the refrigerator. Many people forget to clean behind and under the fridge. Dust and debris builds up. And yours was old, which is another factor. More tests will be done, but it looks like the fire was accidental."

Some consolation that was. Nadine kept her mouth shut as the officer continued.

"You said that your son was home alone. Where were you?"

"I had an errand to run," she said.

"What errand?" the cop pressed.

Thinking fast, Nadine said, "He's been having problems at school." Which wasn't a lie. "And I had a meeting with his teacher." That was a lie. But it wasn't as if she could admit she'd been meeting her drug dealer.

"Hmmm," the officer said, clearly not believing her. "Anyway, your son was plastered. There were several bottles

around the couch. We're assuming that's where he passed out. Where did he get the booze?"

Nadine pressed her lips together. It wasn't illegal for her to have alcohol in the house. She was an adult. And she didn't mind when Stevie drank with her. She was careful to only let him have a little. He needed to learn how to hold his liquor. It would make him a better man.

"Was it yours?"

She shrugged. "Probably. I mean, I had a few bottles in the house. That's not against the law. But he knew not to touch them." That was also a lie, but again, at this point, she needed to do whatever was necessary to make sure she didn't go to jail. How dare this asshole interrogate her when she didn't do anything wrong! He should be talking to the damn firefighter. Demanding to know why it took so long for him to get there and why he hadn't saved Stevie. He should be arresting that asshole, not wasting his time talking to her.

"It's not illegal," the officer agreed.

Nadine tried to look as pathetic as possible. She squeezed a few tears out for good measure.

The man sighed.

Inside, she smirked. Men were suckers for tears. Preston had always hated when she'd cried, and she frequently managed to get a few rocks out of her dealer when she brought on the waterworks.

"Here's what's going to happen," he said. "You'll have to see the judge for your DUI charge from last night. But from what we can tell, you had nothing to do with the fire. It was bad luck that your son decided to experiment with alcohol on

175

the same night the fire started. But you need to use this incident to turn your life around. Stop drinking, and for God's sake, get off the meth. It's going to kill you."

He was wrong. It had already killed her. She was a walking, talking corpse, and without Stevie, she didn't even care. She'd reach over and grab the officer's gun right now and put it to her head if not for one thing.

She had to make sure the firefighter paid for being too late to save her son.

"I will," she lied again.

The officer stared at her for a moment, as if he knew she was still bullshitting him.

"I'm going to give you some pamphlets. Use them. The organizations on them really want to help."

Nadine nodded, knowing she'd throw the damn things away the first chance she got.

Sighing again, the officer stood. Nadine followed suit. "Come on. I'll make sure you have a ride to wherever you want to go."

That was the thing. She had nowhere to go. No house. No husband. No friends. No son.

"I'll be fine," she said with a weak smile.

Thirty minutes later, Nadine left the station with one thing on her mind. Getting to her dealer and getting a hit. Then she'd start researching. She had to be careful. Do things just the right way to cause maximum pain...pain like she was feeling.

. . .

The second the door of the trailer shut behind them, the dealer and his friend began undoing their belts. "You know the drill," her dealer said.

Without a word, Nadine pulled off her clothes and leaned over the sofa. She didn't care what they did as long as she got what she needed out of it.

As one of the men—she didn't know which one— did what he'd come to do, Nadine's mind drifted again, and she remembered the look of frustration on Hudson's face earlier that night. He didn't know what was going on yet, and she loved every second of his uncertainty.

He'd know soon enough.

Then he'd feel as much pain as she did.

Maybe then he'd be sorry.

Maybe then he'd wish that he'd moved a little faster that night.

That he'd gotten to Stevie faster.

Ignoring what was being done to her body, Nadine closed her eyes and got lost in her mind. Lost in the satisfaction she knew she'd finally feel once Hudson understood what was going to happen—and why.

CHAPTER ELEVEN

A few days later, no one was any closer to figuring out who was behind setting Crash's car on fire. It was definitely arson, but other than the "Are you sorry?" note written on the back windshield, they had no concrete evidence.

Nothing else had happened in the ensuing days, and everyone was being cautiously optimistic that maybe it was simply punk kids acting out, and not something more sinister.

Taco planned on picking up Koren around four. She was working on travel details for a group that was going to the Bahamas for a wedding. He'd talked to her that morning when he got off shift and had already been eager to see her.

And that was another new thing for him. He hadn't understood how his friends could spend every waking moment—when not at work—with their women and not get bored. But now he did. Even if he and Koren didn't do anything other than sit in the same room and watch TV together, he felt content.

She didn't constantly hound him about his day or want gory details about calls. She didn't pressure him to try to make up with his parents. She didn't feel the need to go out and party. He knew she'd been trying to spend time with her best friends while he was on shift, so she could spend his off time with him, and that meant the world to Taco.

The bottom line was, being around Koren was relaxing. And he hadn't realized how much he wanted and needed that in a girlfriend until her. Being around Jen hadn't been relaxing in the least. She constantly wanted to be entertained, and she'd always asked him a ton of questions. Now he understood that she'd been fishing for information about Quinn, but at the time, all it had done was make him tense.

Taco still worried a bit about the fires, but since there was no more information, there was nothing he or his friends could do but encourage their women to be safe and alert.

The sound of his cell ringing brought Taco out of his musing. Hoping it was Koren—which was something else he'd rarely done in the past...looked forward to chatting about nothing with his girlfriend—he rushed into the kitchen to answer it.

Seeing it was Beth, and feeling bad about the pang

of disappointment that struck him, Taco clicked it on. "Hello?"

"Hey, Taco. It's Beth."

"Hi. What's up?"

"I…uh…Cade encouraged me to call."

Taco tensed. He couldn't figure out Beth's tone, but it wasn't good. "Why? What's wrong? Did you find out something about the fires?"

"Yes and no."

When she didn't continue for a long moment, Taco huffed out a breath. "Spit it out, Beth."

"Right. In my defense, I was looking into every little thing to try to figure this out. I left no stone unturned. Looked under every nook and cranny. I wouldn't stop until—"

"Beth," Taco warned.

"Sorry, right. After Crash's car, I was trying to figure out what's different *now* than a few weeks ago, before Chief's shed went up in a puff of smoke, since that was the first incident. And really, the only thing different is that you're dating Koren. I had to do it. I didn't have bad intentions and only wanted to protect you and everyone else, but… Iinvestigatedher."

Her last few words were all strung together, and it took a moment for Taco to comprehend what she was saying. When he did, he felt his hackles rising. "What?" he asked.

"I know, I know! It was a shitty thing to do. And I

admit, I started even before Chief's shed caught fire. I was worried about you, Taco. I couldn't stand the thought of you getting screwed over again. But I didn't find anything that worried me at all. Your girl is squeaky clean. She had the all-American upbringing. Two parents with good jobs who everyone seems to admire and like. Koren got good grades in high school and college and hasn't ever been in trouble with the law except for a bunch of parking tickets when she was in college...but who hasn't gotten a parking ticket on a university campus? Parking always sucks. She started out working in a brick-and-mortar travel agency. Can I call it that? You know what I mean. Anyway, she got great annual reviews and eventually she decided to go freelance."

"You investigated Koren?" Taco bit out.

"Well...yeah. That's what I'm telling you."

"You had *no* right."

"Taco—"

"I get it. You're the computer expert. But you violated her privacy, Beth. That's not cool! Not cool at all."

"I know," Beth moaned. "But...she was new to the group. And after Jen, how could I *not*?"

Humiliation swept over Taco in a swift tide. "Right, because I'm the stupid schmuck who was dating the serial killer. I get it."

"It's not like that," Beth replied softly.

"Then explain it to me," Taco said sharply. "I start

dating a nice woman, and you go and stick your nose in where it doesn't belong."

"I did it for you!" Beth said desperately. "And Jen was a bitch, there's no doubt, but you weren't the only one duped by her. We all were. Including me. I didn't particularly like her, but I never suspected she was only with you to get closer to Quinn. None of us did. I'd do anything for you, Taco. Just like I would do anything for the rest of the gang."

"Excuse me if I think violating Koren's privacy is something you should be thanked for."

"She knows," Beth admitted. "I told her that I'd done a background check on her. She wasn't happy, but she said she understood."

"Well, I don't," Taco responded. He knew Beth was a computer genius who had a habit of doing things online that she shouldn't, but he never thought he had to worry about her digging into his personal life. And Koren was definitely a big part of his personal life.

"I know you're pissed at me. I also understand why. I'm sorry for hurting you, but, Taco…I'd probably do it again if it meant keeping the people I love safe."

Taco tried to understand. But the hurt and anger that she'd gone behind his back was too much for him to get over instantly. "So what did you find, then?"

"How do you know I found anything?" she asked.

"Because if you didn't, you wouldn't have called me and admitted to looking into her background."

"Right… Well, before, I just looked at Koren and her

immediate family. But after the fire at Sophie's, and Crash's car going up in smoke, I expanded my search. Then I talked to Cade, and he told me I had to call you."

"Just spill it," Taco said, rubbing a hand over his face in frustration.

"Koren's friend Sue was arrested for setting a car on fire."

"*What*? When?" Taco asked.

"When she was in college," Beth said.

Taco quickly did the math in his head. "So over a decade ago."

"Yeah, but I don't think we can dismiss any information."

"What are the details?"

"She was twenty, and after their basketball team won the conference championships, the campus went a little crazy. She was caught on shitty video, helping to light a car on fire. Her parents hired an expensive lawyer and she got off with probation and community service."

"Let me get this straight," Taco said in a low, even tone that belied how pissed he was. "Koren's friend was all hyped up that her team won a championship, and she was caught on someone's cell participating in vandalism with probably countless others? And now she's in her early thirties, with a family and a steady job, and you think she's decided it might be fun to bring back her college days and start another fire?"

"She has a history with fire," Beth insisted. "It can't be ignored."

"So do you," Taco said flatly.

There was silence on the other end of the phone for a tense second before Beth said, "Okay, I deserved that. But this isn't the same thing, Taco."

"Beth, I've met Sue Butler. She's a very nice woman who would do anything for Koren. But there's no way she'd torch a car and a shed and leave cryptic notes about being sorry. I admit that I don't know her that well, but I'm fairly confident if she had a problem with me, she'd just come right out and tell Koren she was making a mistake in dating me."

"But—"

"I know you didn't mean anything sinister by researching Koren, but from where I'm standing, it feels like a hell of a violation," Taco said quietly. "I appreciate you telling me what you've done, but *don't* do it again, Beth. You've spent so much time behind the screen of your computer, I think you've forgotten the people you're looking into are living, breathing beings with feelings. Would you have appreciated it if Hayden had researched *you* and told Sledge all about what happened to you out in California? Warned him away on the premise that you were too unstable to make a good girlfriend?"

Beth didn't say anything, so Taco went on.

"You wouldn't. I know you wouldn't. I admit that I made a huge mistake with Jen, but Koren isn't anything like her. If you truly cared about me, you'd trust me to have learned my lesson. I'd bet everything I have that neither Koren nor anyone in her life have anything to do with what's happening. We still don't know that the fires have anything to do with *any* of us."

"I'm sorry," Beth said softly. "I just…I've never had friends like the ones I do now, and I felt so awful about what happened to Quinn that I vowed to do everything in my power to keep anything like that from happening to my friends again. I was just trying to keep everyone safe. We've all been through enough stuff, and if I could do anything to keep any more bad stuff from touching us, I was going to do it."

"Apology accepted," Taco told her. "But don't be telling anyone else that shit about Sue. She's a good woman, and I'm sure she'd be embarrassed if that story got out."

"I won't."

"Good."

"Are…are we okay?" Beth asked.

"Of course," Taco said.

"Okay. Cade's standing here frowning at me. For the record, he told me exactly what you did. Then he urged me to call and tell you what I'd done. And I did gladly, because I wanted to protect you."

"I get it. I'll see you later, Beth."

"Bye, Taco."

Taco clicked off the phone and bowed his head, breathing hard.

He was extremely upset. It seemed as if his life lately had been one drama after another, and it was frustrating. He didn't want Beth to feel like she had to protect him. He didn't want Koren to have to deal with whoever was behind the fires.

Looking at his watch, Taco saw that it was still way too early to go over to Koren's condo, but he didn't care. Beth had said Koren knew she'd looked into her. He was kind of upset that she hadn't said anything to him. Koren should've been pissed that one of his friends had looked into her background.

His decision made, Taco pocketed his phone and headed for the door.

Twenty minutes later, he was knocking on Koren's front door. He turned to observe her neighborhood as he waited for her to answer. Her three-story condo was sandwiched in the middle of a row of similar-looking units. Each had their own garage and driveway. Across the street were more condos. They all looked a bit cookie-cutter, but the neighborhood was quiet and well kept. It was very middle class. Suburban. He couldn't say that it fit Koren's personality, but he understood the lure of easy living. And paying a monthly fee to have someone take care of the landscaping, and to have a pool and tennis court to play in and on whenever you wanted, was a good deal.

The door opened behind him and Taco turned.

"Taco! Hi! You're early," Koren said.

"Can I come in?"

She frowned at his tone. "Of course. What's wrong?"

Without answering, Taco moved past her. He went into the living area that was attached to her kitchen, then turned.

She'd closed the door and approached until she was about five feet away.

"Beth called me today."

When he didn't say anything else, she asked, "And?"

"And she told me that she'd investigated you."

"Shit," Koren said under her breath.

"Yeah," Taco agreed.

"I knew you wouldn't be happy she'd done that."

Taco tilted his head and studied her. She didn't look upset in the least. She looked more worried about *him* at the moment than what Beth had done. "You aren't bothered that she looked into your background? That she violated your privacy? Because, make no mistake, she did. She's able to find shit on the Internet that would make your head spin. Hell, the woman can hack into government satellites, for God's sake."

"Seriously?"

"Yes."

Koren took a deep breath. She didn't come any closer. "I'm not thrilled, if I'm being honest. But I've got nothing to hide, Taco. And I understand why she did it. To protect you. If my friends had the abilities Beth does, they'd probably have done the same thing. They're nosy and can be overly protective of me, but that's because they love me. Just like Beth loves you. So yeah, it was a surprise and it made me feel uncomfortable for a bit, but honestly, I'm just me. My life is boring."

"You are not boring," Taco said sternly.

Koren smiled. "I am, but it's okay, I'm perfectly fine with that. Seriously."

Taco stared at her in surprise. But she wasn't aware of the full implications. "Beth told me today that she expanded her search. She not only violated *your* privacy, but she also violated Sue's and Vicky's."

Koren nodded. "Let me guess. She found out that Sue is a hardened criminal who was arrested for vandalism."

Taco nodded.

For the first time, Koren looked worried. "And you think Sue set Crash's car on fire now?"

"No. Of course not. I think Beth's lost her mind, and is clearly desperate to find a reason for the fires."

"I was there too," Koren said softly. "And so was Vicky. But we weren't caught on the video. We got swept up in the excitement of the night and stupidly got involved with setting that car on fire. But, Taco, it was a junker. Placed on campus by some spirit group. It was spray painted and graffitied for the game. It wasn't someone's *actual* car. We wouldn't have done that. And Vicky and I felt so bad that Sue had gotten caught and been arrested when we were there too, that we did her community service with her. Sue didn't set Crash's car on fire. Or Chief's shed. She'd be more apt to get up in someone's face if she had a problem with them.

"And the reason I ultimately don't care that Beth looked into me—other than the facts that I have absolutely nothing to hide, and I had a great childhood and teen years, and even adulthood—is because she did it out of love for *you*."

Taco listened—and realized she wasn't just trying to reassure him. She really *didn't* care that Beth had hacked into her college records, or that she'd violated her privacy.

He slowly closed the distance between them, keeping his eyes on hers. He stopped right in front of her and reached out and took her face in his hands. "How'd I get so lucky?"

Koren immediately gripped his shirt at his sides. "I think that's my line," she teased.

He shook his head. "No. You don't get it."

"Get what?"

"You are the epitome of the perfect girlfriend. You're funny, beautiful, and you have wonderful, supportive friends and family. You aren't into drama, and even when there *is* drama, you somehow let it bounce right off you."

"That's not true," she protested.

"It is. You could've gotten flipped out over the fact that Beth dared to research you. And your friends. I wouldn't have blamed you if you'd gotten spooked and wanted to take some time to think about our relationship. But you didn't. You haven't. You're the *perfect* girlfriend."

"I'm not perfect," Koren protested. "Not even close. In case you haven't noticed, guys aren't exactly beating down my door."

"Their loss is my gain," Taco retorted.

"Taco," she said with a small shake of her head. "I'm not who you think I am."

"Yeah? Who do you think you are?"

She shrugged. "You're seeing me through some sort of distorted glasses or something. I'm just me. Plain ol' Koren. I'm more comfortable hanging out in my fat pants and T-shirts than dressing up and going out. Why do you think I started working from home?"

"And?"

She huffed out a breath. "I can't live up to your expectations of me. It's too much. I'm bound to screw up and you'll wonder what in the world you were thinking."

"You don't get it."

"I know I don't!"

"You've already met and exceeded *all* my expectations, Koren. You can't screw anything up because there's nothing *to* screw up. As I said, I'm the lucky one, and believe me, I'm well aware that you're way too good for me, but I don't care. I'm going to be selfish and do my best to tie you to me anyway."

Her fingers tightened on his T-shirt. "I'm already tied to you," she whispered.

Taco stared down into her blue eyes and brushed a lock of blonde hair behind her ear. How he'd ever thought she looked like Jen was beyond him. Yes, she had similar color hair and eyes, but that was where any resemblance ended.

"I need you, Koren…" Taco started, taking a breath to continue, but she interrupted before he could.

"Yes."

"I was going to say, I need you in my life. Any way I can get you."

"Oh," she said, and her face flamed with a blush and she looked away.

Taco put a finger under her chin and turned her back to face him. "But as usual, you're braver than I am."

She rolled her eyes.

He smiled. "I need you that way too. I've dreamed about nothing else over the last couple of weeks. You have no idea how difficult it is to wake up to the sound of the emergency bell and try to put on a pair of bunker pants over an erection."

Her lips quirked. "Probably as difficult as researching a nice, quiet place for Blythe and Squirrel to have a getaway before she has that baby and thinking about how perfect the place would be to make love to you at." She shook her head. "That didn't come out right."

"I know what you meant," Taco told her. "And I

know I'm early. Did I interrupt anything that can't be picked up later?"

"No."

That was it. A clear and concise answer. Just to be sure they were on the same page, Taco asked, "I want to take you upstairs to your bedroom and make love to you. *With* you. Right now."

"I want that too."

"You sure?"

Koren nodded.

Taco leaned forward and kissed her oh so gently. Her fingernails scraped against his sides, the feel of them muted through the material of his T-shirt. Then, without another word, he grabbed one of her hands and headed for the stairs.

CHAPTER TWELVE

Koren kept her eyes on Taco's ass as he climbed the stairs that led to her bedroom. This was probably the most exciting thing that had happened to her in a very long time. Every other time she'd had sex, it was more of a we've-been-dating-for-six-months-so-it's-time kind of thing.

Taco had come over because he was pissed on her behalf. Not to make love. And it was the middle of the afternoon. She was wearing a pair of sweats and a T-shirt with no bra. It was her normal work outfit. She'd planned on changing before he came over later. But he didn't seem to care about her clothes. Koren never felt as if she had to look perfect when she was with Taco. In fact, the more comfortable she was around him, the more they seemed to click.

He towed her straight to her bedroom, not even

looking into her office, which was an unholy mess. There were books and papers everywhere. She'd been in the middle of researching the best Bahamian resort for her client to have her wedding, but that could definitely wait.

Being with Taco couldn't.

He led her over to the bed, then turned and sat.

Surprised, Koren could only stand there as he wrapped his arms around her and rested his cheek on her belly. She stroked his hair and closed her eyes, absorbing the moment. Yes, she wanted him, but being with him like this felt like something special.

After a while, he looked up at her, running his hands up and down the outside of her thighs. "Are you sure?" he asked.

"Are you?" she countered.

Taco smiled. Then nodded. His hands moved to her waist and his fingers slipped under the waistband of her pants. Slowly, giving her time to object, he pushed the loose cotton off her hips. They fell to her feet without a sound. It felt weird to be standing in front of him in nothing but a T-shirt and panties, but the look in his eyes made it a little better.

"I wasn't expecting you until later," she said shyly. "I was going to put on a nicer pair of underwear, just in case."

"These are perfect," he said, his eyes glued to them.

"They're white cotton," she protested. "There's nothing perfect about them."

"Wrong," Taco said, licking his lips.

"Um…shouldn't we close the curtains?" she asked, looking over to the windows uncertainly.

"We're on the third floor. No one can see in," he responded, not even glancing over to where the afternoon sun was streaming into the room.

"It's weird," she said softly.

He looked up at her then. "What is?"

"It's the middle of the day."

"And?"

"And…I don't know."

"You haven't made love in the afternoon before?"

She shook her head. "Only at night. When it was dark."

He smiled. "It's not dark now, and I'm fucking thrilled. I get to see every inch of you."

"That's what I'm afraid of," she quipped.

"And you get to see me," Taco added.

Hmmm. That definitely had its perks. "True."

Then Taco leaned forward and nuzzled her T-shirt up until his lips touched the bare skin of her belly. Koren inhaled sharply. She wasn't exactly skinny, and she'd never been thrilled with her stomach. But the second his lips touched her, she forgot about the weight she wanted to lose and concentrated on how he was making her feel.

His fingers grabbed hold of her shirt and his thumbs brushed back and forth over the sensitive flesh at her sides. His mouth kissed and caressed the skin around her panty line. Koren shifted restlessly in front of him.

He did this for a long time, ratcheting up her desire. Finally, when she couldn't stand it any longer, she said, "Taco..."

"You smell so good," he mumbled. "I can smell how turned on you are."

She should've been embarrassed, but instead she simply felt impatient. "I'd love to say the same about you, but alas, I can't."

She felt him smile against her belly before he tilted his head back and aimed his grin her way. "Take off your shirt."

Koren blinked. She'd expected him to say something teasing back, or to finally stand up and start stripping. But he wanted her to take off her shirt when he was still fully dressed?

"Please," he added after a few seconds.

Figuring that maybe it would encourage him to speed up his own disrobing process, Koren's hands went to the hem of her shirt, and she whipped it up and over her head in one quick movement, kind of like pulling off a Band-Aid.

Taco's eyes immediately went to her boobs. Since she wasn't wearing a bra, they were hanging loose. In her own critical eye, they were too saggy. Too big. Too...something. But Taco didn't seem to have any problems with what he was seeing.

His pupils dilated and he swallowed hard. Koren thought he'd immediately reach for them, but instead his fingers tightened on her hips, almost hurting with their grip. He pushed her back a step and his eyes roamed from her chest, to her belly, to her hips, then her legs. He licked his lips and brought his eyes up to her face.

"You. Are. So. Beautiful."

Koren simply smiled down at him. She really didn't think so, but it felt good to hear him say it all the same.

"You don't believe me," Taco said with a shake of his head.

"Taco, I'm a naked woman who is more than ready for you to make love to her. Of course you think I'm beautiful," she told him honestly. "I'm a sure thing."

"Fucking hell," Taco breathed then rested his forehead on her belly.

Surprised, Koren just stood there, not sure what to do.

Then his head came up—and her breath froze in her lungs.

The look on his face was so intense, she didn't know if he was about to break up with her, or throw her to the floor and fuck her until she couldn't move.

"I'm not letting you go," he said in a low, rumbly voice. "You're *mine*."

"Okay," Koren said immediately.

"And if it's the last thing I do, I'm gonna make you

see yourself how I see you. You're fucking gorgeous, Koren."

"I'm not sure it's possible for a woman to think she looks good," she griped.

Taco chuckled, and his warm breath wafted over her belly, making her shiver.

"And this is why you are the way you are. If you knew how beautiful you were, you wouldn't be you."

Koren frowned down at him, though he didn't elaborate. His hands moved then, sliding under her panties, his palms hot against her hips. Then he slowly slid his hands down, taking her underwear with them, but his eyes didn't leave hers.

When the scrap of white cotton fell to her ankles, she stepped out of them.

Taco's thumbs brushed against the creases where her legs met her hips, and his hands seemed huge as they gripped her thighs. Then he dropped his head and nuzzled the small strip of hair she'd left the last time she'd shaved.

Jerking in his grasp, she grabbed hold of his shoulders, digging her fingernails into his skin through his shirt and holding on for dear life. "Taco?"

"Hmmm?" he mumbled, as he continued nuzzling her.

"Maybe we should lie down."

"Good idea," he said, standing suddenly.

Koren took a step back and would've fallen if his hands weren't right there to catch her.

"Easy, Kor." Then, instead of turning to help her onto the bed, he led her over to a patch of sunlight on the floor. "Stay right there for a second."

Bemused, Koren watched as he went back to the bed and took her comforter off the top. He came back over to where she was standing and spread it on the floor. Then he whipped his shirt over his head and kneeled down in front of her once more. He pulled her into him, and once again, Koren reached out to grab him for balance.

But this time her fingers touched smooth, warm skin instead of his T-shirt. Taco was *ripped*. His muscles flexed in the light as he moved, and she was almost mesmerized by all of his skin bared to her gaze.

He put his hands on her inner thighs and pressed outward. Shifting where she stood, Koren realized too late that with him on his knees, his face was directly in line with her pussy.

"Taco, I'm not sure—"

"Shhhh," he soothed. "Please. I've been thinking about this for weeks."

She swallowed hard and moved one hand to the back of his head as it lowered.

The first touch of his tongue against her folds made her jerk. But he didn't give her time to protest or try to move away. His hands came up and he took hold of a butt cheek in each one. Then he pressed his mouth to the most intimate part of her and feasted.

There was no other word for what he was doing.

His tongue licked between her folds, then moved upward to flick over her clit. He kneaded her ass cheeks all the while, moving his head one way then the other as he explored her.

"Jesus, Taco," she managed.

He didn't respond, as his mouth was otherwise occupied. Before long, her hips were moving without conscious thought, trying to get his tongue where she needed it most. Koren also used her hands on his head to try to force him to pay more attention to her clit. She felt him smile against her, but he refused to give her what she wanted.

"Taco," she complained.

"What are you supposed to call me?" he asked, before nuzzling her inner thighs with his rough beard.

"Rob! God, please, Rob."

"Please what?" he asked, still smiling. "I'm not a mind reader."

"My clit. Please, harder on my clit."

"With pleasure," he muttered before concentrating all his efforts on the little bundle of nerves between her legs.

Almost shrieking with pleasure, Koren's knees bent a little and she widened her stance. God, this was awkward and a little uncomfortable, but she couldn't complain if her life depended on it. Within seconds, he'd worked her up until she was right on the edge of exploding.

"I'm almost there," she warned him. Her legs started

to tremble and her fingers gripped his hair. Then Taco wrapped his lips around her clit, his tongue flicking as fast as he could, and he hummed.

That was all it took.

"*Unghhhh!*" was all Koren could moan as every muscle in her body seemed to seize up when she came.

One second she was standing with Taco's head between her legs, and the next she was lying on her floor on top of her comforter, looking up at him.

His short beard glistened with her excitement but he didn't bother to wipe his face before he reached for the button on his jeans. Before he shoved them off, he grabbed his wallet out of his back pocket. Without a word, he fished out a condom and ripped it open with his teeth. Then he shoved his pants and boxers down.

Koren could only stare up at him. He was in the sunlight, and she'd never seen anything so perfect in all her life. His dick was standing straight out, and he quickly covered it with the condom. Then he stepped out of his clothes and dropped to his knees, straddling her thighs.

She lay there, exhausted but somehow energized at the same time. The sun was warm on her naked body and it lent an extra sexy element to an already erotic situation. Taking her time, she took in Taco from head to toe. He had a six pack, and she couldn't see an ounce of extra fat on him. He even had those v-muscles leading down to his cock.

Reaching out to touch him, she was surprised when he caught her hand in his.

"Uh-uh," he said with a shake of his head.

"I want to touch you," she complained.

"Not the first time. And not when you have that dazed look in your eye. You have a habit of latching on to any part of me you can reach," he said with a smile. "The last thing I want you digging your fingernails into is my cock."

Koren couldn't help it, she laughed. She tugged on her hand, he let go, and she put it above her head with the other. Then she stretched languorously. "Maybe I'll just take a nap then," she said with a smirk.

"You look like a kitten stretching in the sun," he said. Then shook his head. "No, that's not right at all. You're too sexy to be a kitten. More like a sex goddess."

She grinned and spread her legs as far as she could, which wasn't far at all with him straddling her like he was. "Yeah? Well, this sex goddess would like to request her slave get busy doing more than just staring at her."

"Yes, ma'am," Taco said, then he shifted to lie between her thighs and brace his arms next to her shoulders. Koren could feel him from her hips to her boobs. She took a deep breath and her nipples brushed against his chest.

They both moaned.

"I'm going to take my time and worship your tits...after."

"After?"

"After I make love to you. After you come again. After I come. And after we take a nap."

"Oh. Okay," she said, feeling the tip of his dick brush against her folds.

"Hold on," Taco ordered.

"To what?" she asked.

"Me."

One of his hands moved between them, brushing against her clit as he gripped his cock and pressed it inside her.

Without thought, Koren's hands whipped down and grabbed his biceps. They flexed and moved as Taco did. She felt every inch of his dick ease into her body, and she held her breath until he was seated as far inside her as he could go.

She felt his pubic hairs mesh with hers, felt his balls press up against her ass. Spreading her legs farther apart, she wrapped them around him, hooking her ankles together at his butt.

"You ready?" he asked.

Meeting his gaze, Koren nodded.

Then without another word, Taco began to make love to her. It was as sensual as it was carnal. He alternated between hammering her body and gently easing in and out. Just when she had his rhythm down, he changed it. It was frustrating, but also exciting.

Neither said a word as he pumped into her. Her

eyes closed, and Koren could feel the sunlight, warm against her eyelids. She smiled. This wasn't like her. Making love in the middle of the day in the bright sunlight. It wasn't her, but it felt amazing. Taco made her feel amazing.

She opened her eyes and stared up at him. He was clenching his teeth, making the muscles in his neck stand out in stark relief. Every time he bottomed out inside her, she felt herself shift upward a little bit. She loved that he wasn't treating her as if she were made of glass. His roughness totally did it for her. Turned her on more.

He shifted, balancing himself over her on one hand, and the other snaking between their bodies. He took one of her boobs in his hand and squeezed. She arched into his touch. Then he pinched her nipple before moving lower. His thrusts got shallow as his fingers found her clit.

"Come for me," he ordered. "I want to feel you come on my cock."

His words were carnal, as much for what he'd said as for the fact they were the first words he'd spoken since he'd entered her.

"Faster and harder," she told him breathlessly. "If you want me to come, I need it faster and harder."

He did as she asked, strumming his fingers against her in a perfect combination. It wasn't long before she felt her orgasm looming. Taco stopped thrusting in and out of her, his entire concentration on her clit.

"Oh my God, yes. There...Rob!" And she exploded. Pressing up into him, Koren felt his cock still deep inside her, and it made her orgasm all the more intense.

Taco kept the pressure on her clit for a second, then he removed his hand, braced himself with it once more, and fucked her. *Hard.*

This wasn't making love, and she was more than okay with that. Every time he entered her, she felt the reverberations in her still sensitive clit.

She'd never come without direct stimulation to her clit before, but she knew without a doubt, she was about to.

She shoved her hips up with every thrust and felt the contractions move through her body yet again, just as Taco pressed himself inside her as far as he could go and held still.

"Fucking hell," he muttered as he held himself over her.

When Koren came back to herself, she realized that Taco was still propped on his hands. Opening her eyes, she looked up and blinked at the intense expression in his hazel gaze. His hair was in complete disarray, probably from her fingers running through it, and his beard still glistened with what had to be her juices. His jaw was set and he didn't speak for a long moment.

Just when she was getting worried, he blew out a long breath. "You can take your claws out of me now."

Shocked, Koren looked at his biceps, where she was

holding on for dear life. She gasped and let go, seeing the half-moon marks where her fingernails had bit into his skin.

"I'm so sorry," she whispered.

Taco didn't say a word, merely lowered himself down until he was plastered next to her side. One arm went across her chest and the other went under her neck. He rolled her until she was more on top of him than he was on her.

The floor was hard beneath them, and the sun was now almost too bright and warm, but Koren didn't complain. How could she?

"I love that," Taco said after a while.

"What?"

"You grabbing me as if I'm the only thing holding you together. You do it all the time, and it never fails to make me feel ten feet tall."

Koren wasn't sure what to say. She didn't think she needed to apologize, but she did it anyway. "I'm sorry."

"Don't be. If you ever stop doing that, you're going to be in big trouble," he mumbled.

"Okay."

She shifted against him, feeling the floor digging into her hip bone. As if realizing what the issue was, Taco shifted out from under her and rolled to a sitting position. He stood, seemingly not embarrassed in the least that he was butt naked. He removed the condom and reached for a tissue on a nearby dresser.

Koren knew she was blushing. She'd never seen a

man deal with the aftermath of a condom before. It seemed very intimate.

Then Taco held out a hand. "Come on, the floor's too hard. I love seeing you in the sun, but you'll be more comfortable in bed."

Holding on to the comforter, she let him help her off the floor. He chuckled, as if he knew she was self-conscious, but didn't protest her holding the blanket to her like a shield. He got her settled under the covers, then draped the blanket over the bed once more. He crawled under the sheet with her and pulled her into his arms.

Sighing, Koren melted into him. One hand gripped his shoulder, and the other curled up against his chest.

"That was perfect," she said after a minute.

"Couldn't have said it better myself," Taco said. "Now hush."

"I should get up and work some more," she said sleepily.

"Shhhh. Take a nap. I'll get you up in a bit."

"Okay." Koren trusted him to keep his word. Yeah, he'd said he wanted to make love some more after a nap, but she knew without a doubt that if she said she had to work, he wouldn't get in the way of that. Just as she would never get in the way of his job.

Feeling more comfortable and sated than she had in forever, Koren closed her eyes and was asleep almost immediately.

* * *

Taco didn't sleep. He was too wired. Not only from making love with Koren for the first time, but because of the words that tumbled through his brain over and over.

I love you.

He wanted to say them.

But didn't want to freak her out.

And for some reason, he knew telling her how much she meant to him *would* freak her out.

He needed to be smart.

Patient.

But it was hard.

The most difficult thing he'd ever done.

He'd move at her pace if it killed him.

He'd realized earlier, when she'd said she wasn't pretty, exactly how unsure of her appeal she was. If he had to guess, social media or society's insistence that only skinny people were attractive were responsible for her warped thinking. Koren Garner was the most beautiful woman he'd ever seen. Sure, she carried a little more weight on her frame than was acceptable to some, but from the tips of her toes to the top of her head, she was fucking gorgeous.

And she was *his*.

He'd move heaven and earth to make her realize it too.

Shifting, he lifted his head and kissed her temple. She smiled in her sleep, and the fingers that were wrapped around his shoulder tightened.

Yeah, it was safe to say he was a goner.

And he couldn't be happier.

CHAPTER THIRTEEN

A week later, Taco was sitting in the fire station shooting the shit with his friends. Things had been quiet since Crash's car had gone up in flames. Everyone was being careful. Making sure to keep an ever-watchful eye on what was going on around them.

The fire investigator had said the car fire was definitely arson, but the police weren't any closer to figuring out who had started it than they'd been the night it happened. Whoever had done it was either extremely smart or very lucky.

"How's Pen doing?" Squirrel asked Moose, keeping his voice down. She was in one of the back rooms napping, and he didn't want to wake her up.

He sighed. "Not good. She won't talk to me at all. Has she said anything to you, Sledge?"

"No. I've tried everything I can think of to get her to open up...even going so far as to remind her of when we were little, when she idolized me and told me everything," Sledge said.

"Has she opened up to any of the women?" Driftwood asked. "They all seem to be close."

Moose shook his head. "Not that I know of."

"Maybe the Delta guys up at Fort Hood?" Chief asked.

"No. No one. She comes over to see Smokey and hangs outside in the barn with him for hours. She won't come inside unless I pretty much make her," Moose said.

"Is this normal?" Squirrel asked. "I mean, I know soldiers get PTSD all the time, but it's been quite a while since she was rescued. Why does she seem to be getting worse?"

"PTSD manifests itself differently in everyone," Moose said. "I've been reading up on it so I can try to help her. Sometimes it rears its head right away, and in other cases it can take years."

"Something's got to change," Sledge said. "I love my sister more than anything, but it's starting to affect her work."

Taco nodded. "Did you guys notice at that fire call this morning, she volunteered to stay with the truck and manage the hoses rather than go inside?"

Everyone nodded.

"And at that MVA yesterday, she didn't immediately rush over to the car to help. She farted around getting out of the truck until all the vics were covered. Then she just ran back and forth relaying information," Driftwood added.

"She also no longer hangs out with us in here," Moose said softly.

"I'll talk to her again," Sledge said. "She's gonna end up hesitating at the wrong time and the wrong place and put someone's life in serious danger. She needs to get professional help."

"This sucks," Crash said softly. "She's always been so strong."

"I think it's not that she's *not* strong. Maybe she feels like she can't be weak at all anymore. Because of what happened to her and what she survived. Everyone is always telling her how amazing she is, and sometimes that much praise can be detrimental."

Taco thought about Moose's words. He was right. They were always telling Pen how awesome she was, how unique. And she was. She worked her ass off at the station and they'd never worried that she wouldn't be able to hold her weight. Not to mention, how great of a soldier she'd been and how she'd handled what had happened to her when she'd been a POW. But that would be a ton of pressure to carry around all the time.

"And the anniversary of her friends' deaths is coming up," Moose said. "She mentioned it to me once. I know she still feels guilty about White's and Black's deaths. Not to mention, that other soldier who was with them, and even that Australian bloke. She puts a ton of pressure on herself."

"I'll try to talk to her," Sledge said again.

"Me too," Moose agreed.

The sound of the emergency tones ringing out through the station was always startling, but today they seemed even more so in the somber atmosphere.

Everyone jumped up and ran for bays where the trucks were kept, Penelope right on their heels. As they were putting on their bunker gear, the dispatcher's voice sounded over the speakers in the garage.

Structure fire. Fully involved.

She gave the address—and everyone stopped dead in their tracks.

Taco whipped his head around and stared at Moose.

It was *his* house. Shit.

Shit shit shit!

Caller states she can see smoke but no flames yet. The fire is coming from a small wooden structure southwest of the house.

"That's the barn!" Penelope yelled. "Oh my God! Smokey's in there!"

The firefighters were already moving quickly, but at

her words, they turned it up a notch. Sledge climbed into the driver's seat of the ladder truck and the others jumped onboard. Sledge didn't wait for the others to get strapped in, he flicked on the siren and lights and pulled out of the fire station a lot faster than was protocol.

Taco was right behind him, driving the smaller truck. No one said a word as they drove toward Moose's house. He lived on a couple acres and every single one of the men knew that, considering Penelope's current fragile state, if something happened to her beloved donkey, she might not recover.

Taco also knew that, in the back of their minds, every single one of them were wondering if this was the work of whoever had set Crash's car on fire. Was this an escalation of whatever problem the arsonist had with them?

It took an agonizing fifteen minutes to get to Moose's property. There was black smoke clearly visible as they bounced down his gravel driveway. The second they turned a corner and saw the small barn, Taco swore under his breath.

When he got out of the truck, the most agonizing sound was echoing across the valley.

Smokey.

He was braying as if he was being skinned alive.

It sounded eerily like a woman screaming.

Goose bumps rose on Taco's arms.

"God!" he said under his breath. For a second all he could do was stand there, dumbstruck and horrified.

"*Noooooooooo!*" Penelope screeched, snapping Taco out of it. He saw Moose grab Penelope around the waist and physically restrain her from running into the burning barn.

Ignoring the way Penelope was fighting and begging Moose to let go of her, Taco turned and grabbed an ax off the truck. He saw that Squirrel and Driftwood had done the same thing. Crash and Sledge were getting the hose from the pumper truck ready and charged.

Taco ran toward the small barn, trying to figure out where Smokey's stall was based on the horrendous sounds coming from inside. The smoke was thick, but he didn't even hesitate. He brought the ax up and began chopping at the side of the wooden barn as fast as he could.

He could hear Penelope wailing and crying behind him, which made him work faster. Squirrel and Driftwood joined him and, between the three of them, a hole quickly formed in the side of the barn. Smoke rolled out, and the three men threw down their axes and started ripping the wood boards off with their bare hands.

When they had enough slats removed, Taco looked inside. They'd made a hole big enough for the donkey to get through, but there was a burning piece of the roof lying in the dirt between them and the terrified animal. "I'll get him," he told the others.

Coughing, but knowing he didn't have enough time to go and grab his hood and oxygen tank, Taco fell onto his knees and frantically threw dirt on top of the burning wood. It was extinguished quickly, and he stood up and reached for Smokey's halter.

The donkey threw his head back and screamed. Literally screamed. Smoke was rolling off the small animal's back as the hair on his body began to catch fire from flying sparks.

Knowing he didn't have time to be gentle with the poor animal, Taco leaned over and simply picked up the miniature donkey. Smokey squirmed in his grasp, but Taco held him tightly. He stepped over the beam in the middle of the stall and hightailed it for the hole. Squirrel and Driftwood were still outside waiting for him.

They each grabbed hold of an elbow, steadying Taco as he stepped up and out of the burning barn. Just as he straightened, the roof on the barn collapsed in a shower of sparks, smoke, and orange flames.

The sound of the collapse startled Smokey, and he reared his head back once more and brayed.

Even with the support of Squirrel and Driftwood, Taco stumbled and went to his knees. Smokey twisted his body and managed to escape Taco's hold. The donkey, still braying at the top of his lungs, took off running. His back was still smoldering, and Taco swore in frustration.

"Smokey!" Penelope screamed. Moose let go of her and they all watched as she ran after her beloved pet.

For a second, Smokey continued to run. Then, as if Penelope's voice suddenly registered, he did an about-face and came galloping back toward them.

"Oh, God! Water. I need water!" Penelope yelled as she sank to her knees with her arms outstretched.

Smokey ran right for her, and Taco watched, knowing the animal was going to bowl over the diminutive firefighter. But at the last second, the donkey reined himself in and came to a halt before running over his favorite human.

The sounds Smokey continued to make were horrific. He wasn't screaming anymore, but braying in a long, continuous stream that was almost unearthly.

Crash ran toward them with one of the hoses connected to the pumper truck. He didn't hesitate, just turned it on, dousing Smokey—and Penelope, who was holding on to him for dear life.

The sizzling sound of the water as it made contact with the animal's back was something Taco knew he'd never forget. He hadn't been there when Penelope had found Smokey in the middle of a forest fire, but he imagined that when she'd doused him back then, it had sounded much the same way.

Smokey finally lay down, putting his head in Penelope's lap. His brays sounded like moans now rather than the terrified screams he'd been emitting earlier.

Now that Smokey was safe, the firefighters turned their attention to Moose's barn. Crash brought the hose toward the burning structure, and Sledge brought a second hose over. A few chickens ran out of the hole Taco and the others had made in the side of the barn.

"Any other animals in there?" Chief asked Moose.

"Probably more chickens, but that's it," Moose said. "It's only got two stalls. I was going to tear the thing down, but then we found Smokey."

Taco understood. He'd kept the barn for Penelope. She needed Smokey almost as much as the donkey needed her.

By the time the sheriff's deputies arrived, the fire was extinguished. Penelope and Smokey hadn't moved from their position about a hundred feet off into a small field next to the barn.

The deputies were talking to Crash and Moose about what had transpired.

Taco and the others were walking around what was left of the barn, making sure there weren't any hot spots that would flare up again.

When they walked to the back side of the structure, all four of them froze in shock.

"Shit!" Sledge said.

"Fucking hell," Squirrel swore.

"Damn," Driftwood breathed.

Taco had no words. He could only stare in disbelief.

On the back of the barn were the words, *Are you sorry NOW, Hudson?*

They were spray painted in red letters about a quarter of the way up the back wall of the building.

"Don't touch anything," Sledge warned.

The others nodded and everyone took a giant step backward.

"Well, at least now we know the other fires weren't random," Squirrel said.

"And we know who this person is mad at," Driftwood pointed out.

Taco could barely think. This was *his* fault. He had no idea what he was supposed to be sorry about, but right now, he was *definitely* sorry.

He took another step back, then another, as if backing away from the ugly words could somehow erase them. His chest felt tight and he wanted to throw up. First Chief's shed, then Crash's car. Now this. If something had happened to Smokey, he knew without a doubt Penelope wouldn't have survived it. She was barely hanging on as it was.

Shock swirled through his brain. His fault. This was *his* fault. "I'm sorry," he said, his voice cracking.

"Fuck that shit!" Squirrel said. "This is *not* your fault."

Taco gestured to the side of the barn. "Yeah, it obviously is."

Sledge crossed over to him and put his hands on his

shoulders. "No, man. It's *not*. Someone's fucking with all of us."

"It has to be Jen," Taco said, still feeling sick. "I brought her into our fold and I'm still paying for it. Big time."

"I'm gonna get Beth on this," Sledge told him. "Jen's in jail, but if it's one of her psycho cronies, she'll find out who and get this shit shut down. Come on, we need to step back and let the detectives do their thing. Penelope needs us right now."

"Holy cow. Who's Hudson?" one of the deputies asked as he walked around the corner of the barn.

"Me," Taco said without emotion. He didn't know what to feel. At the moment, he was numb.

"Someone really doesn't like you," the deputy said, then turned to motion toward his fellow officers to come and take a look.

"I'll make sure dispatch is sending an arson investigator out," Sledge said.

Taco nodded, and he turned and woodenly walked back toward their trucks. It didn't matter what his friends said, this *was* his fault. Someone hated him enough to target his entire crew. And he only knew one person who had that kind of hate in her heart.

Jennifer Hale.

He watched as Moose examined Smokey. Then when he picked him up and headed for his house, Penelope hot on his heels. The man was madly in love with Penelope…he had to be, in order to not make a fuss about bringing a barn animal inside his home.

Remembering the sounds the donkey had been making while trapped inside the burning barn, Taco shivered. They'd been lucky today. Extremely lucky. Yes, Moose had lost his barn and a few chickens, but he could've lost a whole lot more. He couldn't lose Penelope.

Thinking about Pen brought his thoughts to Koren and the other women. The arsonist had targeted Crash, Chief, and Moose. Who was next? Sledge? Squirrel? Drift-wood? Was the person responsible saving him for last? And each fire had escalated. So far they'd only suffered a loss of property, but today had been close. Too close.

"Come on, Taco. We're out of here. Sledge called the chief, and he's giving Moose and Penelope the rest of the shift off," Driftwood told him.

Taco nodded and climbed into the truck, letting Squirrel drive back to the station. He knew the others were talking to their women, but he didn't make a move for his phone.

He couldn't. This was all his fault.

There was no way he could drag Koren into this.

The best way to keep her safe was to end things between them.

His heart hurt, but Taco couldn't think of anything else he could do to make sure his drama didn't touch her.

CHAPTER FOURTEEN

Koren paced back and forth. She'd heard about the fire at Moose's house from Adeline. She'd texted Taco to make sure he was all right, but hadn't heard back. That worried her. Taco *always* texted right back. He never made her wait to hear from him.

The last week had been idyllic. She'd stayed at his house the nights he wasn't working, and he came over to her condo to hang out while she worked during the day. They made love every night, and each time was better than the last. She'd never felt closer to another person before. It seemed like she'd known him forever.

But at the moment, she didn't like the ugly feeling growing inside her. She was worried, and he had to know she would be, but he still hadn't gotten in touch with her.

Koren had talked to each and every one of the other women, and they'd all heard from *their* men. She'd had to learn about Smokey almost dying from Sophie. Quinn had told her that Moose and Penelope were holed up in his house with the donkey. Blythe had explained that the men were getting off shift early...

And Beth had texted her a picture of the words that had been painted on the back of Moose's barn.

After seeing that, Koren had immediately tried calling Taco, but it had gone to voice mail. She'd left a message, telling him that she was worried and to please call her as soon as he could, but she still hadn't heard back.

Koren was now past being worried; she'd moved into pissed-off territory. Oh, she was still concerned about where Taco was and what he was thinking, but she was also upset with him. He *had* to know she was worried, but he still didn't call. The others hadn't said he was hurt, so it wasn't like he was lying unconscious in a hospital somewhere.

No. For some reason, he was shutting her out.

She wanted to drive over to his house and confront him, but that wasn't her. She didn't like confrontation or drama. Didn't want to have to get all up in his face so he'd realize that he'd hurt her.

And that was the bottom line. She was hurt.

Trying to tamp down her feelings, Koren continued to pace.

It was almost an agonizing hour later when a knock sounded at her door. She looked out the upstairs window and saw Taco's Silverado in the driveway. For a split second, residual anger made her consider pretending she wasn't home, but deciding it was better to get any confrontation over with sooner rather than later, she headed for the door.

She opened it, but didn't step back to let him in. Koren had been prepared to be tough. To let Taco know exactly how much he'd hurt her, but the look on his face immediately had her wavering.

"Can I come in?" he asked.

Even the tone of his voice was off. He seemed... remote. Almost cold.

Shivering, Koren stepped aside. He walked past her and stopped in the middle of her living room. She slowly shut the door and stared at his back. She'd been so angry with him...but now she was afraid. With the way he was acting, it seemed like...

Like this was it. He was going to break up with her.

She had no idea why, or what she'd done to make him act like this. Had she called too much? Pushed too hard? Was it because she'd talked to the other women about what was happening and not to him? Koren had no idea.

She slowly walked into the living room and waited for him to face her.

When he did, her heart started thumping overtime in her chest.

"I guess you heard about what happened today," he said quietly.

"Yeah. Adeline called me."

He nodded and pressed his lips together. Then he took a deep breath and said, "I think we should take a break for a while."

There it was.

Instead of being devastated, anger rose up in Koren like a tsunami. It built slowly but surely until it overcame all her other thoughts.

"*You* think?"

"Yeah. Not forever. Just…for a while. Things have moved pretty fast between us, and—"

"In all the time I've known you, I haven't thought you were a coward until right this second."

Taco met her gaze for the first time. She could see the shock at her words, but she didn't even care. She was *pissed*.

"We've spent every possible moment together for the last week. You've made me feel more in those seven days than I have in my entire *life*. But you were a dick today, Taco."

He didn't say anything, just stared at her.

"I had to hear about what happened from *Adeline*. Crash had called her and let her know. Not only that, but I heard about Smokey from Quinn. Blythe texted me and told me that you guys were getting off work early. And Beth sent me the picture of what was written on the barn. But you know who I *didn't* hear from today?" He flinched but Koren didn't care. "*You*. I didn't hear from my *boyfriend* that there was another arson directed at one of his friends. That this fire was connected to *him*. You didn't bother to let me know that you were okay. Nothing!"

"Koren, I—"

"You what? You're sorry? I'm not sure that's gonna cut it right now, Taco. How about telling me *why*? Why you let me worry about you all day? Worry about Moose and Penelope and all the others?"

"I just...this is apparently all happening because of *me*. I don't want you in the middle of it. You'll be safer if we just take a break for a while."

"Adeline told me that Crash had their neighbors come over to check on her. Chief called his mom on the reservation so she could perform an emergency protection ritual for Sophie. Blythe told me that Squirrel called her friend Hope to have her come over and spend the day with her, so she wouldn't be alone. Quinn was at work with Sophie, so she had her and their other co-workers to keep them company. Even Moose was with Penelope. But you know who was with me? No one. I was here worrying about you all by myself. It seems to me that if you wanted to keep me safe, you went about it the entirely wrong way. How easy would it have been for someone to knock on my door, pretend he was selling something, and snatch me away? Or set my condo on fire? Shit, Taco, by ignoring me, you actually put me in *more* danger."

The only sound after her words faded away were from the ticking of a clock in the other room. Taco just stared at her, his fists clenching.

"But you know what?" Koren went on. "Maybe this is for the best. Why would I want to be with someone who's so inconsiderate, he doesn't even take the time to call or send a quick text to let his girlfriend know he's okay? Especially after I left a message telling you I was worried. My parents have been married a very long time, and I know for a fact my dad would *never* do that to my mom."

"Koren—" Taco began, the pain easy to hear in his voice.

She took a step back and held up a hand. "No. You're right. It's fine. We'll take a break. That's what you want to hear, right? Okay. You can go now. Don't worry about me. Besides, it's probably better this way. I've never been involved in anything like this. I told you from the get-go that I don't do drama. And this is *definitely* drama. So you can go with a clear conscience. We're good. Great. Peachy."

She saw a muscle in his jaw tic before he took a step toward her. "I changed my mind."

"Nuh-uh. Too late. You can't."

"You're right. I was a dick. I was too stuck in my head. I couldn't see what was right in front of my face."

Koren didn't want to know. She just needed him to *go* so she could break down in peace.

He kept walking toward her, and Koren kept backing away. He couldn't touch her. If he did, she'd break. She knew it. "You wanted to break up with me, and you did. So just go."

"We're not broken up."

"Jesus, Taco! Could you be anymore flakey? Just *go* already! I can't deal with all this drama. I haven't gotten any work done today and I have a ton of emails that I need to get to. I was fielding calls all day from the others. It's obviously not good for my productivity. So you can just tell everyone that we're over and they'll stop calling and texting. I can finally get some work done."

He didn't say anything, just kept stalking her until her back hit the wall next to a large bookcase. Koren put up her hands to try to stop him, but he kept coming. In order to keep from touching him, which would make her give in, Koren flattened her palms on the wall behind her.

Taco was in her personal space now. She could feel his body heat and smell the slight scent of soap. He'd taken a shower recently, and normally the scent of his soap made her weak in the knees. Today it made her weak for an entirely different reason. She was sure this would be the last time she'd be this close to him. Smelling him.

"I'm sorry, Kor."

She shook her head. "Too late, Taco."

"Unacceptable." He looked down at her hands on the wall and frowned. "I hate this."

When he didn't elaborate, she asked, "What?"

"You're not touching me. Not grabbing my shirt as if you'll never let go."

Koren's fingers twitched, but she forced herself not to move.

He lifted a hand and brushed a lock of hair behind her shoulder. "I'm sorry. You're right. All of it. I was a dick. I was inconsiderate and stupid. I thought I was keeping you safe by staying away, but all I was doing was putting you in more danger. We've spent enough time together recently that whoever is doing this probably knows we're a couple. I should've called. I should've let you know what happened. And more importantly, I should've contacted one of your brothers and asked if they could come and stay with you until I got home."

Koren swallowed hard, the huge ball of emotion in her throat making it hard to breathe.

"I know this is all too much fucking drama. Believe me, I *know*. I hate it, probably more than you do, and I feel completely helpless because I don't know what to do about it. If I just knew *why* this was all happening, it'd be easier to deal with. I haven't been a saint, but I've racked my brain to try and figure out what I should be sorry about, and the only thing that comes to mind is my ex. I'm *definitely* sorry that I ever went out with her, that's for sure, but is that what all this is about? I just don't know.

"All I could think about, the whole damn day, was that I was the reason this was happening to my friends. I wanted to keep you out of it. But that's impossible, because you're already in it. Because I've spent every minute with you when I'm not at the station. Because you're mine."

"Please," Koren whispered. "Stop."

"I love you, Koren," Taco said.

A sob escaped, and Koren pressed her lips together and squeezed her eyes shut. Her fingers curled, but she couldn't get a grip on the wall. She felt Taco take her wrists and he placed her hands on his sides.

"I fucked up. Bad. I was trying to be all noble and shit, but breaking up with you is the last thing I want to do. In fact, if I had my way, you'd move in with me, lock, stock, and barrel."

She couldn't help it, her fingers grabbed hold of his shirt at his waist and she held on. She was breathing as fast as if she'd just run a mile, and her heart felt as if it was going to beat out of her chest. Koren kept her eyes closed, not yet ready to face him, to have him say he was kidding.

"It won't happen again," Taco said softly. He framed her face with his hands and his thumbs wiped away the tears that had escaped. "I'm scared, Koren. Fucking *petrified*. Today was a close call. I'm well aware that if something happens to Smokey, we could lose Penelope forever. She wouldn't get over that. And whoever is doing this is escalating. Today it was a few chickens that lost their lives, but what about tomorrow? A shed is one thing. A car another. But now we're talking something more. Bigger. It scared me. I can't lose you, Koren. I just found you. I'm finally happy for the first time in my life. I understand exactly how much I have to lose. And the thought made me crazy."

Koren finally opened her eyes. The look in Taco's made her knees weak.

"You hurt me," she whispered.

"I know. And it won't happen again. I mean, I'll do my best to make sure it doesn't. I'm sure I'll do stupid stuff in the future, but I swear to you that I won't purposely keep you in the dark with what's happening ever again."

Koren didn't want to give in. Wanted to stay mad at him. But ten minutes ago she'd been hoping against hope that she'd hear from Taco soon. And now he was here, and she was being stubborn.

Then what he'd said earlier registered fully. He loved her.

He hadn't said it in a way that made her think he was trying to manipulate her. He'd said it, and then explained what had been going through his head earlier that day.

She wasn't ready to say it back. Not after what he'd put her through. But she had no doubts that Taco wouldn't say the words if he didn't mean them. He hadn't had the best role models in his parents. But he saw how his friends acted with their fiancées.

"Are you hungry?" she asked in a voice that only quivered a little.

He let out a breath, then rested his forehead against hers. "Yeah."

SUSAN STOKER

"We could go out, or I could make stuffed peppers."

"Stuffed peppers," he said immediately.

"Okay."

"Okay," he echoed. Then he picked up his head and wrapped his arms around her. He pulled her into him and simply held her.

The embrace felt good. Koren knew without a doubt that they'd been on the verge of never seeing each other again. If he'd walked out of her condo, that would've been it. They'd fought, but she hoped they were now stronger as a result.

She still didn't want to be in the middle of any kind of drama, but it wasn't like Taco was purposely generating it. No, someone else was orchestrating these attacks.

A thought struck her then. "It seems to me that, with your friends, the dramas they went through involved their girlfriends. Adeline's boss, Beth's agoraphobia, the crazy doctor at Sophie's work, the guys who wanted to get back at Blythe, Quinn's birthmark… but this time, it's *your* drama that's the issue."

Wincing, Koren regretted putting her thoughts to words the second they came out, but Taco didn't get upset with her. He didn't tense up and didn't pull away. He merely huffed out a breath.

"Right. Lucky me."

She smiled and shoved a hand under his shirt and caressed the warm skin of his back. "I'm sorry, Taco. What I meant was, this isn't your fault anymore than

232

their dramas were theirs. And honestly, your drama is *my* drama. I'm sure I'll have my share of it in the future. My parents aren't exactly subtle and my brothers are a pain in my ass. Not to mention, Vicky, Sue and I like our nights out. So you'll have to deal with plenty from me in the future."

"I can't wait," Taco said. "I'm going to do my best to mitigate whatever is happening. I don't want you involved, and I need to make sure you're safe. You were exactly right earlier. I should've been moving heaven and earth to make sure you were covered, instead I had my head up my ass. It won't happen again."

"I hope that doesn't mean you're going to go over-board," Koren warned. "I've lived on my own a long time, and I'm not about to go into lockdown mode over a threat that we don't even understand or know where it's coming from."

Taco frowned. "But that's exactly why you *should* go into lockdown mode."

Koren shook her head. "No. I'm not saying I'm not going to be careful. I am. My doors will stay locked at all times. If I have to go out, I'll carry mace and, if possible, I'll call one of my brothers or my friends to go with me."

"Deal. And when I'm not on duty, I want you to stay with me."

Koren knew she was blushing but she nodded. "I had planned on that regardless."

He smiled. "Good. I like having you in my bed."

"And I like being there," she returned.

"Come on. I'll help you get dinner ready."

Koren nodded, and when he twined his fingers with hers and led the way to the kitchen, she let out a sigh of relief. Everything within her relaxed. She'd come close to being broken. Taco leaving would've broken her. But luckily they'd both been able to meet each other halfway. They'd learned a lot about each other today…and hopefully they wouldn't have another scare like that again.

Koren wanted to be with Taco, but she also needed him to want to be with her right back. She wouldn't settle for being the only one making an effort in a relationship. She needed Taco to fight for her as much as she was willing to fight for him.

CHAPTER FIFTEEN

Three days later, Koren was drinking a glass of white wine and catching up with Sue and Vicky. Taco was on shift, and he'd texted her on and off all day, and she'd talked to him twice.

Beth was doing her best to try to figure out anything and everything she could about Taco's ex-girlfriend's followers. Jen was in jail, but most of the men and women who'd been with her when Quinn had almost been burned alive had gotten off with much lighter sentences or no jail time at all.

Any one of them could be holding a grudge for their leader being locked up, so Beth was digging into all of them. It was slow going, even for Beth, which was frustrating for everyone.

Penelope and Moose were back at work as well, but Smokey was currently being watched by Adeline when Penelope was on shift. There was no way she was going to leave her pet alone again, and from what Koren had heard, Smokey wasn't that thrilled at being separated from Penelope.

If people could suffer from PTSD, Koren had learned that animals could as well. The miniature donkey had been traumatized by once more being caught in a fire. Taco had described the sounds coming from the animal as horrifying and heartbreaking at the same time. Adeline's service dog, Coco, seemed to be the only thing keeping Smokey calm when Penelope wasn't at his side.

Koren knew the other women were either holed up together or visiting relatives. Everyone was taking the threat of more arson attacks seriously, but not knowing who might be next in the line of fire, literally, was unnerving.

Once more, the arson investigators had determined that the barn fire had been deliberately set, but they didn't have any clues as to who might've done it. The police were "looking into it," but Koren had a lot more faith in Beth than she did the cops. Not that they weren't doing everything they could, but Beth didn't follow the same set of rules the police had to obey.

Koren knew it was killing Taco that his friends had been targeted. No one knew if the person behind the fires was going to work his or her way through the rest of his friends, or if Taco himself would be the next target.

Sledge, Squirrel, and Driftwood were on high alert because nothing of theirs had been torched yet.

"I can't believe how crazy all this is," Sue said.

"You don't know the half of it. At one point, your name was brought up as possibly being involved," Koren told her friend.

"Oh, jeez. That thing in college, right?"

"Yup. But I explained what happened back then and admitted that Vicky and I were there too, but we weren't caught."

"It was stupid," Sue said. "We'd all had too much to drink."

"I know," Koren said and patted her friend's knee.

"So they really think it's related to his ex-girlfriend? The one who was setting people on fire to 'save' them?" Vicky asked.

"I guess. Taco doesn't know what else he's supposed to be sorry about. He swears there's no other reason for someone to be pissed at him. And I believe him."

Sue wasn't listening, instead looking down at her phone.

"What are you doing?" Koren asked. "Beth's already on the case. I'm not sure you have the skill set needed to track down crazy Jen's followers," she teased.

"Shut up." Sue grinned. "I'm not looking up Jen or any of her psycho followers. I'm cyber-stalking your boyfriend and his friends."

"Sue!" Koren scolded. "You're married."

"I might be married, but I'm not dead. And if I get

237

turned on by looking at pictures of hot firemen, my husband is the one who benefits."

Vicky and Koren both laughed.

"Seriously. Like, look at this one," Sue said, turning her phone around to show them. "Tell me that's not hot as hell."

Koren had to agree that it was. Sue had found a picture of Moose. It was taken from behind, and he had a hose slung over his shoulder and there was a large fire in the background.

"Or this one," Sue said, quickly turning her phone around, scrolling for a second, then showing her friends again.

This time, she'd found a picture of Sledge and Crash. They were high atop one of the ladders in a bucket, manning a hose. Water was spraying everywhere and the looks of concentration on both men's faces was intense...and hot.

"How are you finding those?" Vicky asked, pulling out her own phone.

"You guys, stop it," Koren scolded.

"I tried a bunch of search words, but the ones that worked the best are 'Station 7 San Antonio' and 'San Antonio firefighter.' Most of the pictures that come up seem to be taken by a local news station, and I can't tell if they're from Station 7 unless the photographer got the helmet in the picture, because they have a big 7 across them, but at this point, a hot firefighter is a hot firefighter."

Koren rolled her eyes at her friends and got up to grab the bottle of wine from the fridge. She came back into the living room and refilled all of their glasses. As much as her friends exasperated her, Koren wouldn't change them for the world.

"Look at this one," Vicky said, showing the others her screen.

"No, this one!" Sue exclaimed.

Koren sat back and put her legs up on the coffee table. She knew better than to try to stop them now. Eventually they'd get tired of their new little game, and they could talk about serious stuff again...like when they were going to have their next girls' night out, and if Koren could invite all the firefighters' fiancées.

Vicky and Sue went on for several minutes more, trying to outdo each other with the pictures they found on the Internet of sexy firefighters. "Okay, this one is a little sad, but... Hey! I think this is Taco," Vicky said, showing her screen to Koren.

Koren grabbed the phone from her friend. Sue came out of her chair and sat on Koren's other side. Both friends looked over her shoulders as she enlarged the picture.

It *was* Taco.

He was carrying a child out of a house. The kid looked unconscious, as the arm not against Taco's body was drooping bonelessly to the side. Taco still had his face mask on, but she could still see the intensity in his eyes when she zoomed in. His last name was blurry on his uniform, but since she knew what she was looking at, she could totally read it.

"Holy shit. When was that?" Sue asked, tilting the screen her way.

"I'm not sure. Hang on, let me read the caption," Koren told her.

She zoomed back out and her eyes scanned the words accompanying the picture. There wasn't much there, but the date was just weeks before she'd had her own accident and had been rescued by Taco. "This was before we met at the grocery store," Koren told her friends. "Not too long before we met, actually."

"Hey, I didn't know his name was Hudson. That's a badass name. How come he doesn't use it?" Sue asked.

Something about her friend's question made Koren hesitate. "What?"

"Hudson Vines. I didn't know that was Taco's name. It's cool. How come he goes by the silly nickname Taco when he has such a great real name?" Sue asked again.

"Bad history with his family and his name," Koren said absently. Then a thought struck—hard. "Holy shit."

"What?" Vicky asked.

Koren quickly saved the picture to her friend's phone, then immediately went to her picture folder and texted it to her own cell. She shoved the phone at Vicky and grabbed up her own.

"Koren?" Sue asked.

Holding up a finger, Koren ignored her friends. She

saved the picture to her phone and immediately sent a text of her own, attaching the picture.

She clicked on Beth's name and brought the phone up to her ear.

"I haven't found anything yet," Beth said in lieu of a greeting.

"I just sent you a text," Koren told her. "I need you to look at it. Maybe it's nothing, but maybe it's something."

"Koren, seriously, I'm in the middle of—"

"Just look at it," Koren interrupted. "I know you're busy, and I wouldn't interrupt you if it wasn't an emergency."

She heard Beth sigh. "Okay. Hang on. Right, it's a picture of Taco."

"Read the caption," Koren told her. She heard Beth reading the caption under her breath.

"Okay, I read it."

"It has Taco's name. His *real* name. I didn't think anything of it until my friends saw it—and were surprised. He doesn't tell *anyone* his real name," Koren said urgently.

"Shit!" Beth said.

"Exactly," Koren replied.

"I'm still confused," Sue said from next to her.

More to her friend than Beth, Koren said, "We thought the only one who really knew Taco's name was Jen. And probably her minions. But, if it was in the paper, then it opens up the suspect list considerably."

"Oh!" Vicky exclaimed.

"But it's more than that," Beth said in Koren's ear.

"What?" She turned her attention back to the phone.

"I remember this fire. That kid Taco's holding died. He'd been inside the burning house too long. He'd been passed out from drinking his mom's alcohol stash."

"Oh, shit. I remember that now too," Koren said.

"Apparently the mother got home just as he was coming out of the house with her son," Beth said. "She was freaking out and yelling all sorts of threats at Taco. I'm not saying she's behind this, but she was *definitely* enraged, and since his real name was in the paper, she could've seen it. She wouldn't know what his nickname was, wouldn't know that he never uses Hudson."

"Why was she mad at Taco?" Koren asked. "He risked his life to go in and try to save her son."

"I have no idea. And maybe this isn't it, but it's worth looking into. I gotta go. I need to call Cade."

"Okay."

"Koren?" Beth asked before she could hang up.

"Yeah?"

"Good job. This could be huge."

"I'm glad I could help."

"Bye."

"Bye."

Koren clicked off the phone and brought the picture of Taco back up. Looking at it now, it was even more tragic than before. The child he was carrying was dead. Had already passed away before Taco could get to him. That had to have hurt Taco.

"Kor, what in the world was that?" Sue asked.

She spent the next few minutes telling her friends what Beth had just told her. "It doesn't mean she's the one doing this, but it gives Beth someone else to look into."

"How're you holding up?" Vicky asked. "I mean, this whole situation is pretty intense."

Koren nodded. "It is. Taco and I got into a fight about it the other day."

"You did?" Sue asked.

"Yeah. He tried to break up with me."

"*What*? That asshole," Vicky said with a scowl.

"He was terrified after Moose's barn was burned down and told me he was doing it to keep me safe," Koren explained.

"Save us from macho men," Sue said with a roll of her eyes.

"What did you tell him?" Vicky asked.

"Well, after getting pissed and telling him off, I agreed and told him to get out."

Both Vicky and Sue gasped.

"You didn't! What'd he say?" Sue asked.

"He changed his mind and wouldn't leave."

"Quit telling us the story in bits and pieces," Vicky complained. "Spit it out."

"Fine. After his friend's barn went up in flames, he didn't call to tell me, the other women did. I learned all about it, and about Smokey, from them. I called and left a message and he still didn't contact me. When he did finally show up here, he was remote, cold. I knew he was going to break up with me, and I was so angry that I was fine with it. I was done. He tried to tell me he was breaking up with me to keep me safe, but that was such bullshit. I mean, if he wanted to keep me safe, he would've been *with* me. But instead, he was throwing me to the wolves, at least that's what it felt like. So I told him that. Then he realized I was right, and when I tried to agree with him that we were done, he said he wasn't leaving."

Koren took a deep breath, remembering how hurt she'd been. "We went back and forth a bit more, and finally I gave in."

"Well, thank God," Sue said.

"Hey! I thought you'd be pissed on my behalf," Koren said.

"I am. But, Kor, I've never seen you as happy as you've been the last month or so. Don't think we don't know how much you crave having someone in your life. You've never begrudged us our husbands and families, but it's obvious you want one of your own. And Taco obviously makes you happy. You stood up to him and let him know he was being a dick. Let him know you wouldn't put up with that bullshit. He reassessed, realized you were right, and fought to keep you. If he'd up and left, you would've known he wasn't the man for you. But he didn't. He realized he'd fucked up and stayed."

Her friend was right. She would've lost all respect for Taco if he'd left, and she wasn't sure she would've accepted him back if he'd changed his mind later. And now, after time to think about it, him wanting to keep her safe *was* nice. He hadn't gone about it in the right way, but the sentiment was nice.

"I really like him," Koren told her friends.

In tandem, both Vicky and Sue rolled their eyes.

"Duh," Vicky said.

"But seriously, I'm glad it's working out," Sue added.

"Me too," Koren said with a smile.

Vicky left shortly thereafter so she could get home to put her son to bed. Sue was going to stay longer, but her husband called and started sweet-talking her, so she left not too long after Vicky did.

Koren made sure all the doors were locked before she went upstairs to bed. Feeling paranoid in light of everything that was going on, she peeked out the window before heading to the bathroom to get ready.

Everything looked normal. The streetlights were on and she didn't see any cars she didn't recognize. There weren't any crazy people running around with pitch-forks or anything.

Chuckling at her overactive imagination, Koren dropped the curtain and headed into her bedroom. She'd call Taco after she was in bed. If he was able to get some privacy, maybe they could have some fun over the phone.

* * *

Nadine parked down the street and turned off her lights. She'd been waiting forever for one of the bitches to leave the girlfriend's condo. She needed to get to Koren, and using one of her friends was just the way to do it.

After the barn fire, the firefighters had been *far* more cautious, which was annoying. Nadine was having a hard time finding opportunities to mess with the rest of them. So she'd decided to forgo her plans and just move on to the grand finale.

She was tired.

Tired of living without Stevie.

Tired of doing whatever her dealer wanted so she could get the drugs her body craved.

She was ready to be done with it all.

Her life sucked.

She'd lost her job, had no money, was living in a piece-of-shit trailer, and she was bending over two or three times a day just to get a fix.

She was done.

But before she went out in a blaze of glory, she had to make sure Hudson suffered.

The woman she'd followed home opened her garage door and pulled her yuppie Highlander inside.

Nadine clenched her teeth. She needed to get ahold of the bitch's cell phone. Had to get her number. The entire plan hinged on it.

She had the perfect way to make Hudson regret he hadn't tried harder to save her son. But she needed to know either this or the other bitch's phone number.

Feeling restless, knowing she had a rock in her car ready to be injected, Nadine pressed her lips together in frustration.

Then, as if a miracle was being delivered from above, a man walked out of the house toward the mailbox. He put a few letters inside and raised the flag before heading back to the house.

Impatiently, Nadine waited another twenty minutes to make sure the occupants of the house were busy. Then she silently climbed out of her car and walked down the sidewalk. She had the mailbox open and the letters in her hand in seconds.

Praying that they were what she needed, she waited until she was back inside her car before glancing at them.

Bingo.

Bills. Three of them. And a check usually accompanied a bill.

Not able to wait a second longer, Nadine tore open the first letter and pulled out the check.

Right there at the top was the bitch's name and address…and a phone number.

Shaking with excitement, Nadine folded the check and placed it in her back pocket.

It was about time something went right in her life.

Not caring that she was in a middle-class neighborhood and anyone could walk by or look out their window and see her, Nadine reached into the glove compartment and pulled out the small bit of meth she'd been saving. She prepared a syringe to slam it into her vein. She knew slamming wasn't safe, but since it took only seconds to get a good high when she injected it straight into her bloodstream, it was preferable to smoking it.

Her hands were shaking by the time she got the meth dissolved she shot it into her arm, and almost immediately, the familiar feeling of euphoria washed over her.

Pulling the needle out, she threw it on the floorboard of the passenger side and started her car. Tomorrow she'd go to the library and log into Spoof-Tel, the website that allowed her to purchase credits to the app. She could then send a text to anyone, masking her number behind someone else's...namely, Hudson's bitch's friend.

Excitement rose up within Nadine. It was almost time. She couldn't wait.

CHAPTER SIXTEEN

"How did we not realize the paper published Taco's real name?" Squirrel asked as he paced back and forth in the large common room in the fire station.

Sledge had just gotten off the phone with Beth, and she'd told him what Koren's friends had innocently discovered.

"No clue," Taco said. "But this isn't exactly good news. It means that instead of just having Jen and her followers to investigate, the possibilities are practically endless. With that picture on the Internet, literally anyone could've seen it."

"I hadn't remembered that crazy lady at the scene where we pulled out that teenage boy until Beth mentioned it," Sledge said. "It could be her."

"It could be," Taco agreed. "But we've been at other scenes with hysterical family members. Remember that car accident the other week with that drunk driver? That girl's mom was yelling at us to do something to save her daughter, and when the police tried to tell her it was no use, that it was too late, she still screamed at us."

"True. But this woman bears looking into," Sledge pressed.

"I agree," Driftwood said. "But the question still remains...why you? What are you, specifically, supposed to be sorry about?" Driftwood asked.

"Sorry he didn't save someone?" Sledge asked.

"Sorry for being too abrupt at a scene?" Squirrel threw out.

"I. Don't. Know!" Taco bit out. "Look, I haven't been Mr. Congeniality at scenes, but none of us are, really. We're too worried about trying to save lives. I've also dated a bunch of girls from all those online dating sites, but I wasn't an asshole. I didn't promise anyone anything, and most of them were only first dates anyway."

"Calm down," Crash said.

"How can I calm down?" Taco seethed, running a hand through his hair in agitation. "I apparently did something I'm supposed to be sorry about, but I have no idea what. Some crazy person is now punishing my friends in order to get back at me. We don't know what they have planned next and who might be their next target. My girlfriend is having a hard time dealing with all the drama I've brought into her life, and I can't say I blame her."

He took a deep breath and collapsed onto one of the couches. "I feel as if someone is going to pop out from behind a corner and tell me I'm on candid camera or something. But whoever is behind this is right about one thing. I'm so sorry that this is affecting all of you." Taco looked at Penelope. "I'm sorry, Tiger. So fucking sorry. If Smokey could understand me, I'd apologize to him too."

"Stop it," Moose ordered. "This is not your fault."

"Apparently it is!" Taco countered. "If not for whatever it was that I did, this wouldn't be happening. Smokey wouldn't be traumatized. Penelope wouldn't be withdrawn and pissed at me. Crash would still have his car, you'd still have a barn and chickens."

"Beth is gonna figure this out," Sledge said from a chair across the room.

"Stop with the pity party, man," Chief threw in.

"I'm not pissed at you," Penelope added.

Taco took a deep breath and looked around at his friends. "How do we keep our women safe? That's what's bothering me the most. What if whoever this is decides to shoot Koren? Or kidnap Blythe? Or somehow hurt any of the others? I feel so *helpless*."

"They know to be careful," Driftwood said. "Unfortunately, we can't just stop our lives and barricade ourselves at home. I get it, the last thing I want is for

Quinn to have to go through anything like what she went through at the hands of that psycho bitch Jen again. But I have to trust her to be smart. To be safe. I know if she feels the slightest bit uneasy, she'll call me. They all know that."

"I know, I just...I have this feeling that the shit's gonna hit the fan, and I hate not being able to do a damn thing about it," Taco said.

"Try feeling that way for months and months at a time," Penelope murmured.

Everyone turned to look at her.

Tiger didn't talk about her feelings. *Ever*. It was as if she'd become a robot after coming back from Turkey and being held captive by ISIS. This was the first time she'd said anything even remotely about her feelings on the ordeal.

"Every time you walk into a store, you wonder if someone's watching you. When you go home at night, you lay awake staring at the ceiling, wondering what it was that you did to deserve to be kidnapped and terrorized. I wish I could tell you that the feeling of helplessness goes away...but I can't," Penelope said softly.

"Tiger—" Taco said, but she held up a hand, stopping him.

"Koren's the lucky one. She's unblemished by the shit life throws at us. She's got a good family, friends, job...the worst she's probably suffered in her lifetime is the death of a grandparent or a pet. And I don't mean that in a bad way. She's lucky. I'm completely envious. But if something happens, she'll be okay. She's got you. And her family."

"You've got us," Sledge said quietly. "I'm your family by blood, but everyone sitting here is your family as well. Whatever you need, we'll bend over backward to make sure you have it."

"I know," Penelope said.

"I don't think you do," Moose said. "You're shutting us out. We all know it. *You* know it. Let us help you, Pen."

"I'm gonna go lie down," she replied instead, standing and avoiding eye contact with everyone.

"Tiger—" Sledge said, but she held up her hand again and walked out of the room.

"Damn it!" Moose said in frustration.

No one else said anything, as they were just as frustrated as Moose. With Penelope. With the fires. With not knowing who was behind them and why. And about not being able to be with their women so they could protect them.

The next day, Beth called to talk to Taco.

"What do you know about this woman whose son was killed in that fire?" she asked.

"That's easy. Nothing. Why?"

"I've been looking into her. Looks like she got divorced a while ago and was raising her son by herself. In the year or so before he was killed, he'd been getting into more and more trouble at school. At first it was petty stuff, but in the last four months before the fire, he'd actually been suspended twice."

"And?" Taco asked.

"And nothing. I'm just saying. Her name is Nadine Patterson, and her husband was having affairs. She took him to the cleaners in the divorce and was awarded a ton of money in both child support and alimony. Preston, the ex, was upset, and claimed she would spend it all on drugs, and when he pressed his lawyers to make her do a blood test, they said he didn't have enough proof of her drug use to get the judge to order one."

"You scare me, Beth," Taco said. "I have no idea how you find this stuff."

"I'm good," she said without conceit. "Anyway, before the fire, Nadine Patterson looked like your normal single mother on paper. She had a fairly good job, and her credit cards weren't maxed out, even though they had pretty good balances on them. But... the money her ex paid her every month was withdrawn almost as soon as it cleared. I can't find any record of where she was spending it."

"*Was* she spending it on drugs?" Taco guessed.

"Possibly. She was given a citation for DUI when

she showed up at the scene of the fire, but because of the circumstances, I think she was let off easy."

"And she was the one who was going crazy that night, right?" Taco asked.

"Right."

"So where is she now?"

"That's the thing. I don't know. She stopped showing up to work, withdrew all her money from her accounts and disappeared."

"No one just disappears," Taco said. "She has to be somewhere."

"That's what I thought too, but honestly, Taco, she hasn't used a credit card, and I can't find her anywhere."

"Do you think it's her?" Taco asked.

Beth sighed. "My gut says yes, but my research says it's unlikely."

"What do the cops say?"

"They're still working on it," Beth said in exasperation. "It's a good thing I work for the government and not the local cops or Texas Rangers. They have so many rules and regulations they have to follow. I get it, I do…privacy rights and all that, but it takes absolutely forever to get anything done."

"All I want to know is if Koren's safe," Taco said. "If this Nadine person is mad at me because of what happened to her son—which doesn't even make sense, as I was there to try to *save* him—then what's her end game? Why start all these fires? And why Crash, Chief,

and Moose? Nothing about this makes sense. And what am I supposed to be sorry about? I don't get it."

"I know. And that's why I'm still digging," Beth said. "I could be wrong. Maybe it *is* Jen or one of her followers and they just want to see you suffer."

"Shit, Beth, why'd you call me if you had no information?" Taco asked in frustration.

"I wanted to see if you knew Nadine, or if you remembered having any contact with her since that fire," she said evenly, not upset with the way Taco was speaking to her.

"I don't."

"Okay. I'll keep digging."

"Beth?"

"Yeah?"

"Thanks. I know you do a lot behind the scenes and probably don't get enough appreciation for it."

"Oh, don't worry. Cade is veeeeery appreciative."

Taco smirked. "Later, Beth. You'll call if you find out anything important?"

"Of course. Later."

Taco clicked off the phone and paced. He wanted to be home. Wanted to be with Koren. Wanted to see for himself that she was okay.

Not thinking beyond needing to hear her voice, he clicked on Koren's name.

She answered after the first ring. "Hi, Taco."

"Hey, Kor. How are you?"

"I'm good."

"Nothing's happened?"

"If you mean has any crazy fire-wielding lunatic knocked on my door, no," she said with a laugh.

"That's not funny," Taco said, not feeling in the mood to joke about the situation.

"I'm sorry," she said contritely. "I'm fine. I've been inside all morning working. I've got Blythe and Squirrel's trip all set up. I finished making the arrangements for that big wedding in the Bahamas, and I've got about half a dozen new clients to research trips for as well. Things are good."

Taco breathed out a sigh of relief, but the feeling of trepidation, that something was lurking around the corner, wouldn't go away. If this was how Penelope felt all the time, no wonder she wasn't sleeping well and was always on edge.

"I should be off shift at the normal time in the morning."

"Are you coming over here?" Koren asked.

"Yeah. If that's all right."

"Of course. You want me to go over to your house instead? You could text me when you leave and I could meet you there."

"No," he said immediately. If someone was targeting him, the last place he wanted Koren was at his house by herself. "I'll come to you. That way you aren't disturbed when you're working."

"I miss your place," she said after a moment. "Your kitchen is bigger than mine, and I love being able to spread all my shit out on your table and not feel as if I'm taking up the entire room."

Taco couldn't deny her words felt good. He liked her in his space too. "I know," was all he said.

"Have you heard anything new from Beth?" she asked.

"Unfortunately, no. But she's doing her illegal best to uncover every dark secret of anyone I've ever met before."

"I'm sorry," Koren said sympathetically. "What can I do to make this better for you?"

"Stay safe," Taco said immediately. "Be smart. If anyone comes to your door, don't answer it. If you smell smoke, get the hell out of your condo. Be hyper-alert for the smallest thing that seems off and call me if you get nervous about anything."

"I can do that."

Taco took a deep breath and tried to lighten the conversation. "What are your plans for tonight?" he asked.

"I'm going to go over to Sophie's house. Blythe and Quinn are coming too."

"You'll text me before you leave and when you get there?" Taco asked.

"Of course."

Taco closed his eyes. He had no idea how he'd gotten so lucky. A lot of women would balk at telling their boyfriends everywhere they went, but not Koren. She understood that he was worried about her and wasn't trying to be creepy about it. "I miss you," he said softly.

"It's only been a day and a half," Koren said with a laugh.

"I know, but I miss you anyway."

"I miss you too," she said.

"I'm gonna let you go and get some work done," he told her.

"Okay. Be safe today," Koren said. "I hope it's a light day for you."

Taco actually hoped they were slammed. It would make time go by faster. "Me too," he said instead. "I'll talk to you later."

"Bye."

"Bye, Kor."

Taco clicked off the phone and resumed his pacing. If anything, talking to Koren made his anxiety ratchet up a notch instead of making him feel better. He couldn't deal with it if something happened to her because of him. Like Penelope had said, she hadn't ever had to deal with anything like this in the past. The last thing he wanted was someone pissed at him and taking it out on *her*.

Just when he didn't think he'd be able to keep from going crazy, the emergency tone rang out. The dispatcher informed them there was an alarm sounding at one of the nursing homes nearby. Most of the time these things were false alarms, but the firefighters didn't treat them differently from any other call.

Taco ran into the garage and met the others there putting on their gear. Within a minute, the first truck was peeling out of the bay with lights and sirens blazing. At least the call would keep his mind occupied for the next hour or so…if he was lucky.

CHAPTER SEVENTEEN

Koren was in the kitchen laughing with Sophie, Blythe, and Quinn. They'd decided to hang out at Sophie's for the simple fact that her shed had already burned down. It was silly, but they kinda thought that since she'd already been targeted by the arsonist, her place might be safer than any of theirs.

There were a hundred ways that their reasoning didn't work, but they didn't care. Besides, Sophie and Chief's house was one story. If something *did* happen, it was super easy to go out a window or the back sliding door to escape.

Koren didn't like that she even had to think about something like that, but the truth was, she couldn't *stop* thinking about it. She hadn't quite reached paranoia level, but every time she talked to Taco and he harped on her being safe, she got more and more nervous about boogeymen lurking around corners.

So far, things had been quiet at Sophie's. They'd finished dinner and were putting the dishes in the sink and cleaning up the kitchen.

"Okay, who here has heard from their man already tonight?" Quinn asked.

Sophie raised her hand.

Blythe raised hers.

Koren grinned and wiggled her fingers.

"Now...who's irritated that their man can't stop worrying about them?"

No one said a word or raised their hands.

"Exactly." Quinn smiled. "I'd always wanted someone who *really* loved me. For a while, I was afraid to admit that John might be that man."

"Afraid?" Sophie scoffed. "Quinn, we practically had to bully you into even giving him a chance!"

"I know, but despite seeing how amazing Chief was with you, the last thing I wanted was to go out with John and realize that, while he was perfect on the outside, inside, maybe he was just like all the other shallow people I'd let into my life in the past."

"I'm happy for you," Sophie said, putting her arm around Quinn's shoulders.

"So..." Blythe said, turning her attention to Koren. "What updates do you have for us about Taco?"

Feeling as if she was suddenly in the hot seat, Koren tried to play dumb. "What do you mean?"

"Oh, no!" Sophie said, pointing her finger at Koren. "We're s-smarter than that. We've all been where you are, and you are not going to deny us juicy details!"

Everyone chuckled. Koren leaned back against the counter. "We're good," she said.

Sophie shook her head. "Nope. M-More."

Koren knew she was blushing. Sophie reminded her a lot of Sue. She pushed and pushed until she got what she wanted. "Seriously, we're good. We had a fight the other day because he thought pushing me away would make me safer."

Quinn rolled her eyes. "As if."

"I know. I was upset at first, but then decided I was done and agreed with him," Koren said.

"Let me guess, then he decided that wasn't what he wanted after all," Blythe said with a smile.

"Exactly. So now he texts me a million times a day to check on me and I talk to him at least two or three times when he's on shift."

"And when he's not?" Sophie asked with a quirk of an eyebrow.

Koren smiled. "Then we're together."

All three of the other women whooped in delight. When they'd quieted down, Koren continued. "Since I work from home, it's easy to just hang out together. Lately he's been coming to my condo because he thinks it's safer than his house. So he stops by after he gets off work in the morning and hangs out while I work. Then if I need to do errands, we do them together. Then we eat in and watch TV or whatever."

"It's the 'whatever' I want to know m-more about," Sophie said suggestively.

"How about you, Soph?" Quinn asked. "Want to tell us more about the wedding you're planning?"

With a smile, Sophie gladly went into detail about the wedding Chief was planning on his reservation. It would be a small affair, with only his native relatives in attendance. But when they got back to Texas, they were planning on having a huge party.

Sophie was in the middle of talking about where she wanted to have her reception when Koren's phone vibrated with a text.

Expecting it to be Taco, she was surprised to see Sue's name on the screen.

Sue: I need you.

Alarmed, Koren immediately texted back.

Koren: What's wrong?
    Sue: I'm at your place.
    Koren: What? Why?
    Sue: I had to get out of my house.
    Koren: OMG. Why? Talk to me.
    Sue: I can't. Not over the phone. Can you come?

Koren: Of course. I'm on my way right now. Did you bring your key?

Sue: No. I left it at the house.

Koren: Okay. My spare is in that secret rock around back by the basement door.

Sue: Thanks.

Koren: I'll be there as soon as I can. Hang in there.

"What's wrong?" Sophie asked.

"I don't know. That was my friend Sue. Something's up. Maybe a fight with her husband? She said she had to get out of her house. She's at my condo now and wants to talk to me," Koren said.

"Well, go!" Quinn said.

"Is there anything we can do?" Blythe asked.

"I don't think so, but thank you," Koren told them. "I appreciate you letting me hang out here tonight."

"Anytime," Sophie said. "And not just because we're trying to hide out from a crazy person."

"Make sure you text Taco and tell him that you're headed home," Quinn said as Koren gathered up her stuff.

Nodding, Koren shot off a quick text.

Koren: I'm headed home. Sue texted. Something's up and she needs me.

Taco: Okay. Be safe.

Koren: I will. C U in the morning.

Taco: Definitely.

With that done, Koren stuffed her phone into her purse and hurried out to her car parked in Sophie's driveway. She took a look around before climbing in, and didn't see anyone or anything out of the ordinary.

She drove faster than she might otherwise and arrived at her condo in record time. Koren pulled into her driveway and opened the garage. She didn't see Sue's car anywhere, but supposed she might've taken a taxi or Uber to get there. If something happened at her house or with her husband, she might've just stormed out without her purse or something.

The garage door closed behind her, and Koren jumped out and headed inside.

"Sue?" she called out when she got inside. No one answered, and Koren put her purse down on the kitchen counter and glanced into the living room.

Dumbfounded, Koren stared at the stranger sitting in one of her chairs. The woman was extremely skinny, and she wore black jeans with a black shirt. She had a pair of ragged sneakers on her feet, which were resting on the coffee table.

"Who are you? Where's Sue?" Koren demanded, instantly on alert.

The woman stood up and pointed a pistol at her.

Koren froze.

Stupid! The second she saw the stranger inside her house, she should've run.

"Sue's not coming," the woman said.

"What'd you do to her?" Koren asked.

The stranger laughed. "Nothing. Your friend is sitting at home safe and sound. No worries."

Now Koren was confused.

"I'm Nadine," the woman said.

When Koren didn't react, the woman seemed to get pissed.

"You don't know who I am?"

Koren shook her head. "Should I?"

"Yeah, bitch, you *should*! Hudson ruined my life, and I would've assumed he'd have talked about it. About what he did! But now it's even more obvious to me that he doesn't give a shit!"

Koren swallowed hard as things clicked in her head. Taco *had* talked to her about a Nadine. In a call earlier that very evening. She was the mother of the kid who had perished in a fire before Koren started dating him. The poor kid in Taco's arms, in the picture in the paper, was this woman's son.

"I'm so sorry about your son," she said softly.

"Don't you talk about my son!" Nadine screamed.

Koren pressed her lips together. Something was drastically wrong with Nadine. She knew she needed to stay calm and not provoke her. Needed to do whatever it took to get out of this without being shot.

"Can I get you something to eat or drink?"

For some reason, Nadine found that extremely funny. She threw her head back and laughed as if she hadn't heard anything funnier in her life.

Terrified now, as it was more than obvious Nadine was on some kind of drug, Koren spun around and bolted for the garage door. If she could get inside, she could maybe hold Nadine off until the garage door opened then get out of there.

But she didn't make it.

Nadine didn't say a word. She didn't yell for Koren to stop. One second Koren was running for her life, and the next, every muscle in her body coiled and she fell to the floor with a thud. She couldn't even put up her hands to stop her fall.

Once Koren was down, Nadine again cackled with laughter.

Koren closed her eyes as pain enveloped her body. This was it. She was dying, and she wouldn't get to tell Taco how much she'd come to love him.

Stupid...so stupid.

"Slow night," Squirrel said.

"Aw, man!"

"Shut the hell up."

"Now you've done it."

The complaints came hard and fast from around Taco. He shook his head and didn't even feel sorry for Squirrel when the others started throwing whatever they had handy at him. A napkin. A pen. A pillow.

"You know better than that," Sledge said with a shake of his head. "Now we're gonna get slammed."

Squirrel smirked. "Just making sure you guys are all still awake. Jeez, it's only eight at night and everyone's ready to go to bed. Our women are making us lazy."

"Not sure that's exactly true," Crash said. "I mean, I'm only speaking for myself. I might go to bed at eight, but I'm not exactly sleeping."

Everyone chuckled and agreed.

Taco leaned back on the couch and smiled. He loved this. Loved getting to hang out with his best friends three to four days a week. There wasn't a better job in the world.

"Anyone hear from their old ladies yet tonight?" Moose asked.

"Beth would kick your ass if she heard you call her an old lady," Sledge said.

"Adeline would just laugh," Crash threw in.

"Koren texted me earlier. She, Sophie, Quinn, and Blythe were over at Soph's house, but her friend Sue texted and needed to see her, so she went home," Taco said.

"Beth's still neck-deep in researching," Crash said.

"She told me to stop bothering her when I checked in last."

"Adeline, Coco, and Smokey were watching *The Secret Life of Pets*," Penelope said quietly.

"How's Smokey?" Chief asked.

"Good. Adeline said he finally settled down. He stole Coco's bed, and Coco simply climbed on top of him and fell asleep."

Everyone smiled at the imagery Penelope's words evoked.

"You hear from the detective?" Taco asked Sledge.

The other man shook his head. "Not today. He said they're looking into every possibility, but that the investigation is slow going."

Taco sighed. "This sucks. I know I can't just take off work indefinitely, but I hate leaving Koren vulnerable. And I feel as if whoever is doing this is just waiting to pounce. On her, or at one of you guys."

"Between the cops and Beth, they're going to find out who's responsible sooner rather than later," Sledge said.

"I hope so," Taco said.

The second the words were out of his mouth, the tones rang out through the fire station. Everyone leaped up as one and ran for the garage to put on their gear. On their way, Chief elbowed Squirrel. "This is your fault."

Squirrel just smirked.

* * *

Koren opened her eyes slowly. She was still lying in the short hallway leading to the garage. She remembered everything that happened. Nadine had Tased her. Her back hurt where the barbs had hit and her mouth was throbbing.

"You awake yet?" Nadine asked impatiently from somewhere nearby.

Koren wanted to say no, wanted to buy herself some time, but that wasn't going to get her out of this situation. Shifting up on her elbows, she brought one hand to her face and touched her chin. Her fingers came away bloody.

"That was fucking hysterical," Nadine said. "The second those prongs hit you, your entire body went stiff as a board and *BAM*, down you went. Right on your face."

Yeah, Koren remembered that. It was the scariest feeling ever. She'd been completely cognizant of everything happening around her, but couldn't do a damn thing to protect herself as she fell. Hitting her shin on the floor hurt. As did the barbs in her back. And the amps moving through her body.

"Come on," Nadine said, leaning down and grabbing hold of one of Koren's biceps. "I need to get you upstairs before you have any more bright ideas."

Koren stumbled and would've fallen again if it wasn't for Nadine's tight hold on her arm. She had no idea how the other woman had the strength to drag her up from the floor, but she did.

Without giving her any time to come up with another plan, Nadine force marched Koren up the stairs. It took a while, because Koren still didn't really have control over her body. She felt as if she'd been run over by a Mack truck. Blood dripped from her chin onto her T-shirt, but that was the least of her problems, and Koren knew it.

Nadine had obviously spent a bit of time looking around her condo before Koren had arrived home because she knew exactly where she was going. She dragged Koren into the master bedroom, and then into the bathroom.

"Sit there," Nadine ordered, pointing to the tile next to the toilet.

Scared out of her mind that Nadine was going to shoot her in the head—with a real gun this time—Koren hesitated.

"Sit the fuck down!" Nadine ordered, sticking one of the butcher knives from Koren's kitchen in her face.

Not wanting to feel the slice of the blade, Koren sat.

"Good girl," Nadine praised. Then she reached into her pocket and pulled something out. She flung them at Koren, and she flinched when the heavy object landed in her lap.

"Put those on."

Looking down, Koren saw a pair of handcuffs. A

tear fell from her eye before she could stop it. "Please don't do this," Koren pleaded.

"Oh, I'm doing it, and your tears aren't gonna stop me, so quit crying. You're so *pathetic*. Put one of the cuffs around that pipe behind the toilet and the other around your wrist."

Koren looked from Nadine to the pipe in question. It was just about the only place in the bathroom where she could restrain her. "Taco did his best to get to your son," Koren said quickly, hoping against hope that she could distract Nadine.

"Who?"

"Um…Hudson."

Nadine leaned down until she was in Koren's face. She used the knife to punctuate the air with each of her words. "You. Don't. Know. What. You're. Talking. About!"

Freaked about how carelessly Nadine was swinging the knife around, Koren pressed her lips together.

"Now, put on the damn cuff!"

Slowly, Koren did as she was told. She tightened one side of it around the pipe and gently eased the other cuff around her wrist.

Nadine laughed once more—then pounced toward her.

Koren jerked back, but there was really nowhere to go. Nadine grabbed her wrist and squeezed the cuff. Koren yelped in pain and tried to jerk her hand away, but all that did was make the metal bite into her wrist more.

As fast as she'd come at her, Nadine backed away. She put the knife down on Koren's bathroom counter and fluffed her short hair.

Panting through the pain in her wrist, Koren didn't take her eyes away from the other woman. "What'd you do to Sue?"

"Nothing."

Koren frowned. "But she texted me."

"So stupid. That was *me*."

"But it came from her number. Did you steal her phone?"

Nadine turned to look at her. "I didn't have to steal it. I'm smart enough to figure out how to clone it."

Koren closed her eyes. She was thankful that Sue probably really was at home, safe and sound and oblivious to what was happening, but she felt stupid that she'd walked right into Nadine's trap.

"So...you know that your boyfriend is a murderer, but you don't care?" Nadine asked in a casual tone.

Koren swallowed hard, trying to acclimate to the abrupt change in topic. She wasn't sure if it was better to say yes or no. So she said nothing.

"I heard him say it himself that night. He was late." Her eyes went to Koren's. "*Late*. Like he was going out for dinner or his alarm didn't go off or something. He was late to my house fire." Nadine put her hands on the counter and leaned forward, her head bowed.

"I'm sorry," Koren whispered.

"Yeah, you will be," Nadine said, straightening up. Then she reached into her back pocket and took out a syringe. Her hand disappeared into the front pocket of her jeans and she pulled out a small baggie.

Koren watched in disbelief and horror as Nadine began preparing the drug. As she spoke, she used a lighter to heat up the small rock on a spoon she'd also pulled from her pocket.

As she got her drugs ready, Nadine kept talking. "I was like you once. Clueless to just about everything but my man. I loved Preston. I would've done anything for him. We had never been happier than when Stevie was born. I quit my job to stay home with him rather than pay for childcare, and that's when things went to shit. I couldn't lose the baby weight, and Preston spent more time with the bimbos at work than at home with his wife and kid.

"But I didn't care. He could fuck his secretary because I had Stevie. He was my life. But then I failed at that too. I don't even think he liked me much there toward the end. My child didn't love me anymore…just like Preston."

Nadine effortlessly transferred the melted drug from the spoon into the syringe and sank the needle into her arm without pause. Her eyes closed, and she tilted her head back as she pushed the plunger and injected the drug into her body. When she was done, she took the needle out and tossed the used syringe into the sink carelessly. She turned to look down at Koren.

"I'm sure he loved you," Koren said desperately.

"Doesn't matter now, does it?" Nadine asked rhetorically. "Hudson was *late* getting to my house, and my baby boy died."

Koren knew the story of what had happened. Knew the teenager had been passed out from drinking too much, that Nadine had left him alone. Now that she'd witnessed the woman shooting up right in front of her, Koren had to believe she'd probably been out trying to get more drugs that night.

"What are you going to do?" Koren asked as bravely as she could.

Nadine smiled then. It was an awful smile, and Koren could see every one of her rotting, gray teeth.

"I'm gonna see how fast Hudson can hustle when someone *he* cares about is in trouble. Wanna put odds on it with me? I'm saying that there's no way he'll be *late* when he hears that his precious girlfriend's condo is on fire."

Koren's eyes widened and she stared at Nadine in horror. Her arm reflexively pulled on the cuff.

Nadine took a step toward Koren, and she couldn't help but flinch back. The strung-out woman laughed and merely patted Koren on the head. "Don't worry. I have some stuff to do to get ready before our fun starts. Stay put, would ya?" Then she cackled again and left the room, closing the bathroom door behind her.

The second Koren was alone, she panicked. She pulled as hard as she could on the handcuff, but there was no way it was going to slip off her wrist, not after Nadine had tightened it so much it was cutting into her skin. And it certainly wasn't going to be coming loose from the pipe going into the wall.

She still had one hand free, and she maneuvered around the toilet to open the door under the sink to see if there was anything she could use as a weapon or to somehow break the handcuff chain. Staring in dismay at the stack of towels, the bottle of toilet cleaner, the extra rolls of toilet paper, and the two bottles of shampoo, Koren had the sinking feeling that she was in big trouble.

Grabbing one of the towels, she pressed it to her chin for a moment, then pulled it away. Bloody. Her chin was still bleeding. Koren figured she probably needed stitches, but that was the least of her worries at the moment. She pressed the towel to her chin again and crawled back to where she was sitting before, between the toilet and the tub.

Closing her eyes, she prayed as she'd never prayed before. She didn't feel her phone in her pocket anymore, Nadine had obviously removed it. There was literally nothing she could do to get help. Her neighbor on the other side of her was on vacation, so even if she pounded on the wall, no one would hear. Her other neighbors were elderly and already hard of hearing, so if she screamed they probably wouldn't hear her either.

The only thing she could hope was that Nadine didn't actually kill her before she did whatever else she had planned. Koren had to stay alive long enough for Taco to get to her.

* * *

"You dick," Driftwood said, smacking Squirrel on the back of the head. "We've been on four calls since you had to go and comment on how quiet it was. Thanks a lot."

"We're not bored though, are we?" Squirrel quipped.

"He's got a point," Chief said. "Calls make the night go by faster. And the faster we can get through the night, the sooner we'll be with our women again."

Taco ignored his friends and pulled out his phone. He clicked on Koren's name and frowned when it rang several times then went to voice mail. It wasn't like her not to answer, but then again, if Sue was having a crisis, she was probably dealing with that.

His thumbs flew over the keyboard as he wrote a text.

Taco: I just thought I'd check in. We've been slammed tonight, but don't worry, all's good.

. . .

It took several minutes, but finally his phone vibrated with a text.

Koren: I'm good.
 Taco: Everything okay with Sue?
 Koren: Yes.

Taco waited for her to elaborate, but when she didn't say anything else, he began to worry.

Taco: Are you sure you're okay?
 Koren: Yes. Just busy.
 Taco: Can I call?
 Koren: No. It's not a good time.
 Koren: I love you.

Taco blinked at the three words on the screen.

Holy shit. She loved him? She hadn't said anything about his own declaration of love when they'd been fighting, but he'd certainly had high hopes that she returned his feelings. And there were the words, in black and white.

His heart raced. Damn, he wished his shift was over so he could go to her place and hear her say it in person.

. . .

Taco: I love you too. So much.
    Koren: I'll see you soon.
    Taco: Not soon enough. :)

Feeling on top of the world, Taco tucked his phone into his back pocket and headed to the kitchen to help Crash finish up the dishes from their earlier dinner.

* * *

After what seemed like forever, but was probably only about thirty minutes, Nadine came back into the bathroom. "Well, that was fun," Nadine said happily.

Koren didn't want to ask. But she didn't have to.

"*Taco* texted you. What a stupid name."

Koren's heart stopped. Shit. What had Nadine said to him?

She pulled out Koren's phone and smiled. "When you were out of it, I used your finger to unlock your phone. I was going to text him later but he beat me to the punch."

She clicked a few buttons then turned the screen around and showed it to Koren.

Koren stared at the stilted conversation with dread. But when she got to the part where Nadine had told Taco that she loved him, she froze.

She *did* love him, but for some reason had been holding back from telling him. And he hadn't repeated the words he'd said the day he'd tried to break up with her.

Some of the horror must've shown on her face, because Nadine laughed, then said with a sneer, "Was that the first time?"

Koren stared up at her.

Without warning, Nadine kicked Koren in the side.

Grunting in pain, Koren dropped the towel from her chin and leaned over protectively. She coughed and it hurt like hell.

"Was that the first time you told dear *Taco* that you loved him?" Nadine asked again.

Koren didn't take her eyes from her as she nodded.

"How adorable and perfect," the strung-out woman said. "That will give him extra incentive to do whatever I tell him to."

Koren opened her mouth to ask Nadine what she was going to do, but didn't get even the first word out before she started bragging about her plan.

"I hope you have good insurance, but it's not really gonna matter when you're dead. You see, there's a fire in your basement. It's small at the moment, but alas, it started next to that fluffy chair downstairs. Oh, and that blanket that's hanging over the back of it will also catch on fire. And of course the curtains, and the shelf of books too. It'll take a bit, which gives me a little time."

"Time for what?" The question came out before Koren could stop it.

Nadine smiled another evil grin and stepped out of the bathroom for a moment. She came back inside holding a bottle of coconut rum that Sue had brought over one night. They hadn't finished it, since it was a bit too strong for any of them.

Nadine held out the bottle. "Drink it."

Koren stared at her in shock. She didn't like alcohol when it was mixed with *juice*; she couldn't just drink rum straight from the bottle.

The other woman's eyes narrowed and she took a step closer. "I said, drink it."

Koren pressed her lips together and shook her head.

Nadine lunged. Koren tried to fight the other woman off, but whatever drug she'd injected must've made her almost inhumanly strong. And with one arm out of commission by the handcuff, Koren was no match for a pissed-off, determined Nadine.

She wrapped an arm around Koren's neck and tilted her head back. She held the bottle to her lips and tipped it upward. Koren thrashed, continuing to fight the best she could with one arm. When it was obvious Nadine wasn't going to succeed in forcing the alcohol down Koren's throat, she stepped back and growled. Then she turned and left the bathroom.

Koren's relief was short-lived when Nadine returned in seconds. But this time she had the gun in her hand. She pointed it at Koren's head and said, *"Drink it."*

"Please, Nadine," Koren pleaded.

"Shut the fuck up and drink!" the crazed woman screamed.

Knowing it was either drink or get shot, Koren chose the obvious. She tilted the bottle of rum and took a sip.

"More," Nadine insisted.

The alcohol burned as it went down, but Koren tipped the bottle once again, this time only pretending to drink.

Nadine took a few steps toward her, whipped her arm back, and then smashed the barrel of the gun against her forehead. "Either drink the damn shit faster, or I'll blow your head off and let your boyfriend find your brains covering the wall!"

Terrified over the idea of Taco finding her like that, she forced the alcohol past her tightening throat.

Once Koren had ingested at least half the remaining alcohol, Nadine grabbed the bottle and stepped away. Laughing, she took a giant swig of the rum then whipped it at the sink, laughing harder when the bottle shattered and glass went flying everywhere.

As quickly as she'd started laughing, Nadine stopped and glared at Koren. "Now your body will react like Stevie's did. Eventually you'll pass out, and you'll die of smoke inhalation long before lover boy can get to you. An eye for an eye," Nadine said in a low, chilling voice. "It's the only way for my Stevie to rest in peace."

She backed up farther. "Oh, and I opened your window a bit...you know, to help draw the smoke upward. I don't care if the flames never reach this floor. The smoke will. That's the important part."

Then with another evil grin, Nadine held up Koren's cell phone and walked out of the bathroom. She placed the cell on the middle of the bed and turned back to Koren. "Too bad you can't get to your phone to call for help. Or to tell Hudson how much you love him one more time." Her eyes narrowed, and she spat on the floor before saying, "A part of me hopes he dies *with* you—but a bigger part hopes he lives. That'll cause him way more pain, knowing he'd failed to get to you in time."

And with those parting words, Nadine walked out of view.

Koren heard her going down the stairs then puttering around in the kitchen. The room was already spinning from the rum, and Koren did her best to stay upright. She'd never had that much straight alcohol at one time, and she knew she was going to be in big trouble.

She opened the lid to the toilet and tried to stick her finger down her throat to make herself throw up, but wasn't successful. Just when she was contemplating drinking some of the water from the tank to try to dilute the effects of the rum, Koren smelled the first whiff of smoke.

Her head came up, and she stared in dismay at the thin white wisps of smoke that curled into her bedroom and lazily wafted toward the open window.

Shit! She'd been hoping Nadine was lying. That she hadn't really started a fire in her basement. But with every second that passed, with more and more smoke filling the bedroom, Koren tried to keep herself from panicking.

Even though Nadine had done it maliciously, she'd actually done Koren a favor. Telling Taco that she loved him took a huge burden off her shoulders. If she did die, at least he'd know.

"I love you, Rob," Koren whispered, as she sank back against the wall between the toilet and the tub. She grabbed the bloody towel and held it up to her face. She tried to slow her breathing. The longer she could stay calm, the better the chance that Taco could get to her in time.

Taco's phone rang. He picked it up and saw the call was from an unknown number. He put it down and turned his attention back to the football game on the television. He never answered phone calls from numbers he didn't recognize. There were just too many scammers out there nowadays. If he didn't have a number programmed into his contacts, he didn't want to talk to whoever was on the other end.

As soon as his phone stopped ringing, it started up again.

The same unknown number appeared. Taco hesitated that time. What were the odds that someone he didn't know or a scammer would call, not wait for voice mail, and call right back?

He hesitated, and the ringing stopped.

Just when he'd brought his eyes back to the game, his phone rang for the third time.

"You gonna answer that or just stare at it?" Sledge asked with a chuckle.

Taco clicked on the green answer button and brought it up to his ear. "Hello?"

"Hello, Hudson," a husky voice said.

"Who is this?" Taco barked.

"*Tsk, tsk*. I can't believe you don't know. But you will soon."

"What does that mean?" he asked, the hair on the back of his neck standing straight up.

By this time, the rest of his friends were on alert and staring at him in concern.

"You don't want to be *late*," the woman said in disdain. "If I were you, I'd start rolling now."

Taco was standing already, as were the others. "Where? What have you done?"

"There may or may not be a fire at your girlfriend's condo. You should probably go check."

He was moving even as he said, "If you've hurt her, I'm going to kill you!"

"I'm counting on it," the woman said, then cut their connection.

Taco was running by this time.

"What's up?" Sledge asked as he stuffed his feet into his boots and bunker pants.

"Koren. That was...I'm guessing Nadine. She said something about a fire at Koren's condo."

The others were all suiting up in their gear as well. "I'll call Dax," Chief said.

"And I'll call dispatch and see if they've heard anything," Penelope called.

"I'll get ahold of Cruz and Quint and get them rolling too," Squirrel added.

Taco couldn't even thank them. All he could do was jump into the back of the fire truck and pray. As they pulled out of the station, he looked down at the phone in his hand. He clicked on the text icon and brought up the last conversation he'd had with Koren.

Reading it again, he couldn't decide if he'd actually been talking to *her* or not.

But her words were like a brand on his brain regardless.

I love you.

. . .

Closing his eyes, he took a deep breath. "Please," he muttered, knowing his words wouldn't be heard above the sound of the siren. "Let her be alive when I get there."

Taco had no idea what Nadine, or whoever was behind this, had done to her. It was entirely possible Koren was already dead, but he was going to hold out hope until the very end that she wasn't.

It was the only thing keeping him from completely losing it.

CHAPTER EIGHTEEN

Sledge must've broken every traffic law getting to Koren's condo, because they arrived in record time. Taco leaped out of the back of the truck and made sure his SCBA tank was secure on his back. He was pulling his mask over his face when a voice rang out across the yard.

"You sure made good time, Hudson."

Turning, he noticed a woman he hadn't seen in the chaos of the flashing lights and his concern about getting inside Koren's condo.

Smoke was pouring out of the open window next to her front door. He couldn't see any flames yet, which was a good sign. Of course, as they all knew, smoke could be just as deadly, or more so, than actual flames.

The woman was standing on Koren's front porch, visible in the lights on either side of the door. She was extremely skinny and her hair had been cut short, but

Taco instantly recognized her from another fire scene not so long ago.

"Nadine Patterson," he said in a voice that was way too calm for how he was feeling inside.

"The one and the same. As I said, you sure made it here quickly. It's different when it's someone *you* care about, isn't it?"

"Step aside, ma'am," Crash said, moving toward her.

Her hands moved out from behind her back—and all of the firefighters stopped in their tracks. She was holding a pistol in one hand and a wicked-looking butcher knife in the other.

"Not so fast. Me and Hudson need to have a little talk first."

"Where are the cops?" Taco hissed to Squirrel.

"On their way. I talked to Quint directly and he said he was getting everyone rolling," Squirrel said, voice low.

"Dispatch said they hadn't gotten any calls about a fire yet," Penelope muttered from his other side. "But that they'd send a unit to investigate."

"Hey! Pay attention to me!" Nadine screeched. After Taco looked back at her, she said a little more calmly, "If you prefer to shoot the shit with your friends while your girlfriend is fighting for air inside, be my guest."

Taco took a step toward her again, and Nadine raised the gun to point at his chest.

For a second, Taco didn't care if she *did* shoot him.

It would give the others time to bum rush her and get to Koren.

"Are you sorry now, Hudson?"

"Yes," he said immediately, not even caring what he was apologizing for. If it got him to Koren faster, he'd admit to just about anything.

"For what? What are you sorry for?" she yelled.

Shit. He took a wild stab. "For your son dying."

"For *killing* my son, you mean!" Nadine screamed. "You said it yourself! You were too late! You should've gotten there faster!"

Taco didn't remember what he'd said at that fire. He'd been to so many other calls since then, there was no way to remember specifics. He did remember Nadine being out of control at that scene. That she'd been drunk or high or something.

Speaking of which…

He took a harder look at the crazed woman on Koren's porch. She was blinking rapidly and her gun hand shook. She was most definitely on something right now.

"I'm sorry we weren't able to save him," Taco tried again. "By the time we got there, he was already gone."

"I know, you asshole!" Nadine spat. "That's what I'm saying. You took too long to get there! If you'd tried a little harder, maybe driven like you did tonight, you would've made it in time!"

"What do you want from me?" Taco asked, ever

aware of the smoke rolling out of the window behind her. He needed to get inside.

"You want to save your girlfriend?"

"Yes."

"You think she's still alive?"

"Yes," Taco said without hesitation. "I think you wanted to keep her alive until I could get here just to mess with me."

Nadine smirked. "You're right."

Taco took a chance and stepped closer. "Then let me inside so I can get to her and see what you've done."

"Take off the oxygen first."

"What?"

"And your pants and jacket. Take it all off."

"Don't, man," Crash said under his breath.

"If you want to get inside, you'll do what I say," Nadine warned. "I can stand out here all night."

"The cops are on their way," Squirrel said.

"I'm not afraid of the cops," Nadine sneered. "Fucking cops are *useless*. Besides, you want to wait for them?" She glanced behind her. "The smoke is getting awfully thick."

He didn't have time to wait for someone to find a weapon. Every second he hesitated was a second longer Koren was inside, possibly dying. He had no idea if Nadine had stashed her downstairs near the flames or farther away.

He shrugged out of the harness holding his SCBA pack and placed it on the ground.

"Taco, man, *don't*," Moose said.

"I have to," Taco answered, not taking his eyes from Nadine. He would do whatever she wanted if it meant getting to Koren.

"This is awesome," Nadine said with a smile. She waved the gun at him. "Hurry up…and give me some hip action while you're at it. I want a good strip tease."

"Come on, Nadine," Driftwood called. "Cut this out and let us inside before the rest of the condos go up too."

"You think I give a shit about them?" Nadine asked, glaring at Driftwood. "News flash. I don't. I don't give a shit about *anything*. Not about the bitch inside. Not about Hudson. Not about any stupid fucking neighbors who haven't gotten the clue that there's a big fucking fire about to happen and still haven't left their homes. Who was there to give a shit about *me*? Huh? No one, that's who! Not Preston, and definitely not *you*."

"Who's Preston?" Chief asked someone behind him, but Taco kept his attention on Nadine.

She continued on. "Tonight's my night. What do they call it? Suicide by cop? That's how I'm gonna go. Not by some disease from the needle. Not from a goddamn overdose. Not from some sexual disease my dealer or his friends give me. Nope. For once in my life, *I'm* in control!"

"Nadine," Taco said, standing up and holding his arms out at his sides. "It's off. Please. Let me go inside."

"You still want to go in?" Nadine asked.

"Yes."

"Even though you don't have any oxygen and you'll probably die?"

"Yes."

For a split second, Taco thought he saw acute pain cross Nadine's face, but the look was gone almost as soon as he noticed.

"Then by all means, kill yourself," she said, and gestured to the door behind her.

"Taco, no!" Moose yelled.

At the same time, Chief said, "Don't let that skin-walker be in control."

Nadine laughed, obviously overhearing the others. "Oh, make no mistake about it. I *am* in control here." She turned to Taco. "Don't try anything. If you do, you won't get to her in time."

"I'm not going to do anything," he swore. Taco knew going inside without his gear was dangerous, but Nadine was underestimating his friends. As soon as they were able, they'd be right on his heels.

Taco walked slowly toward her with his arms outstretched. The barrel of the gun was focused on him the entire time. The last thing he wanted was her shooting him before he could get to Koren. She stepped to the side, giving him room to get to the door, far enough away that he couldn't rush her. When he was close, he glanced down at the weapon she was holding —and blinked.

It wasn't real. It was one of those ultra-realistic BB guns.

He opened his mouth to say something, but she beat him to it.

"It might not be real...but this knife sure is," she muttered.

Taco kept his arms at his sides, trying to look like less of a threat. He didn't know what to say. A part of him felt sorry for Nadine. Yes, she was obviously on drugs, and she wasn't a nice person, but she'd lost her son. She'd lost everything.

"I'm not sure Preston ever would'a gone inside a burning building for *me*," Nadine said. Then she scowled and the hate was back in her eyes. "You still aren't sorry enough, Hudson, but you will be when you're both trying to breathe and can't." She paused for one more second, then waved the knife at the door. "Go."

He went.

The door wasn't hot to the touch, which was another good sign. But the second he opened it, black smoke rolled out.

Taking a deep breath, Taco ran inside, slamming the door behind him.

CHAPTER NINETEEN

Almost as soon as the door shut behind Taco, the cop cars started arriving. Within minutes, the entire building was surrounded by police officers. There were multi-jurisdiction units, from SWAT to sheriff deputies to local SAPD officers.

Moose watched in frustration as he and the other firefighters from Station 7 were ordered to back away from the condo. Smoke continued to escape from every nook and cranny and his internal timer was ticking. Taco's SCBA and bunker gear were sitting on the ground near the porch and his fingers itched to snatch it up, run inside, and find his friend.

"Drop the weapon!" one of the officers yelled from behind the safety of his patrol car.

"No!" Nadine yelled back.

"Drop it, now!" another shouted.

And so it went.

Moose sidled up to Quint. "It's taking too long. We need to get in there. Taco doesn't have his air."

Sweat ran down Quint's temple as he stared at Nadine. "She's holding all the cards here," he said quietly.

"Then fucking shoot her!" Moose said in frustration.

Quint didn't respond. It was obvious the law enforcement officers were doing everything they could to end the standoff peacefully.

"Why don't you shoot me already?" Nadine called out mockingly.

"Just drop the gun and the knife and this can be worked out," another officer said. "No one's been hurt yet. We can fix this."

"Yeah? Can you bring back my Stevie?" Nadine asked. "No, you can't!" she screamed, answering her own question. "He's dead because Hudson didn't try hard enough! He took too long! He's got to *pay*!"

"I think he got the message," the officer said. "Come on, Nadine. Let us help you."

"You want to help me?" Nadine asked in a suddenly calm tone, especially compared to the yelling she'd been doing.

"Yes."

"Then shoot me!" And Nadine lifted her arm, pointing the pistol at the cop who'd been attempting to sneak up on her from the side.

Simultaneously, several shots rang out, echoing around the normally tranquil neighborhood.

"Cease fire! Cease fire!" several officers yelled at the same time.

The second everything was quiet, five SWAT officers rushed toward Nadine. She was lying on her back on Koren's porch. Her arms were outstretched and blood was pouring out of four shots to her chest.

Moose and the others were hot on the heels of the officers. Their concern was the smoke that continued to billow out of the front window of the house—and the occupants inside.

Nadine looked up at the officers and didn't even flinch when the gun and knife were kicked out of her hands. Moose heard one of them swear in disgust and say, "The gun's fake."

"Shit," Quint said from next to Moose.

Nadine was coughing, the sounds making it clear she wasn't going to survive her wounds.

"We need an EMT!" one of the officers shouted.

"No," Quint said. "You need to get the fuck out of the way so these firefighters can get inside and rescue the two people trapped in there."

Nodding, the SWAT officers holstered their weapons and worked together to pick up Nadine and get her off the porch.

Moose heard an ambulance arrive, but his attention was on the fire. He bent down and grabbed Taco's air tank. He turned to Penelope, "Ready?"

Expecting an affirmative response, he was stunned when Penelope simply continued to stare blankly at the front door.

He nudged her. "Tiger?"

Her mask was on top of her head and when she turned to face him, Moose flinched at the look of utter despair on her face. There were several other emotions there as well, but she turned her back on him before he could read them.

"I'm going to help the ambulance crew," she mumbled before running away from Moose and the burning condo.

Still in shock, he could only stand there and stare after Penelope.

She'd done the one thing he never would've thought she'd do. That *any* firefighter would do. She'd turned her back on one of their own.

No, *two* of their own.

Having trouble processing what had just happened, Moose startled when Chief slapped him on the back of the head. "I'm here. Let's go."

Taking a deep breath, Moose nodded. He lowered his face mask, made sure his air was on, then signaled to Chief that he was ready.

He heard Sledge say through the headset in his helmet, "Let us know if you need additional manpower."

"Will do," Chief responded.

Moose couldn't imagine what Sledge must've been

thinking when he saw his sister abandon the fire, but he didn't have time to reflect on it.

Chief headed for the front door and Moose followed close behind, holding Taco's air tank. They had no idea what shape they'd find Koren in, but most likely they'd be doing a scoop and move, getting her out as soon as possible. Without training, she wouldn't know how to use an air tank and would probably panic if they tried to put one on her. Not that they had time to wait while someone ran to get them another tank anyway.

Smoke billowed out around them as they entered, as if the house was swallowing them whole.

* * *

When the door shut behind Taco, he was instantly blinded. The smoke was already so thick he couldn't see anything.

"Koren!" he called out, then immediately started coughing. The smoke burned his eyes and made his chest hurt. He strained to hear anything. The sound of the fire crackling under him was ominous and increased his anxiety. If she was in the basement, there might be nothing he could do.

Tilting his head, Taco thought he heard something upstairs. Thanking God he'd been in her condo enough to have long since memorized the layout, he immediately turned and felt for the stairway. Once he found them, he took the stairs two at a time. Using the wall for guidance, he made his way down the hall.

"Koren?"

"Here!"

That time, he definitely heard her voice. Heaving out a sigh of relief, he hurried to her bedroom. When he felt the doorway, he called her name one more time. "Koren!"

"Bathroom!"

Taco quickly found the door and entered. He slammed it behind him, and flipped the switch for the light and turned on the fan for good measure. It wouldn't clear the air, but he hoped reducing the amount of smoke in the room even a little bit would help her.

The light didn't do anything to break the darkness the smoke had caused though.

"Taco?" she called, then coughed so hard he winced.

Using his hands to follow the counter, he swore when something bit into his hand. "Fuck!"

"Be careful!" she exclaimed. "Nadine broke a bottle and there's a used syringe in the sink."

Hoping like hell he hadn't just pricked himself with her fucking dirty needle, Taco shuffled his feet until he brushed up against Koren. He fell to his knees and hauled her into his embrace.

The second he felt her hand clench his T-shirt, Taco felt better. She was alive. He wasn't too late. He grabbed her face, and even though the light was dim and the air thick with black smoke, he could make out her outline. "Are you hurt? What'd that bitch do to you?"

"I'm okay," she said, her voice wobbling. "I fell on my face when she Tased me. I was trying to run, but she got me. I cut my chin."

"Tased?"

Koren nodded.

"Fuck," Taco said under his breath. He wondered now if the pistol she was holding was simply a Taser. "I can't see you well enough to look at your chin," he told her.

"I think I'm okay. It bled for a while but it stopped."

Taco tilted his head and tried to figure out what seemed off, why her voice sounded off.

Then it hit him. "Do I smell alcohol?"

He felt more than heard Koren let out a sob before she controlled it. "She made me drink! Wanted me to be wasted like her son was."

Yeah, it was safe to say any sympathy Taco had felt for Nadine while out on the porch was officially gone.

"It's okay, Kor." He grabbed her hand in his and went to stand up. "Come on, let's get out of here."

She pulled back. "I can't."

"Yes, you can. Come on. I'm sure the cops will have Nadine under control by now."

"No, I mean, I literally *can't*." She coughed again, and Taco waited impatiently for her to explain. Instead, she took his hand in hers and brought it across her chest to the other side of her body.

Wrinkling his brow in confusion, Taco didn't know what she was trying to say…

Then he felt it.

"Do you have a key?" she asked tentatively between coughs.

Fuck. Fuck. *Fuck!*

Taco reached down and grabbed the chain that connected the cuffs and tugged. Koren cried out in pain, and he immediately stopped.

"Sorry. I'm okay. Keep trying," she urged.

Taco felt her wrist, and he winced when his fingers slipped in what he had to assume was blood. The cuff was way too tight on her hand, so she also had to be losing circulation. He realized that Nadine had attached the handcuff to the pipe leading to the toilet.

If he had his bunker gear on, he would've had a small pair of bolt cutters. He always kept them on him, just in case. But at the moment, he was completely helpless.

He could feel her eyes on him, and he was thankful for the first time that the smoke made seeing each other difficult. He didn't want her to be able to read the despair in his gaze. "I don't have anything on me that can get these off," he told her.

For a second, neither of them moved.

Then Koren was pushing him away. She was

shoving at his chest and his legs with her free hand. "Go!" she exclaimed. "Get out!"

"I'm not leaving you."

"Yes, you have to! I don't want you here!"

"Koren—" Taco began, trying to soothe her.

"No! There's no point in both of us dying. Just *go!*"

She was crying openly now, her sobs interspersed with coughs, and it was as painful a thing as Taco had ever witnessed in his life. "*No*. I'm not fucking leaving you. No way in hell. I love you."

The hand pushing him away switched to grabbing him instead. "Oh, God…"

Knowing the situation was dire, and that there was a very good chance neither of them would come out of this alive, Taco sat on the floor as close to Koren as he could get. He wrapped his arms around her and put one hand on the back of her head, settling it into the space between his head and shoulder.

She latched on to him and shook.

"I've got you," Taco murmured helplessly.

Koren continued to cough, and unfortunately, the smoke in the room wasn't dissipating whatsoever. Taco knew it wasn't safe to stay where they were, but since he couldn't get her free, he wasn't leaving.

"It wasn't me texting," Koren said between coughs. Her voice was low and rough.

Taco's stomach fell, but he shook his head. "I don't care. I love you, Koren."

"That's what I was going to say. It wasn't me, but I

do love you, Taco. I was waiting for the perfect time to tell you, but it never seemed right. I thought it was crazy to have fallen in love so fast, but I did. I do."

"Shhhh," he murmured, because her coughing was getting worse. "Don't talk." His voice wasn't much better, but he'd been in the smoke for a hell of a lot less time than she had. "The others will be here in a minute, just hang on."

Her hand clenched his T-shirt, and he wished Moose and the others would hurry up. He needed to get Koren to a hospital.

"I just—" Her words were cut off with an especially harsh bout of coughing. But this time she wasn't stopping. She coughed so hard, she started to gag.

"Easy, Kor," he told her, rubbing her back.

"Can't...breathe...!" she gasped as she kept coughing.

Swearing, Taco got her up on her knees, supporting her from behind. He grabbed the towel she'd been holding and held it up to her face. "Hang on, Koren. Breathe through the towel."

She pushed the material away as she desperately tried to get air into her lungs.

Taco knew their time was up. He stood and headed for the door when it suddenly came crashing open. Taco literally dove backward to protect Koren from whoever had opened the door. He checked himself quickly, and instead of tackling Koren to the floor, he ended up kneeling in front of her once more.

Then he recognized the beautiful sound of someone breathing through a self-contained breathing apparatus. His friends had finally made it to them.

Moose didn't say a word, just came toward them quickly and put Taco's discarded bottle of air on the floor and handed him the mask.

Without hesitation, Taco turned on the air and felt for Koren. He put the mask over her face.

She tried to push it away, confused and disoriented from lack of oxygen.

"It's fresh air, Koren," he soothed. "Leave it on your face, you need it."

But instead of his words calming her down, they seemed to agitate her more.

"*You,*" she managed to get out between coughs.

Taco understood. "We'll share. Okay?"

She nodded.

Taco didn't want to share. He wanted her to put the fucking mask on her face and breathe. She'd been in the condo a lot longer than he had, and she needed the oxygen more. But he didn't argue with her. Waiting until she took a few lungsful of air between coughing, he then brought the mask up to his own face and took a few deep inhalations. God, the air was heaven. He'd never take his SCBA for granted again.

When he had the mask over Koren's face once more, he looked up at Moose and yelled between coughs, "She's cuffed to the pipe behind the toilet. We need a key or bolt cutters to get her loose."

Moose nodded. Taco knew he was most likely relaying the information to the others. They all had radios in their helmets, and he'd never been more thankful. Moose stepped out of the way, and Taco saw another shape behind him. Chief had arrived.

He didn't speak, just bent over with a flashlight to peer behind the toilet.

Taco realized that Koren hadn't attempted to push the mask away like she had before. He turned his attention back to her...and saw why.

She'd passed out. Her eyes were closed and she was limp in front of him.

"Koren?" he called, not taking the mask off her face.

Nothing.

"Koren!" he yelled, this time shaking her at the same time.

Again, she didn't move at all.

"Hurry!" he told Chief.

The firefighter nodded. His voice was distorted when he spoke, but Taco could still hear and understand him. "There's no time to get one of the officers' keys. Moose called for Crash, he's got his bolt cutters on him."

Taco nodded and hauled Koren's unconscious body onto his lap. He supported her head with one arm and held on to the mask with the other. He could just barely make out her free hand. She'd grabbed hold of his shirt when she'd had her last bout of coughing, and the material was still trapped in her fingers.

But she wasn't holding on. He couldn't feel the familiar clutch of her fingers curling into him.

Swallowing hard and coughing violently himself, and doing his best not to lose it, Taco couldn't take his eyes off the dim outline of her fingers.

"Here!" Moose said, shoving his face mask at Taco.

They both knew that Moose was breaking protocol. No firefighter was supposed to give up their mask to someone else. Period. It could leave both persons weak and vulnerable. But his friend obviously knew that Taco had no intention of removing the mask from Koren's face.

Taco took a few deep breaths, then pushed it back toward his friend.

They buddy breathed like that for the precious minute it took for Crash to appear. The bathroom was getting crowded now, but Taco had never been more glad to see his friends in all his life.

Crash handed the bolt cutters—Taco recognized them from his own bunker pants—to Chief. Within seconds, Koren was free. Her arm fell limply to the tile floor.

Chief reached over and took one of Taco's arms, while Moose grabbed the other and also picked up Taco's air pack. They helped him stand and, as a unit, shuffled out of the bathroom. Koren was dead weight in Taco's arms, but he didn't even feel the strain.

With Crash in front leading the way, Moose right at his back, and Chief bringing up the rear, the four firefighters made their way out of the bedroom, down the hall, and started down the stairs.

The smoke was so thick now, Taco couldn't see Crash, who was right in front of him. At one point, the other firefighter reached back and grabbed hold of Taco's arm to help lead him. The sound of the flames consuming everything in their path was frighteningly loud. Without his helmet and mask to muffle the sound, every crash, every crackle, every whoosh of something falling over seared into his brain.

If they'd been even one minute later, Taco wasn't sure they would've been able to exit the condo through the front door. The fire had reached Koren's living room, and in just seconds more would've made it to the stairway.

Crash was the hero in this situation. It wasn't smart of him to have entered the building, not when it was as unstable as it was, but Taco was more thankful than he'd ever be able to say.

One second they were in hell, and the next they were standing outside on Koren's porch. Taco took a deep breath and promptly coughed as if his lungs were trying to turn themselves inside out.

Ignoring his own discomfort, he rushed down the stairs, his buddies at his sides and back the whole way. Ignoring everyone standing around, Taco carried a limp Koren to the nearest ambulance. Again, Moose, Crash, and Chief helped him step up into the back of the vehicle. He placed the woman he loved more than life down on the gurney and moved around so he was out of the way of the paramedics.

"Here," one said, shoving a mask at him.

Taco immediately removed his firefighter's mask from Koren's face and replaced it with the oxygen mask.

"That was for you," the paramedic said dryly.

Taco ignored him. His throat hurt, he felt a little dizzy, but no way in hell was he going to see to himself until he knew Koren was all right. Taco felt the vehicle start moving, and he was relieved. The sooner they could get to the hospital, the sooner Koren would get the advanced care she needed.

He kept out of the way as much as possible, but didn't take his eyes off Koren's face as the paramedics began to work on her. He needed to see her eyes open. Needed to see the beautiful blue eyes he'd fallen in love with.

Her blonde hair was in disarray and streaked with soot. She had a nasty gash on her chin and blood had oozed from the cut all the way down the front of her shirt. Her hand was blue from the constriction of the cuff.

But all of those things were the least of Taco's worries. He knew what smoke could do to a human body. Smoke killed faster than flames. And obviously, Nadine had also known.

Not sparing any more than that brief thought for the bitch who'd tried to take away the most important person in Taco's life, he gently stroked Koren's hair away from her forehead. Between coughs, he murmured into her ear. Telling her that she was safe. That they were both safe. That they were out and all she had to do was wake up and look at him.

But she didn't open her eyes.

She didn't wake up.

The paramedic had to intubate her, to make sure air was getting into her lungs.

At one point, the paramedic picked up a phone and spoke with the doctors at the hospital, telling them the patient was unresponsive and he suspected acute carbon monoxide poisoning.

Taco finally took an oxygen mask from the other paramedic, but only because he was having trouble talking to Koren through his coughing.

He prayed for a miracle. Prayed that he hadn't gotten to Koren too late, as Nadine had wanted. Prayed that she'd be the same person she'd been when he'd last seen her. Prayed that they could live the rest of their days drama free. He'd had enough drama to last him an entire lifetime.

"Please," he whispered. "Don't leave me. Fight, Kor. Fight for me."

CHAPTER TWENTY

It took two days, but Koren finally opened her eyes.

Taco hadn't left her side the entire time, refusing treatment for his own smoke inhalation, only allowing doctors to examine him at her bedside.

Her parents had arrived, along with her brothers and their families, Vicky and Sue and *their* families, as well as Sophie, Quinn, Adeline, Blythe, and even Beth had come by for a while.

The doctors had induced a coma so her lungs could recover faster. She'd had a few sessions in the hyperbaric oxygenation chamber. Her chin had been sewed up and her wrist cleaned. The nurses gave her a head-to-toe sponge bath to get as much of the smell of smoke off her as possible.

But Taco could still smell it. When he did manage to get a few minutes of sleep, he woke with the scent of the smoke in his nose. He had nightmares that he'd been too late, and he'd found Koren dead on her bathroom floor.

Taco knew he should probably give Koren's family some alone time with her, but he couldn't. He hadn't let go of her hand since she'd been settled in a bed in the ICU, and even though it was silly, he felt as if, should he leave, he'd lose her.

He hated how limp her fingers were. Hated that she wasn't grasping on to him. How he'd ever thought she was anything like his ex was beyond him.

The doctors had said she'd be in the coma for another day before they'd start bringing her out of it. Chief had tried to get him to go home and get a good night's rest, but Taco refused. Crash had brought him some puffy tacos from Henry's, but he'd only been able to eat one before feeling like he was going to throw up. When Sledge and Beth had visited, they'd told him how Nadine had died. The cops had found a four-page suicide note in the rundown trailer she'd been living in that detailed all the shit that had gone on in her life.

Taco didn't care.

He had no sympathy for Nadine Patterson. None.

Yes, she'd lost her husband. And her son. But neither of those things gave her the right to try to take someone else's life.

Sue had been horrified to learn that Nadine had gotten to Koren by cloning her cell number. However, she hadn't been surprised to hear Koren had rushed home to be with her best friend…because that was just the kind of person she was.

Flowers filled the room, their sweet smell mixing with the lingering aroma of smoke, making Taco nauseous. But still he didn't move.

Moose came by without Penelope, and as much as Taco wondered where she was, he didn't ask. Koren was his main concern right now.

It was now eleven-thirty at night. The night-shift nurse had been in to check on Koren and had left. The lights in the ICU were so bright, if he wasn't wearing a watch, Taco would have no idea what time it was. The squeaking of shoes on the linoleum floor was loud as the nurses went from one room to another.

Taco wasn't supposed to be there. Visiting hours had long since ended. But no one said a word. They all knew who he was and what had happened. The local news had gone crazy with the story, plastering the newspapers, Internet, and TV stations with every gory detail. So they let him stay.

Taco's voice was still scratchy from inhaling so much smoke and from not taking care of himself, but he didn't really notice. His thumb brushed back and forth over the back of Koren's hand as he told her all about who had visited that day. He kept up a steady stream of one-sided conversation. He firmly believed that even when unconscious, people could still hear what was going on around them.

"Everyone was here again today. Sue and her

husband. Vicky and hers. She even brought her adorable little boy, but he wasn't allowed up here in ICU. Your parents were here first thing. They're really worried about you, but I told them that you'd be up and running around in no time. Gavin's already talked to your insurance company and said the inspector would be meeting him at your condo tomorrow morning. So don't worry about that. Carter was still super upset this morning, and even Robin couldn't calm him down. He's pissed on your behalf and just wants someone to pay for everything that happened. I guess the fact that Nadine is dead doesn't make it any better, because he can't rail at her.

"Blythe sent an email to your boss and told him what happened, and he said not to worry, that he's watching your email and taking care of any problems with your clients that come up. Your job is safe and secure, you just have to get better so you can go back to helping everyone plan the world's best vacations. Beth feels bad that she wasn't able to track Nadine down faster. I think she also feels guilty, which I told her was crap, but you know how she is."

Taco took a deep breath. "I miss you, Koren. I miss hearing your voice in the mornings. I miss seeing you sigh in contentment after you take your first sip of coffee. I miss your texts. I can't even think about going home because I know everywhere I look, I'll see you. I definitely can't sleep in my bed without you there. It'll hurt too much. So you have to hurry up and get better so we can go home. And you *will* be coming home with me. We love each other, and I want you there. I can't bear the thought of you living anywhere other than right by my side. If you don't like my house, I can sell it and we'll get something else. Whatever you want."

Feeling the tears clog his throat, Taco did his best to force them back, but it was no use. They welled up in his eyes and spilled down his cheeks. "I wish it was me lying in that bed. She hated *me*. It should be me…"

Bowing his head, Taco let the tears fall. It had taken two and a half days, but the sorrow and guilt he felt that Koren had been sucked into the drama that was his life finally overcame him.

He was so lost in his own agony and despair that he missed it at first.

But when her fingers tightened once more around his own, Taco's head whipped up and he stared at Koren's face.

Her eyes were still closed. The tube was still down her throat. She hadn't moved an inch.

Except for her fingers.

Some would say it was simply a muscle spasm.

The doctors would say it was impossible because she was still in the medically induced coma.

His friends would tell him not to get his hopes up.

But at that moment, Taco knew the truth.

Koren was going to be fine. She'd heard him. Knew he was there.

He helped curl her fingers around his and was rewarded with her grip tightening again, just slightly.

Nothing had ever felt better than feeling her latch on to him once more.

"I'm okay," he whispered. "And so are you. I love you, Koren. I'll be right here when you wake up…and we'll start the rest of our lives."

* * *

A month later, Koren threw herself down on Taco's couch and breathed out a long sigh of relief. "I thought they were never going to leave," she exclaimed.

Taco smiled, walked over and sat next to her. The first thing he did was grab her hand.

She'd heard all about how Taco had sat by her side in the ICU and refused to let go of her. She didn't remember much about what happened after Nadine had forced her to drink all that rum and left her in the bathroom, but she'd gotten the story from several different people's perspectives. Apparently, both she and Taco were lucky to be alive.

But the one thing every single person had reiterated was how devoted Taco had been while she was in a coma. He'd held her hand as if it was the only thing keeping her alive. And it might have been. What did she know?

Her first memory was waking up and seeing Taco's beautiful hazel eyes looking down at her.

Her condo was completely ruined. As were the two on either side of hers. She had literally nothing other than the odds and ends she'd left over at Taco's house and what had been in her car. That had been the weirdest thing, to go to the bathroom to brush her teeth and realize that she didn't even have her own toothbrush anymore.

Towels, socks, underwear, a comb, tampons, a pot to heat water in...nothing. It was all gone. Either burned, or completely ruined from the smoke and the water used to put out the fire.

But every time she turned around, her friends and family were bringing over stuff. Vicky just happened to be shopping and had seen a beautiful shirt she knew Koren would love. Sue knew how much she adored the color blue, and had brought by a full set of towels. She'd tried to protest, explaining that Taco had towels at his place, but of course her friend had ignored her and brought them over anyway. Her parents had bought her a new laptop. Carter and Liam had sent their wives to the store with instructions to buy whatever they thought she might like as far as a whole new wardrobe.

Even the firefighters and their wives and girlfriends had gotten into the act, holding a fundraiser and, in the end, giving her a check for almost ten thousand dollars.

Nothing would replace the priceless quilt that her grandmother had made that had been on the couch in the basement. Or the photo albums that had burnt to a crisp. But the thoughtfulness of her friends and family went a long way toward making Koren understand that the only important thing in life was loved ones.

Taco had taken it upon himself to throw a "welcome home" party, even though she'd been out of the hospital and living with him for at least three weeks. He'd said he wanted to wait until she was one hundred percent better. And Koren had to admit that he'd been right. She'd slept a lot the first week after getting out of the hospital, and it had taken another two weeks for her to feel more like her old self.

"Happy?" Taco asked.

Koren sighed again and gripped his hand hard. "Yes. Although, you know who wasn't here today?"

Taco nodded. "Penelope."

"Where is she? I've only talked to her once, and it was only for like two seconds. She called to make sure I was all right, then said she had to go right after I said I was fine."

"She's been working alternate shifts than us," Taco admitted.

"What does Moose say?"

"Not much. He's as worried about her as we are. And she's avoiding him too. I think she thinks you're mad at her," Taco said.

"Me? Why?"

"Because, from what I understand, she balked at going into your condo with Moose. She took one look at the smoke rolling out the front door and turned and ran away."

Koren knew that already. "Is that it?"

"Is what it?"

"That's why she thinks I'm mad at her? Good Lord, I wouldn't go into my condo either if I was her."

"You don't understand," Taco said. "She's a firefighter. When everyone else is running out of a burning building, we run in."

"She might be a firefighter, but she's so much more than that," Koren said softly. "She's human. A human who has seen and experienced so much more than any of us have. I'm sure she feels as if she's let all of you guys down. And for that to happen in front of her brother had to have sucked. And Moose. The one person she always wants to look strong in front of. I'm not surprised she's lying low and avoiding all of you."

"How'd you get so smart?"

"I'm not smart," Koren protested. "I just thought about how I'd feel if that was me in her shoes…and you were Moose."

"I love you," Taco said gently.

Koren smiled and fell into him. His arm went around her, and she lay her head on his shoulder. She grabbed a fistful of his T-shirt and gripped it hard. "I love you too. What are we going to do with all this stuff?" she asked, talking about the additional gifts their friends and family had brought to the party. "We don't need it, and it's beginning to stress me out that they keep buying me things."

"They just want to do something nice for you," Taco said.

"I know, but it's time for it to stop. I should be getting the check from the insurance company soon, and anything I've needed in the meantime, you've gone out of your way to get for me."

"They love you."

"Yeah." Koren looked up at Taco. "You know what… when I was in the hospital and learned that everything I owned was gone, it hit me hard."

"I remember."

Koren winced. She'd been almost inconsolable when Taco had explained that her condo was a pile of rubble. "But you know what I realized?"

"What?"

"That it's just stuff. I thought I had nothing. I was having the biggest pity party anyone could ever have, and then Vicky came in and made me laugh. Sue arrived not too much later than that. And then Beth came, even though I could tell she'd rather be anywhere else. The parade of people didn't stop all day, either. It took my mind off what I'd lost and made me concentrate on what I still had. People. People in my life who loved me no matter if I was wearing four hundred dollar shoes or two dollar flip-flops from Walmart. I might've had nothing, but in reality, I had everything. I think that's what Nadine was missing."

"No. Do *not* be sympathetic toward that bitch," Taco growled.

"Hear me out," Koren pleaded.

Taco sighed, but he didn't protest any further.

"She didn't seem to have any friends. She didn't have a family support system. She only had Stevie. And when he died, she literally had no one. She'd lost all her belongings and she had no friends. It's sad."

"No, baby. She had a chance to make friends, but she chose to do drugs instead. She could've gotten involved in parent programs at school, put her son in sports, something. But she spent her time shooting meth and isolating herself. Stevie died because she was negligent. Plain and simple."

"It's sad."

She felt Taco kiss the top of her head. "I love your big heart, but seriously, Koren, she doesn't deserve one ounce of sympathy. She almost killed you. I'll never forgive her for that. Never."

"Okay, Taco."

"Okay. Now...don't think I didn't notice Sue gave you those silk sheets, and then you distracted me so she could go upstairs and put them on our bed. How about if we go up and try them out?"

Koren laughed. "Oh, you're subtle...not!"

He chuckled and stood, pulling her up after him. "Besides, you look tired. I'm thinking you need to take a nap."

"You do, huh?" she asked with a grin.

"Definitely."

She let him pull her toward the stairs to their bedroom. When she'd gotten out of the hospital, there hadn't been any discussion about where she was going to live. He'd brought her back to his house and that had been that.

Honestly, Koren hadn't wanted to be anywhere else. She'd had nightmares the first few nights, but Taco had been there every time. Soothing her.

Keeping her safe.

An hour and a half later, Koren lay sated in Taco's arms. He'd made slow, sweet love to her, making sure she knew exactly how much he adored and cherished her. There would be times when they'd fuck, but tonight wasn't one of them.

Reflecting back over the last month, Koren knew she was one lucky woman. Taco had done everything in his power to make her feel safe in his house. He'd given her a handcuff key to put on her keychain and, as a joke—even though they both knew it wasn't *really* a joke—had hidden them all over the house. There was an emergency ladder next to every window on the second floor, and he'd even gotten her a panic button thing to carry with her as well. He'd also had a security system installed after she'd come home from the hospital.

Koren couldn't help but think about poor Nadine. She felt a little sorry for the woman. She'd had nothing, and even with no possessions, Koren still had the world.

"I love you, Rob," she whispered.

"Love you too, Kor," he mumbled back, already half asleep.

He wasn't wearing a stitch of clothing, but Koren just grabbed his biceps as she snuggled against him.

Sighing in contentment, Taco tightened his hold around her before relaxing completely.

Penelope sat on the floor of her small rental house. It was dark, she hadn't bothered to turn on any lights. The only illumination coming from the night-light in the wall next to the front door. Smokey, her miniature donkey, was asleep with his head in her lap, snoring slightly with every exhale.

She knew her friends were upset with her, and she couldn't blame them. She was upset with herself too. She'd failed in the worst way she ever could've failed. At the moment when she should've been a hero, she'd balked.

But thinking back to that day, and how she'd felt staring at the door, smoke rolling out between the cracks, and seeing Moose standing there waiting for her, something inside her had snapped.

She couldn't do it.

She couldn't be responsible for anyone else's life.

She'd been struggling with the feeling for a while

now, but standing there, knowing Taco, Koren, and Moose were relying on her, made the feelings of failure move over her like a death shroud. They shouldn't rely on her for anything. She wasn't a hero. Wasn't *anyone's* hero.

She didn't remember exactly what happened when Henry White and Thomas Black had been captured with her in Turkey. But she couldn't help but feel a sense of dread that she'd done something wrong. Then they'd been beheaded and burned at the stake.

She wasn't there for that, but sometimes when she was fighting a fire, she wondered what they'd gone through. What their last thoughts had been before the sword removed their heads from their bodies.

And then when Robert Wilson had been set on fire while still alive, that was Penelope's worst nightmare. She'd been in enough fires to know it wouldn't have been pleasant.

Had they died cursing her name for not somehow preventing them from being taken? Had she done something to piss the terrorists off and make them kill her friends?

And the last straw had been the poor Australian soldier. She didn't even know his name. He'd been so scared, and she could tell he'd been pleading with her with his eyes to do something. They both knew he was going to be killed. And yet, she'd done nothing. Had sat there and watched as he was strapped down, screaming and struggling, begging for mercy.

Afterward, she'd read the manifesto the terrorists wanted her to read without protest.

Everyone said the American Princess was a hero. They thought her being a firefighter was noble and brave.

Fuck that.

She was held together by strings, and that night at Koren's condo had finally broken her. She couldn't have set foot inside that building if her life had depended on it...and sadly, Koren and Taco's lives *had* depended on it. And she'd still turned around and left like the fucking coward she was.

Knowing she was only delaying the inevitable, Penelope eased out from under Smokey and headed for the kitchen table. She opened her laptop, read what she'd written earlier that day, made a few tweaks, then printed it out.

* * *

The next morning, Penelope headed into the fire station, glad that she'd arrived right after a call so the building was empty. She didn't have to see anyone. Pretend that she wasn't broken inside. She slipped into the chief's office and placed the resignation letter on his desk.

Then she went to the room she always used when she was there and cleared out all of her personal belongings from her locker. She stopped on her way out to look around the large common area. She'd had a lot of good times there with the guys...with Moose... but it was time to go. She couldn't be relied on anymore, and the last thing she wanted to do was have someone else die or be injured because of her cowardice.

She needed space.

Space to think.

Space to breathe.

Needed to go where no one knew who she was and wouldn't expect anything from her.

Knowing Moose and her brother would be hunting her down as soon as they heard she'd quit, Penelope took a deep breath and hurried out of the building. Smokey was sitting in the car waiting for her. She'd packed enough so they could stay on the road for months. It was better for everyone if she just disappeared for a while.

She needed to get her head on straight. Needed to figure out what the hell she was supposed to do with her life now.

Smokey brayed a bit and nodded his head up and down when she approached the car.

At the moment, the donkey was the only thing keeping her together. He needed her. She couldn't let him down, as it seemed she'd let down everyone else in her life.

Penelope climbed into the car and scratched Smokey behind the ears. "Ready, boy?"

He brayed again and nodded.

"Right. Then we're off."

Penelope pulled out of the parking lot of Station 7 without a backward glance. She didn't know when she'd see it again, and she knew she was still being a coward by leaving without telling anyone, but it was what it was.

* * *

Look for the last book in the Badge of Honor series, *Shelter for Penelope* to find out where Penelope goes and if she can work through her issues to return to San Antonio.

And if you want to catch up with her story and you haven't read *Protecting the Future,* do that while you're waiting for Penelope's story to go live!

JOIN my Newsletter and find out about sales, free books, contests and new releases before anyone else!! Click HERE

Want to know when my books go on sale? Follow me on Bookbub HERE!

Also by Susan Stoker

Badge of Honor: Texas Heroes Series

Justice for Mackenzie

Justice for Mickie

Justice for Corrie

Justice for Laine (novella)

Shelter for Elizabeth

Justice for Boone

Shelter for Adeline

Shelter for Sophie

Justice for Erin

Justice for Milena

Shelter for Blythe

Justice for Hope

Shelter for Quinn

Shelter for Koren

Shelter for Penelope

Delta Team Two Series

Shielding Gillian

Shielding Kinley (Aug 2020)

Shielding Aspen (Oct 2020)

Shielding Riley (Jan 2021)

Shielding Devyn (TBA)

Shielding Ember (TBA)

Shielding Sierra (TBA)

Delta Force Heroes Series

Rescuing Rayne

Rescuing Aimee (novella)

Rescuing Emily

Rescuing Harley

Marrying Emily (novella)

Rescuing Kassie

Rescuing Bryn

Rescuing Casey

Rescuing Sadie (novella)

Rescuing Wendy

Rescuing Mary

Rescuing Macie (novella)

SEAL of Protection: Legacy Series

Securing Caite

Securing Brenae (novella)

Securing Sidney

Securing Piper

Securing Zoey

Securing Avery (May 2020)

Securing Kalee (Sept 2020)

Ace Security Series

Claiming Grace

Claiming Alexis

Claiming Bailey

Claiming Felicity

Claiming Sarah

Mountain Mercenaries Series

Defending Allye

Defending Chloe

Defending Morgan

Defending Harlow

Defending Everly

Defending Zara

Defending Raven (June 2020)

Silverstone Series

Trusting Skylar (Dec 2020)

Trusting Taylor (TBA)

Trusting Molly (TBA)

Trusting Cassidy (TBA)

SEAL of Protection Series

Protecting Caroline

Protecting Alabama

Protecting Fiona

Marrying Caroline (novella)

Protecting Summer

Protecting Cheyenne

Protecting Jessyka

Protecting Julie (novella)

Protecting Melody

Protecting the Future

Protecting Kiera (novella)

Protecting Alabama's Kids (novella)

Protecting Dakota

ALSO BY SUSAN STOKER

Stand Alone

The Guardian Mist

Nature's Rift

A Princess for Cale

A Moment in Time- A Collection of Short Stories

Lambert's Lady

Special Operations Fan Fiction

http://www.AcesPress.com

Beyond Reality Series

Outback Hearts

Flaming Hearts

Frozen Hearts

Writing as Annie George:

Stepbrother Virgin (erotic novella)

ABOUT THE AUTHOR

New York Times, USA Today and *Wall Street Journal* Bestselling Author Susan Stoker has a heart as big as the state of Tennessee where she lives, but this all American girl has also spent the last twenty years living in Missouri, California, Colorado, Indiana, and Texas. She's married to a retired Army man who now gets to follow *her* around the country.

She debuted her first series in 2014 and quickly followed that up with the SEAL of Protection Series, which solidified her love of writing and creating stories readers can get lost in.

If you enjoyed this book, or any book, please consider leaving a review. It's appreciated by authors more than you'll know.

www.stokeraces.com
susan@stokeraces.com

facebook.com/authorsusanstoker

twitter.com/Susan_Stoker

instagram.com/authorsusanstoker

goodreads.com/SusanStoker

bookbub.com/authors/susan-stoker

amazon.com/author/susanstoker

Made in United States
Orlando, FL
26 May 2022

18217942R00185